DOMINATE

PAM GODWIN

DISCLAIMER

The books in the DELIVER series are stand-alones, but they should be read in order.

PROLOGUE

Pecos River Bridge
Langtry, Texas
Ten years ago

There were many reasons to jump, but Rylee Sutton only needed one to step off the ledge.

He was her one.

Her only.

Her first love, her best friend, her husband.

He *had been* her ever after.

Now there was no future. No do-overs. Nothing left but inconsolable pain.

She couldn't breathe. Couldn't see through the searing blur of tears that poured from the damage inside her.

Goddammit, she was a mess. How had she ended up here?

Perched on the bridge high above the Pecos River gorge, she dangled her feet over the yawning black abyss, her flip-flops clinging precariously to her toes. Another sob shuddered up, and she angrily kicked off the sandals, sending them tumbling into the dark.

Plunging.

A silent, insignificant drop.

She would be next.

After a four-second fall at seventy-five miles per hour, she would crash into the Pecos River with the force of a speeding truck colliding with a concrete building.

She'd thought about this a lot, had done the research, and knew this was the one thing she would *not* fail.

She was done. Done failing at life. Done failing her husband.

If she only knew where she'd gone so terribly wrong.

She'd supported Mason through thirteen years of medical school and residency, worked multiple jobs to pay off his student loans, and delayed her own career pursuits to assist the startup of his private practice.

Together, they'd been an unstoppable team. The power couple that all others envied. She'd helped him become an orthopedic surgeon, and now, he was supposed to be at her side while she studied criminal justice.

Only he wasn't with her.

He was with someone else.

Anguish surged faster, harder, wracking her body in vicious waves. She clapped a hand over her mouth and sobbed against her fingers.

She loved him so much it hurt. She hurt so badly she couldn't see past it. Couldn't see anything but the images of him with another woman.

"I knew, Mason," she cried, yelling at the moonless, unfeeling sky. "I've known for months and refused to believe it."

She was an idiot.

His late nights at work, shady excuses, casual flirting with other women, disinterest in sex with her — all the signs had been there, glaring at her. So two nights ago, she followed him. Watched him enter an unfamiliar house without knocking. Waited for him to come back out.

When he didn't, she stormed right up to the front door and opened it.

No amount of suspicion could've prepared her for the sight of her husband banging a woman against the wall. He hadn't even made it past the front room before shoving his dick inside her.

Rylee had lost her shit. Utterly. Maniacally. She'd screamed. He'd begged for forgiveness. She'd left in her car, and he'd chased on foot.

The devastation was so complete she couldn't remember the last two days. She hadn't gone home. Instead, she'd driven five hours through the desert, stayed in a motel, and found herself in Nowhere, Texas, staring over the side of a bridge.

She couldn't pull herself away from the ledge. Revenge was gnawing. Consuming. Demanding that she hurt him as deeply as he'd hurt her.

Her death would destroy him.

Lifting her phone, she glanced at the twenty new texts and missed calls. He'd left hundreds of messages over the past two days, ranging the spectrum from denial and anger to guilt and fear. He was sorry. He wanted her back. He would do anything for her. Blah, blah, blah.

If she went home, maybe he would wear her down and convince her to stay. But she would never forgive him. Never forget. He'd decimated the very foundation of her existence. She didn't have the energy to rebuild. Couldn't fathom starting over at age thirty-one.

She didn't want a life without him.

His messages would go unanswered. But she wouldn't depart this world without the final word.

Tears fell in steady streams down her cheeks as she opened the camera on her phone, switched to video mode, and pressed record.

"Mason, you dumb son of a bitch. You fucked up. You fucked around, and you fucking lost me. I'd say that I hope it was worth it, but I know it wasn't. The moment you put your dick in her, you ruined both of our lives."

The light post across the bridge illuminated a halo behind her, but the screen showed only her face. A ghastly, puffy-eyed, *old* face. She stared at the image for several seconds, shocked by her reflection.

"The face staring back at me isn't mine. It's the face of a defeated woman. I don't recognize her. I don't accept her, and I fucking despise her for the things she cannot change." She swiped at the torrent of tears, unable to rein in the fury in her voice. "I read your messages and listened to your voicemails. You claim it was just sex with that woman, that it meant nothing. If that were true, why do I feel so dead? I used to get tingles every time I thought of you. Now I just feel cold and sick with this slimy, hateful sensation stuck in my gut. That's never going away. So I have a choice. I can live with the pain. Or I can end it."

Her hands trembled so violently she jostled the phone. Readjusting her grip, she swallowed. Blinked.

Cleared her voice.

"Maybe I feel too much. Do I? I think I do. I think I loved you too much. Certainly more than you deserved. So I'm going to stop that. I'm just going to stop feeling. I gave you thirteen years, and what did I ask for in return? Fidelity? I wish you would've told me that was too much to ask. Maybe you didn't know. But you should have. You're a fucking doctor. All that schooling to learn how to heal people, and in the end, you hurt the person who loved you the most. Well, you can just fuck right off. You did your thing, and now I'm going to finally do something for me. I'll see you in hell."

Numb, she stopped the recording. She was spent. Empty. There was nothing left.

She had no living family. No one to mourn her death.

Except him.

He would watch the video after she was gone, and maybe it would wreck him so completely he would eventually follow her off the bridge. It was the cruelest, most selfish thing she could do. The person she was before would've never been so vindictive.

But that person was already dead.

She opened her email to forward the video to him. By the time he received it, she would be at the bottom of the river.

The tightness in her chest choked her breaths. Her eyes were so hot and swollen it was like looking through ripped scabs. She rubbed her lashes and squinted at the screen.

A new email had popped up. *Weird.* It wasn't in her inbox but in the unknown account she'd logged into weeks ago.

Her finger hovered over it.

No. Forget it. She should just send the video and be done with this.

But that account… Why was it receiving an email now? It had never been used. No incoming or outgoing messages ever.

A month ago, she bought a jacket at a thrift store in El Paso. In the pocket, she'd found the email address and password scribbled on a scrap of paper. At the time, the romantic in her had been drawn to the username.

Tommysgirl.

Someone had created it a few months before she'd acquired the jacket. They seemed to have forgotten about the account.

She'd forgotten about it, too.

"It's not important. Just delete the account and erase everything."

She didn't want anyone thinking she'd been having an affair with a guy named Tommy.

As she switched to the account to remove it, her attention snagged on the subject line of the message.

I need you.

Three words, so simple and ambiguous, yet they sneaked beneath her desolation and shone a blinding light on the most broken parts of her.

She desperately needed to be needed.

The fog in her head lifted as she quickly opened the message and read the first line.

I know you're dead, but you're still my girl. I need you.

Her gaze skipped to the bottom of the letter and landed on the signature.

Tommy.

Who was he? Who was Tommy's girl?

Her heart hammered as she absorbed the rest of the email.

I've been avoiding this email account. I mean, I created it and gave it to you the day I lost you. It's like I knew I would need to write this letter to your ghost.

Maybe that's fucked-up, but I need you to hear me. I don't think I can keep going if you're not out there, somewhere in the ether, listening.

They said you died in that car accident, but your spirit is too bright, too big, to just vanish. You always smiled at me like you were part of a better world, so I think that's why you left. You were destined for something greater.

I wish you could tell me where you went. Is it nice? Are you alone?

It's dark here. Everything feels haunted. All I see is shadows, the ones you left behind. They're in the hallways at school, on the trails we walked between our houses, and in the rocks we climbed in the desert.

Your ghost belongs to me. It's the only thing I got to keep. All your possessions were snatched up by extended family and sold off. But your ghost is mine. Except I can't wrap my arms around it. I don't know how to hold it and kiss it.

I miss your lips.

I just want to be with you.

You were supposed to grow up and become the strong woman you were meant to be. I couldn't wait for you to grow up with me.

How could you leave me here to live without you? I want to be mad at you, but I miss you too much. I miss you.

I just...miss you.

It's not fair what happened to you and your family. Or what's happened to me. I guess I can be angry about it forever, or I can just try to...be.

You've been gone for six months. Did you know that? Does time move the same where you are?

My mom makes me see a therapist because I won't talk to her. Funny how, when bad things happen, people make it worse by feeling sorry for you. I see the pity in their eyes, the shared looks of concern. What they're thinking and not saying is that I'm horribly fucked-up and make everyone uncomfortable.

Grownups are clueless. They think they can fix things, like I need someone to take care of me, but mostly they just want me to act normal.

I can act normal and feel brave and still find myself falling.

Maybe that's what love does. It gives you hope then throws you off the cliff into terrible darkness so that every memory stays with you into infinity.

I'm drowning in memories. I remember when you were born, when you started walking, talking, and running faster than me. Jesus, you were fast. I was always chasing you, wasn't I?

Now I'm chasing shadows.

You know what really messes me up? The fact that I've been waiting my entire life for you to get older, and now you never will.

You'll always be fourteen. Three years younger than me this year. Four years younger than me next year. The year after that, five years younger. I have to graduate from high school in the spring, knowing that you will never join me on the other side.

All the dreams we talked about — college, marriage, the

dogs, the kids, the house with the pond, everything we planned... Our future died with you. We did everything right, and it all turned around on us.

You're mine, but you're not. Mine to protect, but I can't do that, can I?

I guess you don't need protection where you are. You're free from danger and pain. Congratulations on being free. But I'm still here, reaching for you and waiting for you to reach back.

Losing you feels like I lost myself. When I try to talk about it, I hear a noiseless hush. Echoes, maybe. Like strangled screaming from somewhere inside me. That really sucks, you know? I can't talk to the therapist. It's a waste of goddamn time.

But writing the words to you... I don't know. This is easier. I don't feel so helpless and weird. Because I know you're listening without judgment. Even when you don't like what I say, you've always listened.

Maybe if I keep writing, if I tell you about the guy who misses his girl, no matter how bad it is, I won't be stuck in this story anymore. I'll be the author of it.

Authors have the ultimate power. They can save a character. Or kill him off. I like that idea.

Shit, I need to go. My mom's calling for me. I think she's lying about how bad her cancer is. I'll tell you about that another time.

Thank you for listening.
I wish you were here.
Yours,
Tommy

A lump knotted in her throat, and her tears cascaded with a vengeance. She read through the email again and again, hurting for him through every word. He was only seventeen. Just a kid. Yet he had more strength and maturity than she did at thirty-one.

Boy, did that put her pathetic life into perspective. What the hell was she doing?

She sat back against the guardrail and pointed her toes toward the black nothingness below. Nighttime insects buzzed around her, and in the distance, the rushing river beckoned.

"Mason cheated on me." She spat the words off the bridge.

She repeated it over and over. Every time she screamed it, the statement was no less true, but it started to lose its power over her.

So he cheated on her. Was that really worth killing herself over?

Yes.

She thought about it and asked the question again. *Maybe. I don't know.*

Mason hadn't died in a car accident. His life hadn't been stolen from her. He was an unfaithful husband. A dirtbag. A man who didn't love her enough to be faithful.

This kid, Tommy, was dealing with something far more tragic, and she didn't sense a hint of suicide in his email. He was powering through it, pushing forward, despite the excruciating pain and loneliness.

If he loved his girlfriend even a fraction as much as she loved Mason, he was hurting. Inconsolably. The more a person loved something, the harder it was to lose it.

She felt that loss at the center of her bones. It was a winless battle she didn't want to fight.

Until she'd read that message.

Now she didn't know what to do. She couldn't email the boy. If she did, he would stop writing to his girlfriend and lose that outlet to express his feelings.

He needed someone to hear him, and deep down, she knew she needed to listen. She couldn't compare his misery to hers. It wasn't even in the same realm. But she related to his words and felt his insecurities like they were her own.

He gave her strength. But was she strong enough to start over? She wasn't seventeen anymore.

She wasn't ninety, either. Age was just a number. An excuse to give up.

Mending a broken heart felt impossible. But that was life, wasn't it? Everyone got their heart broken at least once. Now that she'd experienced it, she knew how to avoid it.

She wouldn't go home. She would never fall in love again. She could focus on a career. Did she still want that?

Did she still want to jump?

It would be easier.

Since when did she ever take the easy route?

Fuck, she was just so tired. Exhaustion pushed in from every direction, pulling on her limbs and straining her insides. It hurt to breathe.

Maybe she should go back to the motel and sleep on it. But if she stepped away from this bridge, she knew she wouldn't return.

So she stayed. Deliberated. Reread Tommy's email. Listened to Mason's new voicemail messages. Then she watched her video through a fresh sheen of tears.

On the screen, she looked like a raving lunatic. A sad, pitiful victim crying out for help. That wasn't her. It was just a moment, one she'd needed to give herself. If she was brave enough, she could put the video and all thoughts of suicide behind her.

She deleted the recording. Then she sat in the silence and allowed herself to grieve.

Hours passed. She remained on the bridge until the first rays of dawn broke over the horizon.

She hadn't slept. Hadn't jumped. But she was no longer crying.

After spending the evening imagining what her life would look like without Mason, she had a plan. It wasn't dreamy or exciting, but it was obtainable. She could get by with a broken heart, and maybe someday, she might find a way to be happy as a single woman.

The sunrise stretched pink and lavender fingers across the rippling surface of the river below. In the light, a fall at this height felt a lot more daunting.

Her moment to jump had come and gone.

Woodenly, she gathered her things into her bag and checked her phone.

Another email had been sent to *Tommysgirl* ten minutes ago. She opened the message.

Me again.
I fought with my mom last night. Turns out, I was right about her cancer.
The doctors give her six months to live.
I really need you.
Are you there?

"Yeah." She stepped away from the ledge and trudged to her car on bare feet. "I'm here, Tommy."

ONE

Eldorado, Texas
Present Day

"I'll only be gone a month, Evan." Rylee breezed past him, her mind running in a million different directions. "The lights are on timers, so don't mess with the switches."

"At least tell me where you're going." Evan caught her arm, stopping her at the front door. "You owe me that much."

"Bullshit." Anger flared as she whirled on him. "I had one rule."

"I never agreed —"

"No expectations. No commitments. No possessive behavior."

"That's three."

"All synonymous with *no clinging*."

"I'm not..." He followed her narrowed gaze to his

grip on her arm. "Jesus." His fingers sprung open, releasing her. "Don't break my balls because I give a shit."

"Stop."

"Stop what? Caring about you?"

"Yes." She grabbed her backpack and slung it over her shoulder on her way out the door. "My bills are paid through next month. You're listed as my emergency contact, but nothing is going to happen. It's just a sabbatical. My first vacation *ever*."

"Rylee." He stepped in front of her, blocking her exit off the porch.

"Evan." Impatience clipped her voice.

His bright blue eyes searched her face as his hand crept along her jaw, soft yet demanding. "Let me in."

She'd let him in her bed, and that was enough.

More than enough.

In the ten years since her divorce, she made it a point only to have sex with strangers. She didn't do relationships. Never slept with the same man twice. She didn't let people in.

Then Evan moved into the house next door.

For the first few years, she turned down his persistent sexual advances. Didn't matter how goddamn good-looking he was. A one-night stand with a guy who lived twenty feet away was a terrible idea.

But Evan was confident and aggressive and gorgeous in all the ways that spoke to her. So it happened—late one evening, after too many beers and a long bout of loneliness.

Drunken stupidity had been her excuse the first time. But the sex was good. So she let it continue. With one rule.

No clingy attachment.

Except they were together a lot. His place. Her place. Several nights a week. Until she woke one morning and realized he was the only man who had been in her bed in over a year.

She'd broken her own damned rule.

Not only did she have sex with her next-door neighbor, but she'd also become monogamous with him. That was dangerously close to a relationship.

"I need to go." She tried to step around him.

"You have no obligations for the next month." He stayed with her, sliding a hand into the back pocket of her jeans, his fingers squeezing her butt as he tucked their hips together. "Give me a few minutes."

She pulled in a calming breath, which inadvertently drew his sexy, masculine scent into her lungs. He smelled amazing, but she was immune. Damaged. Closed off to anything beyond a casual hookup.

Ten years hadn't dulled the thorns inside her. If anything, time had made her harder, icier, more set in her ways. She wasn't looking to change. Detachment suited her career and safeguarded the life she'd built for herself.

But it didn't negate the fact that Evan was her friend. Her only friend. He didn't deserve to be stonewalled.

She lowered the backpack to the porch and rested her hands on his biceps. Thick, corded muscle stretched the sleeves of his shirt, every inch honed through manual labor in his construction job.

At age forty-three, he was two years her senior, divorced, and living paycheck to paycheck just like her. His modest two-bedroom house was well-kept like hers.

He drank cheap, domestic beer like her. His life was humble, unsophisticated, and honest. Like hers.

But unlike her, he had no reservations about putting himself out there—his generosity, his vulnerabilities, and his overprotective heart.

Evan was a catch, and every unattached woman in their small Texan town wanted him. He needed to stop wasting his time with her.

"All right." She straightened her spine, wishing she were anywhere but here. "I'm listening."

"You should see the look on your face. It's as if a conversation with me makes you physically ill. It's not like I'm asking you to marry me."

Blood drained from her cheeks, and she suddenly felt lightheaded and shaky.

"Fuck, Rylee." He cupped her neck, eyes blazing and mouth twisting with malevolence. "I'm going to kill that son of a bitch."

She never told him about Mason, never even mentioned she was divorced. But over the years, Evan had put it together. Every time she shut him out, he blamed a man she tried to forget.

"Are you going to slay all my demons?" she asked.

"If you let me."

"Because I'm not strong enough to fight them myself?"

"Don't put words in my mouth. You've been fighting for years, proving to the world that you're an impenetrable badass. I get it. You don't need me or anyone else. But dammit, if you let me in, you won't have to fight alone."

With a sigh, she rested her cheek on his chest. "You're a good man."

"The best you'll find this side of the Rio Grande. You should be chasing me, not the other way around."

The only thing she chased was her career, but she wouldn't insult him by voicing what he already knew.

His hand settled on the back of her head, holding her against him. "Tell me where you're going."

"Three hours from here."

"Which direction?"

"West."

"The desert?" He tensed. "Have you lost your mind? A beautiful woman in no man's land? *Alone*? It's crawling with rattlesnakes and scorpions and hell knows what else. Not to mention there's no cell service. No hospitals. What in God's name is out there worth risking your life?"

"Closure."

"So this is about the ex-husband." His fingers angrily fisted in her hair.

"Not exactly." She shut her eyes, searching for an ambiguous version of the truth. "I need to deal with some things. Personal issues I should've put to rest a long time ago."

More specifically, she needed to deal with the boy who had been writing to her—or rather, his dead girlfriend—for ten years.

Except Tommy wasn't a boy anymore. He was twenty-seven. *And dangerous.*

It was never her intention to announce herself to him, let alone meet him in person. Hell, she never should've logged into his girlfriend's account. But if she hadn't, she wouldn't be alive today to contemplate whether or not she was doing the right thing.

He'd been there for her on that bridge without

knowing it, and she'd been here for him ever since.

For over a decade, weekly emails arrived in the *Tommysgirl* account. Each message came from a different anonymous address, but they were all from Tommy. After she read each one, she snapped a photo of it, marked it as unread, and deleted her IP address from the activity log.

The day after sending each message, he always went in and erased it. He only needed to change the password on the account once, and she would've been locked out. But he never did. Because that would've locked out his beloved ghost.

An absurd thought, but she knew how his mind worked, perhaps better than he did. He was smart. Too smart to believe that dead people read emails.

But sometimes, beneath his brave, self-assured words, she sensed the lasting sorrow of the boy he'd been. A boy who'd lost his girlfriend in a car accident, his only parent to cancer, and had been abducted and raped by a heartless sex trafficker, all at the age of seventeen.

He'd survived things that most people couldn't fathom and found the courage to write down his trauma in harrowing detail. She never wanted him to learn she'd invaded his privacy. His emails hadn't been meant for her, and responding to them would've been cruel. But when he sent that last message a week ago, she had no choice.

"What the fuck are you going to do in the desert for a month?" Evan leaned down, putting his scowl in her face. "Sprinkle sage on some coals, trip on peyote, and take a revelatory journey until you've vanquished these issues you think you have?"

"Something like that, but without the

psychedelics." She pursed her lips. "And we both know I have issues."

Almost as many as Tommy.

First off, he was going undercover to infiltrate a Mexican cartel, which was by far the most reckless, idiotic thing he'd ever attempted. He had training and experience with his vigilante team, but not enough. Not to take down an entire cartel.

When he made that announcement in his last email, she panicked. Then he ended the message, stating he wouldn't write again.

It was a final goodbye.

A sucker punch to the gut.

No more emails. No more contact. He was going to shut down the account.

If she hadn't written him back, she would've lost him. She might've lost him anyway.

It had been a week without a response to her email. She worried herself sick, wondering if she would ever hear from him again. He used so many different accounts. What if he didn't check them all?

No, he was too meticulous. He probably didn't read her message until he was deep undercover. Man oh man, his reaction must've been boiling, volcanic fury. No question, he was plotting her death at this very moment.

She'd violated his most private thoughts, infringed upon his darkest moments, stole his secrets out from under him, and he didn't even know she existed.

Until now.

It was such a fucked-up situation. From her perspective, he was familiar and intimate. A friend she dropped everything for. Someone she cared about and fretted over. It was the only relationship that worked for her because she didn't have to give any part of herself in return. He couldn't hurt her as long as he didn't know she was there.

She didn't need a degree in psychology to recognize how unhealthy that was. Every time she read his emails, she knew exactly what she was doing. She also understood the consequences of responding to the last one.

He was coming for her.

While that scared the ever-loving piss out of her, it'd been the only way to draw him out of the life-threatening operation he was undertaking with the cartel.

He'd saved her life on the Pecos River Bridge, and now it was her turn to save him.

So she'd devised a plan. An insane, treacherous, terrifying plan. Then she emailed him back, confessed to reading his emails, and told him when and where to meet her.

Evan knew none of this. He didn't know about the bridge or the *Tommysgirl* account or the man, whose name she learned a few years ago was Tomas Owen Dine.

God, if Evan even suspected what she planned to do, he would tie her up and never let her leave.

"I'm going with you." His hands ghosted along her back.

"Oh, really? You're going to take off work for a month?"

"For as long as you need me."

She didn't need him. The thought made her feel like a bitch, but this was something she had to do alone.

"I need you to look after my house." She pinched his rigid jaw and gave him a stern look. "You're not going. That's non-negotiable."

"I figured you'd say that." He eyed the camping gear in her pickup truck in the driveway. "What happens when a hungry bobcat attacks your campsite?"

"Mosquitoes are a greater risk to humans than bobcats."

"Because most humans don't camp out in wildcat territory."

"I have a shotgun."

He already knew that. He'd gone target shooting with her at the range.

"I guess there's just one thing left to say." He gripped the backs of her legs and hooked them around his hips, holding her so close his breath kissed her lips. "And one thing only—"

"Just say it."

He smiled, his teeth blinding white in his suntanned face. "I'm going to miss your hot body."

With a quick dip, he claimed her mouth. Warm tongue, firm lips, clean taste, his kisses were always agreeable. Pleasing. Yet something was missing. Nothing she could label. Just an itch at the back of her mind.

It was her, not him.

She tried to lower her feet to the ground, but he tightened his grip. She leaned away, but his mouth chased hers, intent on recapture.

"Evan."

"One for the road." He pulled her tight against his erection, grinding seductively. "I'll settle for a quickie."

"No."

"Come on, Rylee. How am I going to go without you for an entire month?"

"You have plenty of booty calls." She snatched the

phone from his back pocket and pulled up his contact list. "Who do you want? Addy? Amy? Ashley? Ava? Wow, so many options, and I haven't even made it past the *A* names."

"You're the only one I want." He ripped the phone from her hand and tossed it onto the porch swing. "And you're the reason those women are in my contact list."

That was true. She pushed him onto every unwed lady she encountered.

Somehow, she'd fallen into monogamy while making sure he didn't. She needed to see those women slipping out of his house in the mornings, so that each one could add another mile of emotional distance between her and her charming neighbor.

"I told you no expectations." She squirmed in his arms. "I suck at this."

"Yeah, you do." He set her on her feet. "Only because you want to suck at it." He grabbed her backpack and slung it over her shoulders. Then he fisted the straps, yanked her close, and stole a kiss from her lips. "Get out of here before I carry you into the bedroom and delay your trip."

"Thank you." She stepped back, gave him a small smile, and headed to the truck.

"Rylee."

"Yeah?" She glanced back.

"I'm going to be pissed if anything happens to you."

"I'll take that under advisement."

But no promises.

She hoped to stop Tommy from killing her, but there were no guarantees he wouldn't hurt her before she convinced him to see reason. She didn't know what he looked, sounded, or smelled like. Didn't know anything about him in the physical sense. She wouldn't even be able to pick him out in a crowd.

But she knew his psychological and criminal profile like the back of her hand.

Heaven has no rage like love to hatred turned.

She imagined that summed up his current state of mind. By reading what he'd written to the girl he loved, she'd stained his words. He would regret revealing so much of himself and view the letters as weapons turned against him, his secrets and insecurities wrongfully exposed.

Hell has no fury like a man deceived.

She anticipated his wrath, feared it, but she wouldn't run. She had a month off of work.

A month in the desert with a livid, deadly criminal.

She would survive this, or she wouldn't. But she owed it to both of them to see it through.

TWO

The charred structure protruded from the dry, crusty earth. Rylee's chest tightened as she shaded her eyes, squinting at the rubble around her, trying to make out what was left of the Milton house.

Caroline Milton.

Tommy's girl.

Two exterior walls jutted in misshapen pieces, weathered by years of dust storms. A fire had devoured the rest. Arson. The conflagration had burned so hotly it had melted the stone foundation.

A shiver ran up her spine. With zero cover and nothing but buttes, craters, and searing sand in every direction, it felt as though she were standing amid ancient ruins on an alien moon.

This barren part of the Chihuahuan Desert promised hardship to anyone living here, which was why Caroline's house had sat empty for years after the family died.

Until Tommy bought it and burnt it to the ground.

His own childhood home stood two miles away. A grueling distance for two kids to trek to see each other. The next closest neighbor was thirty minutes by car, so maybe that two-mile hike was a blessing.

The unforgiving sun beat down on her neck, burning her fair skin as she pushed sand over the bag she'd buried in the remains of Caroline's house. The duffel contained her ID, credit card, phone, and license plates from her truck—everything she carried that could identify her. The phone was the hardest to relinquish, but without cell service, it was useless.

Sweat trickled between her breasts, her body temperature rising to unbearable levels. She released her ponytail and shook out her hair, using the length to cover her shoulders and arms. She wouldn't last an hour out here without turning into a blistered tomato.

The heat chased her back into the cab of the air-conditioned truck. She leaned toward the vent, absorbing the cold air as her mind drifted to the next task.

Was Tommy already at his house, waiting for her? What if he hadn't made it out of the cartel's headquarters? She'd only given him a week's notice.

He had the resources to learn who she was and everything about her. The man on his team, Cole, had some sort of military background that enabled him to erase their identities from existence. With time, that guy would've found her. But probably not within the week she'd given. And not while Tommy was undercover and unable to make contact with him.

Tommy's emails never disclosed last names. Not his, Caroline's, or any of his friends'. Rylee only discovered his identity, and that of the Milton family, by piecing together the clues he'd provided, such as the

26

descriptions of his rural home, the details of Caroline's car accident, and the fire he'd set to her family's property.

After she determined where he grew up, she'd driven by a couple of times to check out the place. But not recently, and she'd never dared to step out of her truck and peek inside for fear of being discovered.

Her nerves coiled as she put the truck into motion. In a few moments, she would finally come face to face with the one person she knew better than anyone in the world.

The first few seconds would be critical. He would either listen to her introduction or shoot her in the head.

She'd discarded all her identification because she didn't want him investigating her without talking to her. It would be safer for her and everyone in her life if she defused his anger before giving him too much information.

Navigating along the bumpy terrain, she white-knuckled the steering wheel and swallowed her rising trepidation. There were no roads or tracks. Every landmark looked the same, from the tufts of desert growth to the steep, flat-top hills. It was a wonder she'd found this place the first time.

When the one-story adobe brick building came into view, her entire body began to shake. Adrenaline flooded her system, her senses firing on high alert.

He kept company with a gang of violent criminals and could've brought a few of those terrifying friends along. Except she knew he wouldn't. In his rage, he would regard her as *his* problem, one he'd created, a horrible mistake he needed to clean up.

Tomas Dine—complicated man and lone wolf— would walk through hell to resolve his dilemmas on his own.

What concerned her was that while she knew him, he didn't know her. She was the stranger.

From his perspective, she was the enemy.

Sweeping her gaze over the abandoned house, she found it just as creepy and unkempt as the first time she visited. An old tractor rusted on rotting tires in the unfertilized, parched soil. A windmill canted off-balance, missing most of its blades.

Heavy drapes covered the small square windows. The satellite dish on the roof appeared to be in working condition. But was the electricity on to power it?

Nothing had changed. No vehicles. No signs of life.

Her heart sank.

She drove a wide circuit around the house, surveying the lot from all angles. If Tommy were here, he'd hiked in or caught a ride.

Returning to the front of the property, she parked the truck, shut off the engine, and... *Holy shit.* The front door stood open. No way had she missed that a minute ago. It had been shut. She was sure of it.

Her pulse exploded, her gaze darting back and forth, probing the windows, the perimeter, searching for movement.

Nothing.

He was inside the house.

The jacket that once belonged to Caroline Milton sat on the seat beside her. She grabbed it and slowly stepped out, her boots crunching the baked dirt. Her palms slicked with sweat, her stomach a wasteland of nauseating energy.

Despite the covered windows, she felt eyes on her as she tramped across the trackless sand to the door. The hair on her arms rose at the unnerving feeling of being watched. Whispers of dust spun up beneath her feet. And the hush... It was deafening, thrashing in her ears.

If she screamed, no one would hear. If he fired a gun, no one would come. If he buried her body out here, no one would know where to look.

Any outsider would think she was batshit crazy for walking in alone, unarmed, and without a phone. Maybe she *was* crazy. But she trusted her instinct. Her training and in-depth understanding of Tommy's personality had guided her here. Her wits and intuition would keep her alive.

"Tommy," she called out a few feet from the door. "I'm alone."

Silence greeted her.

He'd often mentioned how the unfathomable quiet served as a protective barrier around his home. When something penetrated the stillness, he heard it. No one could sneak onto his property.

No doubt he'd detected her approach long before she'd driven into view. She'd anticipated that. Just like she knew the left floorboard would groan when she entered the house. She knew a small kitchen sat off to one side, opening to the sitting room where his mother lost her fight to cancer.

Two bedrooms in the back shared the bathroom between them, and a problematic hole above the shower let in geckos and scorpions. He'd patched it dozens of times, and the creatures still found a way in.

She knew every nook and cranny of his childhood home, thanks to his detailed descriptions over the years. So many dreams had been conjured within these walls. So many hopes crushed. But not forgotten. He chased their shadows through the rooms, the ghosts of those he loved, which was why he hadn't set it afire like the Milton's home.

"I'm not armed." She held up her hands and stepped over the threshold into darkness. "This is Caroline's jacket. Since you don't have any of her possessions, I thought you'd want this. I'm just going to set it down."

A track of clean wood gleamed along the otherwise dusty floor, tracing a path from the threshold to somewhere beyond the shadows. A trail recently made by footsteps. She toed the dust layer around it, noting the thickness. No one had moved outside that track for months. Probably years.

Placing the jacket on the clean path, she straightened and returned her hands to the air. "I'm standing directly in the sunlight. No weapons. No phone. You can see for yourself."

No response.

Her heart slammed against her ribs, her breaths quickening with the rush of her words.

"My name is Rylee. Originally from El Paso. I moved from there ten years ago because…uh… Well, I'll get to that. I know you have a gun trained on me. I don't blame you since you don't know me or trust me. But believe me when I say I'm more afraid than you are right now. I mean, I can't see you, but you can see me. That puts me at a disadvantage. So I'm just going to keep my hands up and slowly step inside. You said this floorboard creaks so…" She put her boot on it, listening to it protest beneath her slight weight. "Don't shoot."

With the windows covered and the door wide open, a single beam of sunlight stabbed through the darkness, illuminating dust particles like sparkles of glitter.

They made their way into her lungs, and she coughed, cringing as the hacking sound echoed through the house. Dusty boards, dusty drapes, dusty furniture. In the middle of the desert, there was no escape from the powdered sand that covered every surface and filled every crack. She coughed again, stirring up a maelstrom of dirt into the torpid air.

"I know you're here, Tommy." She squinted at the impenetrable shadows, her scalp crawling with dread. "Please, talk to me."

A rustling sound swished on her left, and she spun toward it, gulping. "Tommy?"

Another soft noise whispered behind her. She whirled again, and the door slammed shut, dousing her in pitch blackness.

Sharp, icy fear shot through her, stiffening her joints and freezing her lungs. She tried to speak, but her voice abandoned her. She needed to move to a window and rip off the drapes, but her legs wouldn't work.

Why hadn't she thought to bring the flashlight from the truck?

Another dry cough erupted from her chest, and the wheezing unleashed her voice.

"I'm just going to start talking and try to explain, okay?" She cleared her throat, trembling with unease. "I married the love of my life twenty-three years ago. We had a beautiful life, a promising future, yadda, yadda, lots of superfluous words." She hugged her waist, fighting down old anger as her senses strained in the dark. "Ten years ago, I walked in on him banging another woman. Maybe it's not the same loss you experienced with Caroline, but I loved him. Every breath in my body was his. You know what it feels like to lose your entire world. But I'm not as strong as you. I wasn't. I died that day and had every intention of killing myself for good. I told you how I acquired Caroline's jacket. I never should've logged into the account you created for her. But there I was, standing on the edge of the Pecos River Bridge, when you sent the first email. I wasn't going to read it. I was just going to delete the account and jump. I was going to die, Tommy. I had no reason to live. Until I saw the subject line of your message. *I need you.* Do you remember it?"

Her question hung in the dry air, her eyes wide and unblinking. The memory still hurt. The sticky, hateful slime in her stomach never faded. But she'd managed to keep breathing, keep functioning, even if she was dysfunctional as fuck.

She held still, listening for the sounds of his breaths, footsteps, anything to give away his location.

Seconds of tingling silence passed. He hadn't shot her in the head yet, so that was *something*.

"You must think I'm a nutjob." She wiped at the sweat gathering on her brow. "Anyone would think that if I told them about you. I haven't. No one has seen your emails. But here's the thing, Tommy. I'm not suicidal anymore. I want to walk out of here unharmed. So I made copies of your messages. They won't be discovered *unless* I go missing. If I don't return home when I'm expected, the authorities will find those copies and know that I drove here to meet with Tomas Owen Dine. I don't want that to happen. I'm not here to hurt you. I have nothing to gain from that. I just want to talk." She caught her breath. "Turn on the lights."

Please, don't kill me. Please, don't kill me.

He didn't make a sound. Nothing.

The longer he kept her in the dark, the more fearful and furious she became.

"I know you're pissed." She forced bravado into her tone. "Fine. Yell at me. Let me hear it. Act like a fucking adult and confront me."

He still had some anonymity because she didn't know what he looked like. But this wasn't about him hiding his face. He was fucking with her.

"I know what you're doing with the silent treatment. The bullshit intimidation tactics are beneath you. It's a dick move and a waste of time. Don't forget, whether you like it or not, I know you better than anyone."

"Are you familiar with the rule of threes?" His deep, gruff voice came from behind her.

With a gasp, she pivoted, reaching out and grabbing only air. "You're talking about the rules for survival?"

Where the hell was he? She stumbled through the dark, arms out, and bumped into the back of the couch.

The bastard was playing with her. Not unexpected. If he terrorized her enough, he could break her down to her most basic instinct. Survival. A human could only endure so much before they surrendered.

But she'd come here prepared to endure a lot.

Where were the windows? Or the light switch? The sheer absence of sight and sound disorientated her. She needed to keep him talking.

"Tell me about the rule of threes." She moved on shaky legs, hopefully in the direction of the door.

"It takes three seconds to make a life-or-death

decision." His breath licked across her nape. "Three."

"You won't hurt me." She shivered, uncertain.

"Two."

"I'm not your enemy." She reached for the door, seeking light. Or momentary escape.

"One."

Her fingers caught the knob just as his hands clamped over her mouth and nose.

She bucked, fighting on instinct. She grabbed at his fingers and twisted, thrashing her body and going nowhere against the powerful strength of his.

Jesus fuck, he was huge and brawny and utterly immovable. She'd always pictured him as a gangly, pimple-faced, seventeen-year-old boy. But the beast who was restraining her and cutting off her oxygen was nothing short of terrifying.

Her frantic struggling bumped her back against a hard-muscled frame. A frame that towered over her by a foot. He stood like a concrete pillar behind her, no part of him jostling or shifting as she jerked and kicked and wore herself out.

"You can survive three minutes without air." The cadence of his timbre glided over her like velvet.

Three minutes? No fucking way. Maybe if she was unconscious. Even then, the asphyxiation could cause brain damage.

Her lungs burned, and her chest raged with fiery panic. Had it even been a minute?

She renewed her efforts to escape, flailing for air and trying to bite his hand.

"Two weeks ago, I watched my friend do this to a girl hanging on a meat hook." He adjusted his grip, pinching her nose while smothering her mouth. "She was innocent. Unlike you."

Tears leaked from her eyes and gathered at his fingers. She surpassed discomfort and denial and plummeted headlong into frenzied desperation. She was going to die, right here in the dark, in the arms of a man who never showed her his face. With each second that passed, she was certain it was her last.

"You can survive three hours in the extreme heat of a harsh environment." His stony voice penetrated her agony, torturing her dying heart. "Three days without water. Three weeks without food. Three months without hope." His lips brushed her ear. "Welcome to my world, Rylee from El Paso."

Her lungs gave out, and shadows crept in on all sides, raiding all conscious thought until nothing remained.

No bright light. No life flash. No euphoria.

Just an endless absence of being.

THREE

"Did you kill her?"

"Who fucking cares?" Tomas snarled into the phone and nudged the woman's limp body with his boot.

Calling Cole Hartman was the last thing he wanted to do, but he needed information. Who did she work for? What were her connections? Who would miss her? Why had she really come here?

The woman had an agenda, and she'd been diligent about not giving it away.

He needed Cole to do the investigative work, but when his friend answered the phone, the first thing Tomas asked was, *Are Luke and Vera alive?*

Last time he'd seen or heard from Luke was in the limo before the cartel had escorted Tomas off the property.

Not only had Luke and Vera survived, but apparently, she'd strapped herself with weapons, including a grenade, and taken down the whole fucking La Rocha family. Christ almighty, Tomas adored her. She was beautiful, ferocious, and the perfect match for Luke. Hearing that they were both safe in Colombia almost lifted his murderous mood.

Almost.

He grimaced at the brunette laid out on the floor. Killing her was the cleanest way to handle this, but first, he needed to know who she was.

When he'd received her email a week ago, he intended to hunt her down *before* she showed up here. But that plan was fucked to hell when the cartel forced him out of the limo at gunpoint. He'd found himself stranded in California without money, transportation, or an untraceable phone.

By the time he stole a car, stole another one when he ran out of gas, dumped the last car, and hiked the rest of the way to the house, he'd run out of time. With only a day to spare, he'd spent those hours preparing for the woman's arrival.

Electricity to the house was kept on to power the security cameras and satellite. The latter allowed him to contact Cole. But the moment he hiked out of range of the house, the outside world would be inaccessible.

That was ideal for what he had planned.

He couldn't kill her right away, and considering the seemingly harmless, but insidious manner in which she'd been spying on him for ten goddamn years, he knew it would take some effort to crack her.

So when she'd stopped breathing against his hand, he'd resuscitated her.

"Did you receive the photo I sent of her?" He swept his gaze over the unconscious body, ignoring all the sinful dips and curves and focusing on the fragile bones that would shatter beneath his fists.

"Yeah, I got it," Cole said. "She looks dead. Tell me she's not."

He crouched beside her and touched the pulse point on her throat. "She's not. For now."

"Listen up. If she has copies of your emails, you need her alive and compliant. Don't fuck this up. The lives of your entire team are on the line."

Of course, he fucking knew that. He'd made a mistake sending those emails. A horrendous, mortifying mistake that started when he was seventeen. He hadn't known any better then. But he couldn't use that excuse ten years later.

He *would* fix this.

"She's not carrying ID?" Cole asked.

"Nothing. I searched her pockets, her truck, and all the gear inside it. No phone. She even removed the license plates."

"She's smart."

"She doesn't look so smart now." He glared at her sulky lips which, just moments ago, had been sucking for air against his hand like a dying fish.

"Any tattoos, scars, or birthmarks?"

"None that I can see."

"You haven't stripped her yet?"

"I'm not a pervert."

"Right." Cole's disbelieving tone grated. "How long ago did you knock her out? She shouldn't still be unconscious."

"I gave her a sedative."

Cole didn't need to ask where the tranquilizer came from. When Tomas and his roommates sold their house in Austin, Texas and moved to the Restrepo headquarters in Colombia, he'd transferred their weapons, electronics, burner phones, and medical supplies here, along with nonperishables, bottled water, and petty cash. It had been Cole's idea. A precautionary measure to ensure the team had a safe house in Texas.

Tomas had enough equipment in this house to restrain and torture the woman for months.

"Okay, so next steps..." Cole exhaled into the phone. "I don't condone the kidnapping of innocent —"

"She trespassed on my property, willingly walked into my house, and she's far from innocent."

"She's guilty of invading your privacy. She hasn't killed anyone."

"That we know of. She has a cheating ex-husband." He updated Cole on everything she'd said when she walked in. "I don't know why she disclosed the details of the affair."

"I'll find out. Just stay put and keep her restrained."

"Where are you?"

"Almost there."

"What the fuck? No, turn back. You don't need to be here." Goddammit, he should've known Cole would show up. "I don't need a babysitter or anyone to clean up my mess. I just need information, and you can dig that up at the headquarters."

"I've been working with Luke and Tate for the past week trying to do just that. We scoured the IP addresses of all the activity on the email account. There's no forwarded mail. No suspicious logins. She knows how to erase her tracks."

"She's in law enforcement."

"Her email implied that, but it's not confirmed. I'll stop in El Paso to do some digging before heading your way. Might take me a few days. In the meantime—"

"I'll call you when she starts spilling secrets."

Tomas hung up, seething with frustration.

He couldn't stop Cole from coming to the house. But it didn't matter. His plan to break down Rylee piece by piece would begin out there. He turned toward the open door, sweating in the heat that blasted in from outside.

Four hours until sunset.

He spent the next few minutes unloading her truck. On his way back inside, he tore off his sweat-drenched shirt and checked her breathing.

The cuff on her wrist attached to a chain that restrained her to a post. But she wouldn't be waking any time soon.

He sat back on his heels and let himself fully look at her for the first time.

Long brown hair framed a pixie face. A tiny turned-up nose, cupid lips, and symmetrical features rounded out her delicate bone structure. Flawless porcelain skin and a toned physique gave her the appearance of a woman in her twenties. But she married twenty-three years ago? If that were true, Tomas would've been four at the time.

That would put her in her forties now. Hard to believe.

Maybe she had laugh lines when she smiled or crow's feet when she squinted. But with the muscles relaxed in her face, there were no wrinkles or sunspots. No indication that she was older than him.

Her tits sat high. Her waist tucked in, and her jeans molded to slender hips and legs, leaving little to the imagination. The woman was built. Easily fuckable.

Insanely gorgeous.

That only made him hate her more.

Shifting away, he turned his attention to the denim jacket that lay near the door. He remembered it well—the soft texture beneath his hands, the scent of vanilla on the collar, and the small front pocket, where he watched Caroline slip the scrap of paper he'd given her the day she died.

If he hadn't written down the account information, he wouldn't be in this mess. Hell, he should've never written down any of his secrets.

Not just his secrets. He'd spewed an unedited, unfiltered stream of consciousness in those emails. He'd detailed his fears, his regrets, every internal battle, every ridiculous notion in his head, every terrible thing that happened to him, and his desires... Fucking hell, she knew his darkest cravings, his filthy fantasies, his obsession with fucking and dominating and his inability to emotionally connect to sex.

He'd confessed every shameful thought to his girl. Because she was dead. He never imagined anyone reading it. Why would they want to?

What a dumb fucking asshole.

Except the writing had helped him. It had given him a sense of control over a life that had spiraled wildly and dangerously into chaos.

He lifted the jacket to his nose and inhaled deeply. Caroline's vanilla scent was long gone. In its place lingered the aroma of an unfamiliar woman. Undertones of lavender drowned in years of deceit.

He hated her with a blinding passion.

Fury burned anew as he stored the jacket safely in his old bedroom.

DOMINATE

Then he loaded the woman into the truck and drove her into the desert.

FOUR

Rylee woke with a hangover.

In the middle of the godforsaken desert.

The sun's unblinking eye glared down at her, scorching her from the inside out. Nausea, headache, crushing heat… She rolled to her stomach and retched precious fluid, groaning miserably.

Fresh pain seeped into her palms, where she'd planted them on the ground.

"Ow, ow, fuck!" She pushed to her knees and shook out her blazing hands.

The sand was the sky's co-conspirator, cooking her as viciously as the sun. And there were miles of it in every direction.

He hadn't just dumped her in this desolate wasteland alone.

He'd shackled her.

A thick leather cuff clamped around her wrist, secured with a tiny padlock. The ring connected to a chain that snaked through the sand and circled the base of an old telephone pole.

From one horizon to the other, that pole was the only sign of human civilization.

Deep cracks forked through the parched earth beneath her, burnt into a hard crust, no more hospitable than a sunbaked rock. If Tommy had driven her here in her truck, the tires had made no impression on the ground.

She felt sick. Aside from her churning stomach, dusty throat, pounding headache, achy muscles, and feverish flu-like symptoms, she was frying in this heat, and that worried her more than anything.

How far would he take this?

She remembered dying. Suffocating beneath his hand. Had he killed her and revived her?

Would he kill her again?

Consumed with panic, she stumbled to her feet and jerked uselessly on the chain. The desert stretched out around her, tufted with shrubs and punctuated with small boulders and tall columns of cacti.

Black vultures circled overhead, eying her like carrion. Reptiles sought shelter in the shadows of the rocks where the sand wouldn't roast them. There was no shade close enough nor large enough to protect her. No water. No breeze. Not a cloud in the sky to filter the harsh rays.

Each searing breath sank into her lungs, drowning her chest in lava.

"You fucking prick! Where are you?" Her scream echoed across the barren terrain. "This isn't how an adult faces his problems. You're a goddamn coward!"

She didn't believe that. A coward would've left her for dead. While he seemed to be doing precisely that, he wouldn't have gone through this trouble after asphyxiating her. What was his plan?

The rule of threes.

She cast her mind back to their ominous conversation, recalling the first and only words he'd spoken to her.

Three seconds to make a life-or-death decision.

Three minutes without air.

Three hours in extreme heat.

Three days without water.

Three weeks without food.

Three months without hope.

Dread swelled, as thick and hot as the air.

He'd already enacted the first two. And now...

"Three hours in extreme heat." She gripped her lurching stomach and fought back tears. "Three fucking hours of this? Are you kidding me?"

She couldn't even think about the remaining rules. First, she had to survive the relentless sun.

How long had she been out here?

Pressing a finger against her forearm, she watched the indentation flash from white to pink. Her skin didn't appear to be burnt. Yet.

She'd arrived at his house with maybe four or five hours left of daylight. Would he leave her out here until dusk? Or all night? Shackled and unprotected?

Predators came out after dark. If she didn't perish from sun-poisoning, she'd make an easy meal for a coyote or snake.

Tommy had done some stomach-turning shit over the years. He'd killed people. Evil people. But he wasn't cruel enough to let her die like this.

The sun perched too high in the sky, but maybe it

was an illusion. Maybe dusk was only an hour away. She could make it until then. She had no choice.

Sitting with her back to the pole, she lowered her head to her bent knees and adjusted her hair to cover her face, neck, and bare arms. Her jeans and boots should protect the rest of her.

The danger lurked in the unrelenting heat. What was the lethal temperature to the human body? How long could she survive out here?

Tommy seemed to think the limit was three hours. But she wasn't a hardened, outdoorsy girl. She camped infrequently and always in campgrounds with shade and running water.

God, she needed water. Her throat felt so raw and sandy it hurt to swallow.

She hated him for this. It was unnecessarily cruel and inhumane. But her clinical mind tried to analyze his behavior from an unbiased angle.

He'd witnessed and experienced the worst of human depravity. The torture he'd endured and inflicted on others had desensitized him. She remembered a story about how his team had injected a man with Krokodil, a flesh-eating cocktail that rotted the skin off the bones while he was still alive.

In Tommy's world, brutality and death were as common as nightfall.

He'd been separated from gentle affection and normalcy for so long he'd lost sight of what normal looked like. He could camouflage himself in society, but he would have to undergo a great deal of therapy and self-help to create a lasting positive change. Especially if he ever wanted to engage in a healthy romantic relationship.

She didn't judge him for his psychological shortfalls. She had her own litany of issues. But she would never do something so ruthless as chaining a person in the desert, even if her issues were the reason she was in this predicament in the first place.

Time passed in a blistering haze. She held still within the dark curtain of her hair, sweating in the oven of her clothes. With each second, the withered shag of the earth blurred into a weird, dehumanized hue. Neither taupe nor gray nor sandy brown, the land was the color of death, reflecting back at her.

She tried to keep her spirits up, giving herself pep talks and tracking the descent of the sun. But her nemesis barely moved, its everlasting rays blasting down on her, diminishing her morale.

Salty sweat rolled off her brow and stung her eyes, her clothes unbearably hot and sticky. Gritty sand worked its way into her hair and mouth and coated her tongue with stiff fur. She avoided licking her lips, knowing it would only chap them further.

God, she ached for crystal, cold water. The thought tormented her until she became mad with the craving.

Unbidden, she wet her lips and tasted… *Strange.* She did it again, flooding her mouth with a chemical flavor.

Wiping at the perspiration around her eyes, she held up her hand and stared at a milky residue. Was her facial lotion melting? It should've rubbed off hours ago.

She raised an arm to her mouth and licked. Same chemical taste.

Her heart hammered as she ran her hands over her face and neck. She hadn't noticed it before, but there was definitely a thick layer of cream on her skin.

He'd lathered her with sunscreen.

Oh, Tommy, you miserable, thoughtful, misguided man.

He'd probably done it as an afterthought, telling himself he didn't want to deal with a blistered body. Misguided reasoning, to be sure.

But she remembered the outpouring of devotion and selflessness in the words of the teenage boy before his abduction. He loved a girl with all his heart. He loved his mother and respected the life she'd given him. Following their unimaginable deaths, he'd remained steadfast, never veering into substance abuse or self-destruction. That kind of inner strength didn't just go away. It was innate, sewn into the fabric of his being.

It gave her hope.

A gentle breeze stirred up the wispy sand and brushed across her skin like drafts from a fire. There was no escape from the hellacious temperature. It sat heavily on her chest, making every breath an exhausting effort.

Gradually, the heat chased her into a fitful slumber. Each time she woke, she felt disoriented and confused. In and out of sleep, she fumbled between reality and hallucination until everything smeared together, plunging her into a nebulous hinterland.

At some point, the fog lifted, as did the torrential heat. She rubbed her eyes, drowsy and weak, squinting in the dark.

Twilight had arrived in the desert. The huge, pale moon rose over the edge of the desolate landscape, its beams falling on the murky outline of a vehicle.

Her truck.

It parked several yards away, pointed in the opposite direction.

Her heart pounded, and her skin shivered, for

perched on the open tailgate was the silhouette of a man.

A cowboy hat angled low on his brow, casting his face in shadow. But it didn't hide the bristling tension surrounding him nor the rage in his unmitigated stare, burning as hot as the Texan sun.

Tommy hadn't left her for dead, but she might wish for that before he was done with her.

FIVE

Rylee lay on her side, her hair stuck to her face and stiff with sand. As she slowly rose to sit, her head swam with fuzz. Dehydration. But her arm was free. Tommy had removed the cuff.

He lifted a water bottle to his lips and drank deeply, watching her, taunting her.

She followed the movement of his throat with longing, swishing her tongue in her mouth, trying to gather moisture where there was none.

"I need water," she croaked, her voice covered in dust.

The plastic crinkled in his hand, and he tossed the empty bottle in the truck bed behind him.

"You think I can survive out here for three days without water?" Her anger fired on all cylinders as she attempted to stand. "Is this my punishment for reading your emails?" Her legs gave out, sending her back to the prickly earth. "Fucking harsh, don't you think?"

He stretched out along the tailgate, crossed his

cowboy boots at the ankles, and reclined against the side of the truck bed.

Hard to make out his form in the blackness of night, but there was something about his presence that intrigued and allured. Maybe it was his brooding silence. Or the cocksure tilt of his hat. Or the dark, intimidating confidence that radiated from his posture.

Whatever it was, she had no business admiring him with female appreciation. She wasn't here for that. Besides, the motherfucker had just put her through ungodly hell, and he wasn't finished.

"You're going to regret this someday." She ran her hands over her hair and clothes, attempting to put herself back together. "I know you're ruthless, but you've never harmed an innocent woman. I'm no one, Tommy. I'm sure as hell not your enemy."

"Tell me your full name and date of birth." His gravelly voice rumbled from the shadow of his hat as he produced another bottle of water and set it beside him.

So this was his plan. Take away the basic requirements for survival and dangle them piece by piece as a trade for information.

"What did you do while I roasted in the desert for the past three hours?" she asked. "Did you contact Cole to initiate an investigation on me?"

As expected, he gave no answer.

All they had to go on was her first name and the city where she grew up. There were a lot of Rylees in El Paso. It would take time to identify her and those she cared about.

She had an ex-husband who never remarried and a neighbor with benefits. That was the extent of her liabilities.

But the moment he learned her occupation, address, and boring background, the mystery would be over. He would send her home with a threat to kill her loved ones if she ever leaked information about him. Then he would disappear forever.

That outcome was inevitable, but before that happened, she had a desperate, reckless need to help him.

She cared about him. Deeply. It was a one-sided sentiment, a motivation he couldn't possibly understand because he didn't know her the way she knew him.

He wasn't happy. Not today, not last week, not one second in the past ten years. His friends, the family of ex-captives who had his back, didn't know the extent of his suffering. He concealed it from them because he didn't want to be a burden. He didn't even know how to open up to someone. For a decade, he carried around a terrible weight in his soul, confiding in no one. Except a dead girl.

That in and of itself troubled her.

After his abduction, he lived with his vigilante team. But over the years, his roommates found partners, some of them married, and the dynamics of their tight-knit clan changed. They were moving on.

Unless something changed since his last email, he and Luke were the only bachelors left.

"What happened with the cartel?" She squinted at his shadow, unable to see his eyes in the dark.

Silence.

Exasperated, she glanced around and spotted a black smudge on the ground several feet away. She crawled toward it, marveling at how quickly the sand had already cooled.

"I assume the cartel bought your undercover story? Either that or you escaped." She focused on the dark object and quickened her movements when she realized it was her backpack. "Where's Luke?"

She pulled the pack onto her lap and dug through the contents while watching him out of the corner of her eye. His silhouette didn't twitch. No sound. No attempt to take away her belongings.

It occurred to her that his undercover operation might've gone terribly wrong. They went in to find Tula's sister. Tula, who had fallen in love with Martin and Ricky during a mission in a Mexican prison.

What if Luke hadn't made it out of the cartel headquarters? What if he'd been forced to kill Vera, Tula's sister?

"You said your friend killed an innocent girl on a meat hook." She shivered, her voice wavering. "Tommy? Is Luke okay? And Vera? Please, you have to tell me."

"Why the fuck do you care?"

Her pulse skipped at the sound of his voice. "I'm invested. For ten years—"

"You've been collecting intel on my team. Tell me what you're doing with that information."

"Nothing."

"Bullshit."

"You needed someone to hear you. So I listened. Through every word, no matter how uncomfortable or horrifying, I silently supported you, rooted for you and your friends. I'm still doing that. It's the *only* reason I'm here."

"You're a liar."

"I speak the truth. You're just not ready to hear it."

She took an inventory of the supplies in her pack.

Some of her belongings were here. The first-aid kit. Sunscreen. Extra clothes. But he'd removed the rest, the things she needed most, such as water, food, weapons, maps, and the compass.

But he'd left the small lantern and its solar-powered charger. She grabbed it, turned it on, and wobbled to her feet.

Thirst was her loudest ache. It screamed from her stomach and clouded her head. Fatigue and fear followed closely behind, making every step to the truck feel like a mile.

The lantern's dim light helped her navigate the uneven terrain. She didn't have a plan beyond the imperative to be in that vehicle when it left.

Halfway there, a startling, ear-splitting bang ricocheted through her skull. Gravel sprayed beside her boots, and she screamed, staggering backward and falling on her butt.

For a moment, she thought he'd shot her. But the sudden pain in her chest was just her heart ramming against her ribs.

"Have you lost your mind?" she roared, swinging the lantern toward him. "If you don't want me to approach, use your fucking words, not a—"

The light snagged on a long, scaly body beside her. Four feet in length, a diamondback rattlesnake lay unmoving, bleeding from the head.

"Oh, my God." She scrambled to her feet, tripping over a deep crack to get away from it. "Fucking shit. Fuck, fuck, fuck."

Her breathing rampaged as full-body tremors robbed her balance. That venomous thing had been right next to her! And he'd shot it with impossible accuracy.

He'd saved her life.

Maybe she should thank him.

Should she thank him for chaining her in the desert, too?

Fuck that.

"Where's my shotgun?" She thrust the lantern out before her.

"Afraid of snakes?"

"Well, I'm not fucking friends with them."

"Who are you friends with?"

"Just you, as crazy as that sounds." She staggered the remaining few paces to the tailgate.

"You're a stranger. That's a long way from *friend*."

"Give me my shotgun."

"So you can shoot me?"

"So I can defend myself against things like that." She pointed at the dead snake.

"No." He hadn't shifted from his sprawled position, the hat still dipping over his eyes. But a handgun now rested on his lap.

He didn't move the gun or the water out of her reach. But she wasn't stupid. If she went for either, he would stop her, and he wouldn't be gentle about it.

Instead, she focused on the view.

The lantern's glow picked out the contoured muscles of his legs and accentuated his trim waist, V-shaped torso, and broad shoulders. Sun-bronzed skin sheathed his biceps and forearms, emphasizing the flex of sinewy strength.

He wore snug jeans, a faded t-shirt, and the rugged hat and boots. The shirt rode up, and the denim rode low, drawing her gaze to the thin strip of brown hair that disappeared beneath his fly.

She swallowed hard and moved the light higher, capturing the arrogant cut of his jaw, the bold line of his nose, and the cruel taunt of chiseled lips.

As fate would have it, he was astoundingly, inconceivably gorgeous. Even with his face etched in godlike fury, he was the most beautiful man she'd ever seen. But she wasn't besotted into thinking that was all he was.

This virile, handsome devil was a dangerous vigilante and killer. He was also a sexual deviant, a kinky freak with an insatiable appetite, who'd lured hundreds of unsuspecting women into his bed.

He'd written about his explorations, and she'd devoured the tantalizing words with flushed cheeks and quivering breaths. She'd also noticed a disturbing progression of depravity over the years, his cravings growing darker, bolder, more painful, veering into dubious territory.

She wasn't a guileless victim. But she was curious enough to slowly reach out and lift the brim of his cowboy hat.

Their stares caught and held, transfixed as the atmosphere shuddered between them. Crackling energy. Red-hot voltage. She felt it everywhere, curling fingers of warmth into parts of her he would never physically touch. He would never try because what she saw in the depths of his gaze was enough to know that he despised her with every jagged shard of his soul.

She'd always been told she had silver eyes. They just looked colorless and gray to her. But his eyes were like that of a tiger, shimmering in hues of molten metallic gold.

They dipped, as though he couldn't help himself,

to chase the rise and fall of her breasts. When they returned, she was once again imprisoned in the magnetic beauty of his face.

From the clean, soapy scent wafting off him and the spotless appearance of his clothes, she assumed he hadn't spent the past few hours in the desert heat like she had. A small part of her had hoped he'd been watching her from afar, growing sick with guilt over what he'd done to her.

But the formidable man who reclined on her tailgate didn't care about her wellbeing. Instead, he glared at her like a stranger he wanted to murder.

"Tell me who you are, and this ends now." The dangerous, silky tone of his words cut through the dense night air.

"You hate lies and insincerity because it goes against everything you believe." She licked her chapped lips and rested a hip against the tailgate near his legs. "I'm known for my ability to keep secrets. It's a fault, really. Foolish, most times. Because I'll keep the truth to myself just to protect someone else's feelings."

"I don't need anyone to protect my fucking feelings."

"I'm not." She held his impatient gaze. "I'm telling you who I am."

"That's—"

"You have an incredible heart and are always willing to help your friends and even people you don't know, like all those innocent, enslaved girls. My heart, on the other hand, is subtle. I don't show it or share it with anyone. Not anymore."

Grabbing the gun and the water, he sat up, swung his powerfully muscled legs off the tailgate, and stood.

Scowling down at her, he looked alarmingly tall, horrifyingly lethal, and unapologetically mean.

He was going to leave.

Without her.

She dropped the lantern and ran. Around the truck and to the driver's door, she yanked it open and threw herself behind the steering wheel. The keys, her gun, water, food… She frantically searched the cab for something, anything that could save her.

Until a fist caught her hair and wrenched her out of the truck.

He tossed the water onto the seat and shoved the gun under her chin. "If you move, I'll shoot and deal with the fallout of your copied emails. That option is shaking out to be a whole lot easier than playing your games."

"This isn't a game." Her chin lifted above the press of the barrel. "I've known you for ten years, dammit. You're important to me."

He snarled and shoved her away with enough force to send her stumbling onto her back. Sharp rocks broke her fall, and she cried out in pain and frustration.

By the time she hobbled to her feet, he was already in the truck with the engine running.

"Don't leave me." She ran to the window and flattened a palm against the glass while yanking on the locked door. "Please, Tommy. I'm not tough or outdoorsy or equipped for this. I don't know how to survive out here."

He gripped the wheel and stared straight ahead, his jaw carved in stone.

"I won't make it through the night. I need water and…" She lurched toward the back of the truck, keeping her hands on the metal side as if that could stop him wrenching away her lifeline.

A quick scan of the truck bed confirmed her supply of water had been removed. Flooded with fear, she pushed up to climb in.

He hit the gas. The tires spun up sand, and the vehicle bolted forward. She tried to hang on, but her fingers lost purchase, her palms sliding off the edge as he sped away.

"Tommy! Don't leave!" She chased him, pumping her legs, heaving for air, and running as fast as she was physically able.

Until she twisted her ankle on a rock.

"Fuck!" A sob rose up, but she pushed through the agony, her eyes bleeding hot tears. "Tommy, wait! Don't leave me. Please, don't leave me."

She sprinted as the sound of the engine faded. She kept moving, limping, long after the taillights vanished over the hill. Then she fell.

Alone.

No water.

No food.

In the desert.

Three days.

She was fucked.

Rolling to her back, she lay in the sand and cried. The moon watched, pitiless, as she mourned her situation and every miserable second leading up to it.

He could've listened to her. Interrogated her. Tried to get to know her beyond a name and date of birth.

Instead, he chose to let her die.

He'd made his decision.

It hurt. Fucking hell, it hurt deep in her soul. But

she'd put herself here. She'd known the risks.

She'd expected too much from him. The man who poured his heart into his emails kept those feelings close. He didn't open up to his closest friends. Why did she think he'd open up to a stranger?

He hadn't given her enough time. Or maybe she'd said the wrong things. Either way, she'd let herself get hurt.

Again.

There was no romantic attachment this time. No broken heart. But she'd allowed pieces of herself to get involved with a man she'd never met.

Even when she closed herself off, she became attached. She was impulsive. Careless with her life. Stuck in a vicious cycle. *Attachment, pain, death, repeat.*

It didn't have to end in death.

Ten years ago, she'd walked off that bridge when it seemed impossible.

Could she walk out of this desert in three days? Without water? Without a map? With no sense of direction?

Impossible.

But if she traveled at night and found shade during the day, maybe?

It wasn't an impossible decision. She could lie here and die. Or she could try.

Rising to her feet, she hobbled back to the telephone pole. The pain in her ankle dulled by the time she gathered the lantern and the rest of her measly supplies.

The truck had headed west. There lay more desert. A black, undulating sea of sand at night. Vast and lonely, with its excruciating heat looming on the horizon.

She started walking.

SIX

Away to the west, the sun sank toward the unreachable edge of the desert. Dusk was approaching for the third time since Rylee had arrived.

Listless, she lay on her stomach at the rear of a narrow cave, her cheek pressing against the cool limestone bedrock. She might as well have been shackled. Exhaustion, heat, and extreme thirst had held her in the same position since dawn.

If she hadn't found this dark hole last night, she would already be dead.

By her estimation, it had been fifty-three hours since she had food or water.

Fifty-one hours in the desert.

Two full days and nights.

It occurred to her that she'd never truly been thirsty until now. It was an agony like she'd never known. Her skull squeezed around a banging, inconsolable migraine. She couldn't produce saliva or tears. Her throat was so raw it felt as though the lining had been flayed and stretched out in the sun to dry.

In normal conditions, she could've lasted much longer without drinking. But the boiling heat had cut her survival rate in half.

It tormented her until all she could focus on was finding something cool to relieve her suffering. She'd spent the first night and the next day wandering the desert scrublands, searching for a puddle, discarded bottle, underground cave, anything that might contain a drop of liquid.

No luck.

She'd heard of survivalists drinking their urine. By the time she'd reached that level of desperation, she had nothing left in her body to excrete.

To escape the heat, she'd holed up in the cave all day and thought of nothing but the taste of water. Sparkling, flavored, natural spring, ice jangling, with little rivulets of condensation running down the sides. She'd give anything for a cool sip. Even a splash of hot, stagnant water would be a godsend.

Now that the sun was setting, the urge to venture out of the cave and find liquid dominated her mind. She didn't know how far she'd already walked or how close she'd come to civilization. Everything looked the same, from the towering buttes and dry ravines to the pattern of stars overhead. For all she knew, she'd been roaming in circles.

As she lay there, ordering her boneless limbs to move, a noise sounded in the distance. Her heart took off at a gallop, and her head shot up, pounding with the boom of her pulse.

She tried to listen past the cacophony of her aches. Then she heard it. The undeniable purr of an engine, growing louder, closer.

Digging her elbows into the dirt, she crawled through the narrow space and dragged her pack behind her. When she reached the mouth of the cave, she squinted into the fading light.

There, on the hazy horizon, two headlights bobbed along the bumpy terrain.

She didn't have three seconds to make a life-or-death decision. Frantic to be seen, she grabbed the lantern from where it'd charged in the sun, flicked it on, and thrust it into the air.

Her arm shook with the effort, her body too weak to run.

"Help!" She crawled, stumbled a few steps on her feet, tripped, and crawled again. "Help me! Here! Please, help!"

Her voice had no strength, coughing and hacking with disuse. But the motorist seemed to see her, making a beeline in her direction. She didn't care if it was Tommy or Hannibal Fucking Lecter. If she didn't get water soon, she was dead anyway.

The vehicle slowed, stopping some fifty feet away. As the dust settled around the tires, she made out the silver paint and the silhouette of a cowboy hat inside.

Tommy had stolen her truck again.

Rage warred with desperation. If he'd come to help her, she'd let him without hesitation. But her amicability was long gone. She had a thing about grudges, as in when she held onto one, she held onto it forever.

He'd hurt her irreparably, thereby destroying any concern she'd felt toward him. She no longer wished to help him. She wanted to forget the last ten years and just go home.

Dropping the lantern, she centered all her energy on dragging her legs beneath her to stand. It required more strength than she had, but she did it. Eyes on the truck, she swayed, floundered, and slowly staggered forward.

The passenger-side door opened, and she realized he wasn't alone.

A man stepped out.

No, he was shoved.

His hands waved around as he yelled, trying to right his balance.

What was he saying? Who was he? Why was he shirtless? She couldn't see his face at this distance, but he sounded pissed off.

She quickened her tottering steps, picking over rocks and slanted earth. It was all she could do to remain upright.

"Tommy." She tried to raise her voice. "Tommy!"

Goddammit, she needed help. It was too far to walk. She'd never make it.

The man shouted something and charged toward the truck.

A shot fired, and she faltered.

More shots followed, each pelleting the sand around the man's feet. He reeled backward, dancing around the bullets and screaming.

Tommy shot at him twice more, deliberately missing. Then he yanked the door shut and spun the truck around, facing in the direction he'd come.

"No! Wait!" She shrieked at the top of her lungs, pushing her legs faster, trying to close the distance. "Don't you fucking leave me! Please! I'm begging you!"

He drove off, taking his time around the ruts in the

ground, knowing she'd never catch up.

Bursts of dizzying light blotted her vision, smeared with tears and the unshakable pain behind her eyes. Her knees gave out, hitting the ground with crushing agony. She collapsed, catching herself on elbows and fists.

He was gone.

And he'd left her with a stranger whose life meant as little to him as hers.

The man charged toward her, his hands balled at his sides and his unrecognizable face twisted in a snarl.

"How do you know that crazy motherfucker?" He stopped beside her, kicking up dust in her eyes.

"Do you have water?" She coughed, her throat so sore it felt as though it were bleeding. "Anything to drink?"

"Yeah, I'm carrying a jug in my back pocket." He spat a wad of saliva next to his leather loafers. "No, I don't fucking have water. He stripped me down and took everything, including my goddamn shirt."

"No food? Nothing?"

He huffed and gripped the back of his neck, looking around.

They were both dead.

Her stomach clamped around a gnawing knot, and she rolled to her back, staring up at him through a blur of pain.

Blood trickled from the tight black curls that covered his head. More rivers of red ran from gashes around his eyes, mouth, and bare chest. Suit pants clung to his legs, smudged with dust and ripped at the knee.

"How do *you* know him?" She pushed herself to a sitting position, woozy and unsteady.

"I don't."

"Then why did he beat you up and leave you in the desert?"

His eyes crinkled, squinting as he studied her. "Something doesn't add up."

She couldn't guess what he was thinking, but Tommy didn't throw punches without reason. This man must've threatened him, trespassed on his property, or endangered his friends. Whoever the man was, Tommy considered him an enemy, just like her.

He was average size and build, if not a little stocky and soft around the middle. A few years younger than her. Maybe late-thirties. His eyes sat a bit too far apart, but most women would probably find his looks adequate.

She found him completely unfamiliar. "You seem to know me, but I don't know you."

"Where are we?" He spun around, scanning the desert in all directions. "Which way is out?"

"You tell me. You just rode in from somewhere."

"He tied my hands and blindfolded me. He removed that shit right before he kicked me out of the truck." His tongue darted out, licking the blood on his lip. "How did you locate the tracker?"

"What?"

"The tracking device on your truck. Did you know it was there? Or did he find it?"

"Why is there a tracker on my truck?" Her heart rate hit a breakneck speed, thudding in her throat. "Who put it there?"

What had she gotten herself into? Tommy didn't even know she existed a week ago. How would he have been able to find her and arrange to have her tracked?

He wouldn't. But he'd know how to spot that sort

of device if he was looking for it.

"*You* put it there." Suddenly wary, she crab-walked backward and scrambled to her feet. "Why? Who the fuck are you?"

"You have no idea, do you?" He clicked his tongue. "Fucking clueless."

"Start talking." She shoved back her shoulders, and the world spun. She braced her legs, and they buckled out from under her, sending her back to the ground with her cheek in the sand. "Fuck!"

He stepped toward her.

"Don't come near me!" She shoved out a hand as if she had the strength to fight him off.

"You've been out here for two days." He crossed his arms over his chest. "Might as well tell me who that man is. Seems he wants you dead more than I do."

He knew how long she'd been here?

Because he'd been tracking her.

"Why do you want me dead?" A chill swept through her bones.

"Didn't say I did." He pivoted and strode toward the cave.

"What are you doing?"

"Getting the hell out of this desert." He snatched her pack and slung it over his shoulder. "Fuck this shit. No job is worth dying for."

"Job?" Her words slurred, her brain chugging on sputtering fumes. "Someone paid you to put a tracker on my truck?"

"Sweetheart, I've been monitoring you for six months." He prowled back to her, pausing just out of reach. "It's been a pleasure watching your sexy ass through my binoculars. Hell, even hours from death, you look good enough to eat."

Dread sank in with the implication of his words. If he wanted to attack her, she wouldn't be able to stop him. She couldn't even lift her head from the dirt.

"What's your name?" Every sound she made caused her pain, every thought an excruciating effort.

"Paul."

"I assume you know my name."

"I know everything about you, Rylee Catherine Sutton."

Not everything. He didn't know how she was connected to Tommy.

"Who paid you to watch me?"

"Someone who is obsessed with every detail of your life—what you eat, where you go, who you talk to, and most of all, who you're banging."

The words bounced around in her head, jumbling into nonsensical mush. She couldn't think past the declining state of her body.

"Who hired you?" she asked again.

"Who are your enemies?"

Tommy. His friends. Maybe one of them had discovered her six months ago and was working behind Tommy's back to learn who she was. It was the only answer that fit.

"Give me a name," she said.

"My contracts are anonymous, and even if I knew, I wouldn't tell you."

She pressed a finger against her pounding temple. There was one aspirin left in the first-aid kit. She wouldn't be able to swallow it, but if it sat in the back of her throat, maybe it would melt.

"Give me my pack." She held out a trembling

hand.

"Can't do that." He glanced at the vast wasteland behind him and turned back, grimacing. "I'd carry you, but it'll slow me down. You're as good as dead anyway."

She dropped her hand, unable to fight or stand or do anything but watch him amble away.

Whatever information he had on her would be useless after she was dead. He was a mystery that would go unsolved, because as she lay there, staring at his retreating form, she suspected he wouldn't make it out of the desert alive.

SEVEN

Rylee woke on her stomach with her face in the prickly sand. The nighttime air spread goosebumps across her arms. But the sky was warming, paling into shades of pink and gray.

She'd made it through another night.

And she wasn't alone.

Hot breath brushed along her spine. Hands gripped the hem of her shirt, lifting the cotton up her torso.

With a gasp, she jerked and tried to roll. But a heavy body came down on her back, pinning her in the dirt.

"Stop." She wheezed, clawing at loose rocks and tufts of plant growth, her voice hoarse, barely a whisper. "Get off me."

"I've been walking around all night," a masculine voice rasped at her ear, "trying to find my way out." A hand wedged beneath her hips and yanked open the fly of her jeans. "Trying not to think about your sweet cunt."

"Paul…" Fear raged through her veins, but her body refused to respond. It couldn't. It had used the last of its energy just keeping her heart beating. "Don't do this."

"For six months, I've wanted nothing more than to do this." He ground his erection against her backside. "If I'm going to die out here, I'm going to satisfy this fucking infatuation once and for all."

"No! You can't!" Despite her terror, she remained calm enough to scan the dirt beneath her face, her fingers digging through the sand, searching for a small rock.

"I can."

"I'm filthy."

"Damn straight, you're filthy. I've watched you fuck your neighbor on the back porch, in your car, and on every surface in your house. Seeing a woman take it in the ass does something to a man. Christ, you don't even know how fucking hot you are."

He'd invaded her privacy. If she had it in her, she might've laughed.

Wasn't Karma a vindictive bitch?

Maybe she deserved to be spied on, but she didn't deserve to spend the last minutes of her life being raped.

He lifted his hips and yanked her jeans and underwear to her knees. Her heart stopped, and her fingers latched onto a skinny stone with a jagged edge. She fisted it and rolled to her back.

With his gaze locked on the exposed apex of her legs, he didn't see her hand moving until it was too late.

She stabbed the rock into his eye.

Direct hit. But not enough strength. Instead of blood, she got his seething, roaring rage.

"Stupid bitch!" He clapped a hand over his eye and

smacked the rock from her grip. "You're going to pay for that."

Teeth bared, he rose up and wrenched her jeans past her knees.

She kicked her legs and slapped at his face, but the struggle was clumsy and ineffective. She couldn't stop him from opening his pants and crawling between her thighs.

He gripped her throat and flashed a manic smile. "Your cunt is mine."

His face blurred, fading with the deprivation of air. Darkness closed in, and a loud ringing sounded in her ears.

Then a boom.

Paul's head exploded, spraying the sky with blood, bits of bone, and brain matter.

He toppled to the side, and the pressure released from her throat.

Stunned, she gulped for oxygen, gripped her neck, and snapped her gaze toward the gray horizon, searching for the threat.

Someone had shot him. Killed him. Was it Tommy? Or the person who'd hired Paul?

She whimpered, heaving frenzied breaths, and fumbled to pull up her jeans.

The rev of an engine approached.

Splattered in blood and scared out of her mind, she moved. Muscle memory took over, her limbs bending and dragging her body across the sand.

The cave. She could hide in the narrow hole.

Tires crunched behind her, shoving her panic into the red zone. Her vision began to fade, but she could still hear.

Footsteps.

A slow gait.

Chasing her.

"Please." She cried, crawling on her stomach, desperate to get away. "Please, don't."

She didn't know when she'd stopped moving, but her arms wouldn't work anymore. She continued to fight, mentally reaching for the cave, willing herself to become invisible.

Hands gripped her back and legs, and she flinched, crying harder. Arms lifted her, and she glimpsed a whiskered jaw. A flash of light brown hair.

Her eyes shut, her face pressed against a warm neck. "Tommy?"

He was walking, the sand grinding noisily beneath his steps. But his breaths were louder, sawing in and out next to her ear.

"Hate you." Her limbs weighed a thousand pounds. Everything hurt.

He laid her on a soft bench seat, and she blinked, trying to adjust her foggy vision.

A dashboard. Air vents. Condensation. Beads of it clinging to the plastic. She was in her truck.

Reaching out, she tried to collect those precious drops. But her movements were uncoordinated, the effort too great.

He bent over her, his body heat invading, too close, too much.

Until a trickle of water ran over her lips. The incredible taste startled her. She choked, lapped at it greedily, and tried to grab the source.

He yanked the bottle away and tossed it into the back of the truck.

"Please. Need more." She was fading. Dying. He slammed the door shut.

EIGHT

The woman passed out. Just as well. Tomas was in no mood to listen to her crying.

The risks he'd taken with her life had been necessary. Not everyone would see it that way, but when it came to his friends, he would accept their anger and disappointment over needlessly putting their lives in harm's way.

Rylee Sutton was a threat. Well, she *had been* a threat. Now he didn't know what she was.

Most people wouldn't last a day out here. The fact that she'd survived without his interference was shocking. He'd watched her like a hawk and skipped sleep, waiting for her to give up or do something stupid like fall into a nest of rattlesnakes.

With the windows rolled down, he navigated her truck across the uneven terrain, holding her head on his lap to prevent it from bouncing.

Sand and blood stiffened her hair, her clothes saturated in grime. Her complexion was too pale for this

climate, ephemeral beyond any hope of tanning. Yet the
smooth alabaster glow complimented her dark lashes,
wing-tipped brows, and long hair. Wild ribbons of brown
hung past her breasts, the color as rich and variegated as
spalted sweetgum.

Her nose was too delicate, her bones too slender,
and her cheeks too silky to have been exposed to the
harsh sun. And her mouth… Those lips were far too
pouty for his liking. They made a man want to taste and
bruise and test how far they stretched around a hungry
cock.

Underneath the gore and desert grit, she was
outrageously beautiful. A goddamn knockout.

And when she was at her weakest, he'd left her
alone with a rapist.

"Fuck!" He slammed a hand against the steering
wheel, boiling with anger.

At himself.

At the bastard who'd touched her.

At the fucking shitstorm that had blown into his
life.

For the next thirty miles, he forced his eyes on the
unpaved wasteland, trying to ignore the guilt and
resentment that rode him.

When his childhood home finally came into view,
he approached slowly, surveying the property for
intruders. Everything appeared in order. Except…

Motherfucker.

A motorcycle sat around the side of the house. Not
the sporty, rubber-burning kind that Luke rode. No, this
beast was throaty and heavy, made for long hauls on
desolate roads. He only knew one guy who was arrogant
enough to take an iconic Harley off-road in the desert.

As he parked the truck, the front door opened. Cole Hartman stepped out and leaned against the door frame, tattooed arms folded across his chest and eyes stony in the twilight.

Every time Tomas saw him, the man had more ink on his skin and hair on his face. He looked hard around the edges, fearsome even, like a one-percenter in an outlaw motorcycle club.

"I turned on the air-conditioning in the house." Cole stalked toward him. "I don't know how you can stand this fucking heat."

"I told you not to come." He rolled up the windows and stepped out.

Cole tilted his head, and when he caught a glimpse of the unconscious cargo, his nostrils stiffened. The cords in his neck protruded, and his face turned red above the beard. "What the fuck did you do?

"Tested her." He strode around to the other side and dragged her out.

"Tested her how exactly? She looks more dead now than she did in the photo you sent."

"Here's an idea. Instead of standing around like a smacked ass, make yourself useful." He cradled her against his chest and shoved past Cole. "Grab a couple of bags of sodium chloride from the bunker."

"She's covered in blood."

"Hadn't noticed." He carried her into the house, and the sudden cold air shot a chill through him. Pausing at the control box on the wall, he raised the temperature. "Don't fuck with the thermostat."

"You've gone off the fucking rails, Tomas."

"The IV drip, Cole. I need it yesterday."

The bunker beneath the house maintained a mild

temperature year-round. It was where they kept all the medical supplies and anything that might perish in the heat.

Cole grunted and treaded toward the interior door that led underground. Tomas headed to his old bedroom.

The bed was narrow like the room, but he had everything he needed to bring her back to life. Settling her on the mattress, he gave her limp body a quick perusal, probing for injuries he might've missed.

Minor scratches and bruises marred her fair skin. No deep gashes or burns. She'd used the sunscreen and kept to the shade when she could.

Blood streaked her face and arms, her shirt soaked and clinging to her firm little tits.

She needed a bath. But fluids first.

Using the supplies he'd already laid out, he cleaned her arm, washed his hands, and prepped the IV tubing and equipment.

When the sound of heavy boots entered the room, Tomas kept his gaze on his task. "What did you find on Paul Kissinger?"

"Nothing yet." Cole handed over two bags of sodium chloride. "He returned to her house yesterday morning, snooping around. Then he left Eldorado and dropped out of signal range. Did he show up here?"

"He tried to rape her."

"What? When?"

"An hour ago." Tomas bent over her arm, hunting for a vein for the IV drip. Hard to do when her little vessels were deprived of fluid. "Goddammit."

"The vein collapsed." Cole crouched beside him, taking up too much room in the small space. "Slow down and try another one."

Neither of them had gone to school to study medicine. They'd learned basic shit in the field, jumping in whenever the cartel's medical staff needed help.

Knowing how to stitch a wound and insert a peripheral IV proved invaluable in their job. Tomas and Kate had taken the most interest in it. Kate wanted to be a doctor and help people. But not him. He just wanted to mend his wounds without depending on others to do it.

He finally accessed a vein, and once the drip started delivering fluid, he sat on the bed and blew out a breath. The intravenous route was the fastest way to rehydrate her body. She would recover quickly. *Physically.*

In other ways, she might never fully heal.

He knew the feeling.

"That's not her blood." Cole leaned over her, picking at the sticky gunk on her throat. "Tell me what happened."

"I found Paul Kissinger lurking on my property. You were right. He put the tracker on her truck."

"What did you do to him?

"Tied him up. Smacked him around."

"And he confessed? Just like that?"

"No. He told *her.*"

Cole's brows knitted, his gaze shifting from Rylee to the doorway. "Where is he?"

"In the desert."

"Idiot. I have a million methods to make a man talk."

"So do I." Tomas grabbed the container of soap and water and gently ran a wet cloth over her face. "Before he showed up, I bugged her pack and dumped her in the desert, too."

"What part of *stay put and keep her restrained* did you not understand?"

"I *did* restrain her. The scrubland is inescapable to anyone who doesn't know its secrets. I was monitoring her. Watching and listening."

"How did you watch me?" Her eyes snapped open, bloodshot and glinting silver. "Were you there?"

He should've given her a sedative. How long had she been eavesdropping?

"Spying again?" He made a tsking sound. "That's a terrible habit of yours."

She kicked her leg, trying to knock him from the bed. A pathetic attempt, given the weakness in her body. She glanced at the cloth in his hand, the IV in her arm, and the blood on her shirt.

"You were there? The whole time?" Her gaze made an uneasy pass over Cole and returned to Tomas. "You watched me suffer for days and did nothing?"

"I stepped in when I needed to."

"When *you* needed." She coughed a dry, raw sound. "Well, now you can step out, let me change clothes, and I'll be on my way and gone from your life."

She tried to sit and failed.

"My backpack." She scanned the room. None of her belongings were in here.

Her attention landed on Cole, tracing his tattoos and lingering on his beard. Tomas waited for her to voice the man's name and spout every incriminating thing she'd read about him in the emails.

Instead, she pressed her lips together and directed a disgusted glare at Tomas.

He glared back, daring her to open her deceitful mouth. He'd written enough about Cole that she could easily identify him. He'd also outlined his assumptions about Cole's background, his shady military training, his ability to slip in and out of any fortress, computer system, or security infrastructure. No one was that good unless they were hiding some scary shit.

The most concerning thing about Cole was his motivation. He wasn't like the rest of them. He'd never spent a night in Van's attic, never had his freedom ripped away, never experienced the kind of loss and hopelessness that made a man long for death. Not that Tomas knew, anyway.

That was the problem. None of them *knew* Cole Hartman. Yet here he was, mired in their lives, and fighting alongside them. For what? Van and Matias stopped paying him a dozen jobs ago. Now he was what? Contracting for them pro bono?

Whenever he was asked about his past life and current endeavors outside of the team, he just smiled or gave vague non-answers. The bastard was as closed-off as Tomas. Perhaps more so.

Tomas didn't trust him. But he'd contacted him anyway, because he was the best at digging up secrets. If Rylee was hiding skeletons, Cole would find them along with every dirty person connected to her.

Eyes locked, she watched Tomas as he watched her. He hated that she knew all of his secrets. His skeletons, regrets, desires, every thought in his head. She also knew that Cole's presence in Texas meant they'd already learned some things about her.

"You were in the desert with me?" Her gaze lost focus, her momentary spurt of awareness dwindling by the second. "I never heard the truck."

He'd parked it out of hearing range and hiked in

close enough to watch her through the scope of his rifle. Only once, he'd left her unattended to return to the house and call Cole. That was when he found Paul Kissinger on his property.

"Fine. Don't answer me." She weakly flexed her hand. "That man…Paul. He must be connected to you and your friends somehow. But you don't believe that, so you put him in the desert to spy on our conversation."

Cole leaned against the jamb of the doorway and squinted at Tomas. "What did you learn?"

She was fucking her neighbor. On the back porch, in her car, on every surface in her house.

Seeing a woman take it in the ass does something to a man.

His stomach hardened against the stirring images. "Paul monitored her for six months. She didn't know him."

"*Didn't?*" A muscle flexed in Cole's jaw, twitching his beard. "You killed him?"

"Like I said, he attacked her."

Pulling the trigger hadn't been planned. It just happened. They'd needed the son of a bitch alive to get answers. Oddly, the only regret he had about his impulsiveness was the looming task of driving back and dealing with the body.

"We could've pulled information from him." Cole gripped his nape, his expression etched in frustration. "Now we don't know who he was working for, why he was following her, or how it's connected to us."

"She'll tell me." Tomas met her eyes.

"*She* doesn't know anything." Her jaw set. She didn't look away, fidget, or show any signs of dishonesty.

Maybe she was good at lying.

"Did you find anything on the ex-husband?" Tomas asked Cole without breaking eye contact with her.

"He's clean. Except one thing. She has a restraining order against him."

"*Ex*-husband." Her eyelids hooded over silver pools of fatigue and anger.

There was no surprise in her expression. She'd anticipated them investigating the people in her life once they learned who she was. That was why she'd shown up without identification.

"Tell me about Mason Sutton," Tomas said.

"He's a jealous nuisance. Way too jealous to hire another man to watch me. Where are the keys to my truck?" She touched the catheter in her arm, likely debating the best way to yank it out.

"You're not leaving." He caught her probing hand, stopping her.

"You're not keeping me here for three weeks without food."

"What is she talking about?" Cole straightened.

"Give us a minute." His head throbbed, magnified by exhaustion.

"No." She twisted her wrist out of his grip. "You had your minute. You had two days, you heartless cunt."

He'd prepared an intravenous sedative, just in case. If he restrained her to the bed, she would struggle and risk dislodging the IV.

Mostly, he just needed her to sleep so he could close his eyes for the first time in two days. He was operating on three-percent battery life and rapidly draining.

He reached toward the dangling IV bags and began the flow of the sedation drug, titrating the dose to give her just enough to relax her back into dreamland.

"What are you doing?" Her eyes widened, glazed and unfocused, trying to follow his movements.

"Who are your enemies?"

"The only enemies I've made are in this room. What did you do to the IV? What are you giving me?"

"I know who you are, Rylee Sutton."

She glanced at Cole and back to him. "You should've talked to me instead of starving me in the desert. It would've saved you the trouble of calling in your friend. So what have you learned? That I'm a stupid woman, who waltzed in here alone thinking I could do some good and instead, ended up getting myself hurt? Go, Rylee. Another failure." She exhaled a tired breath. "Look, Tommy, I've learned my lesson, okay? Believe me when I say I'm done. I don't want any part of this or *you*. I just want to go home."

"It's too late for that." He leaned over her, bracing an elbow on his knee. "You wanted me. Now you're stuck with me."

NINE

Tomas had reached a level of worn-out that hurt. Every muscle wanted to surrender to gravity. What he needed was sleep. Any horizontal surface would do.

But there was a corpse rotting in the desert. An unfinished conversation with Cole. An IV drip that required monitoring. An unwashed, blood-splattered woman in his bed. And too many unanswered questions.

"I'll ask again." He put his face in hers. "Who are your enemies?"

Her teeth ground together. "I already told you—"

"We know you're a criminal psychologist, Rylee." Cole gripped the upper frame of the doorway, leaning into the small bedroom. "You aid in apprehending scoundrels and testify against them in court. I'd say you make more enemies than we do."

"Since you know my occupation, you also know that I contract for small-town law enforcement." More teeth grinding. "I deal with petty thieves and potheads. Tracking devices are a part of *your* world, not mine."

"You must be bored out of your mind." Tomas scrutinized her bleary eyes, willing the sedative to kick in faster. "So you show up here with your fancy, underutilized degree, hoping to dissect a real criminal mind."

Her mouth stopped grinding, her jaw falling slack. Her head lolled to the side, losing strength. Then she snapped it back, her tone deadened. "You're the reason I chose that field of study."

"Excuse me?"

"I went to school for criminal justice, but as I got to know you…" Her words slurred, fighting the sedation. "Your emails…changed my major." A long, lethargic blink. "I don't…feel…right. You…drugged…"

Next thing from her mouth was an angry, muttering exhale. Her lashes drooped over her cheekbones, and the tension visibly left her body. She was out.

Finally.

He turned off the drip of the narcotic and swapped the sodium chloride with a new bag.

"She's taken a lot of interest in you." Cole approached the bed.

"That's her problem."

"She's making it *your* problem. Seems she's in the habit of getting mixed up with the wrong men. Nine months ago, she filed a protective order against Mason Sutton. Three months later, Paul Kissinger started watching her."

"You think Mason and Paul are connected?"

"Maybe."

"We need eyes and ears on Mason. Find out what he knows about us."

"I'm on it. He's an orthopedic surgeon. Runs a booming practice. On the surface, he seems too busy to get involved with a troublesome ex-wife. What would be his motivation?"

"Jealousy. Obsession. He never remarried and has more than enough money to hire people to monitor the object of his obsession. Especially since she lives five hours away from him." He let the weight of his head hang, fighting exhaustion. "She's sexually involved with one of her neighbors."

"Evan Phillips?"

"Who?"

"The single guy who lives next door to her. Divorced. Forty-something. Good-looking. Works construction. He's collecting her mail and looking after her house while she's on sabbatical. I'll dig deeper, see what I can find on him." Cole narrowed his eyes. "You look like shit. When was the last time you slept?"

"I need to deal with the stiff in the desert." Sleep closed in, heavy and persistent. He slumped onto his side in the narrow space next to Rylee. "In a minute."

"The stiff can wait." Cole rubbed his whiskers and stared at Rylee's unconscious form. "Go grab a few hours of sleep in the other bedroom. I'll clean her up."

"You're *not* touching her." Christ, that came out sharper than he'd intended. He softened his voice. "This is my mess. I got it."

"Yeah, I see that. Suit yourself." With a grunt, Cole left the room and shut off the light. "Stubborn fuck."

Within seconds, Tomas passed out.

He slept hard and deep, but not long. An hour maybe?

When he woke in the dark, he registered Rylee's

93

body pressed against the front of his. With his arm around her tiny waist and her head tucked beneath his chin, he didn't move.

Had she rolled into him? Or had he subconsciously grabbed her to keep her from escaping?

His eyes slowly adjusted to the dimness, bringing the room into focus. A new bag hung from the IV pole. Cole must've slipped in and swapped out her fluids. Her boots were off her feet. Cole must've done that, too.

She still wore her grimy clothes and reeked of sweat and desert dirt. Or maybe the odor was coming from him.

He removed the phone from his pocket and stared at the locked screen, stunned. He'd slept three hours? *Jesus.*

Without waking her, he untangled himself from her soft, small body. Then he checked her vitals and headed to the bathroom.

After a quick shower, he set out bottles of water and apple juice on the nightstand, checked her breathing, and left her sleeping to go deal with his other unwanted visitor.

Cole perched on the couch in the front room, eyes glued to a laptop.

"Feeling better, princess?" The man idly flipped a black coin-sized disk back and forth between his fingers, his gaze never leaving the computer screen. "You two looked so cozy in there I didn't want to disturb you."

Tomas didn't acknowledge the dig as he lowered into the armchair. "Any updates?"

"The guy she's banging, Evan Phillips, walked through her house an hour ago. In and out in ten minutes. No other movement."

94

"You think he knows something?"

"I think we can't rule out pillow talk. If they're fucking on the regular, she's telling him things, sharing secrets, like how she's been reading the incriminating ramblings of a dumbass vigilante for ten years."

Pounding heat flared beneath his skin, his system flooding with the ire he'd been holding back for days.

"You have something to say to me, fucking say it." He shot from the chair and stood over Cole, hands clenching. "Better yet, use your fists. You're the one who taught me how to fight. We both know you can kick my ass. If you're going to do it, fucking do it already!"

Cole slowly shifted his gaze from the computer screen, moved it over Tomas' rigid stance, and stopped on his eyes.

The air thinned, and the tension in Cole's lethal glare grew taut. Then he blinked.

"Nah." He returned to the laptop. "You're beating yourself up enough for the both of us."

Irritation twitched through Tomas' muscles. He spun away and paced the room, noticing the lack of dust on the surfaces. Cole had kept himself busy for the past few hours.

Everything that once filled these rooms had been replaced with new furnishings. Nothing remained from his childhood. No photos. No keepsakes. He'd moved it all to the Milton house and burned it.

His mother's home and the land it sat on was the only tether he allowed himself to keep.

"I was seventeen when I sent the first email." Tomas paused at the kitchen table and rubbed his brow. "It started out harmless. Just the words of a boy who missed his dead girlfriend."

After his mother died, he'd spent two weeks alone in this house. That time in his life left a black hole in his memory, the grief more than he could bear. The only thing he could recall was his urgency to leave, to go somewhere, to be anywhere but here. So he'd left.

"Two weeks after my mother was put in the ground, I drove east. Ended up in Austin." He laughed hollowly. "A small-town kid in a big city. I'd never seen anything like it. So many tall buildings, flashing lights, loud noises, and the people... Christ, they were everywhere, packed together on the streets in every size, color, and creed. I was so fucking out of my element. It's no wonder I didn't last a week."

"That's when Van captured you?"

"I was easy prey. A young, naive boy with a decent physique and no sense of danger, wandering the streets, utterly lost." *Lost in life.* "I walked right up to Van's car and asked for directions. Next thing I knew, I was chained in his attic."

"No one blames you for continuing the emails after your captivity. If writing to her was therapeutic..."

"She was the only one I could talk to. A dead girl. I know that's fucked up. I knew it then, too. But it kept me sane." He released a slow breath and turned to face Cole. "I fucked up when I started writing about you and the team. As much as I covered my tracks and meticulously monitored the account, it was still reckless. Fucking careless. And I'm paying for it now."

"Maybe it's not as bad as it seems." Cole typed something on his laptop. "I hacked into the neighbor's home network. Look at this."

He joined Cole on the couch as the image of a shockingly gorgeous woman filled the screen.

His heart stopped, and his breath fell on a gobsmacked groan. "Holy fuck."

"Yeah. There's more." Cole flipped from one photo to the next, each candid snapshot of Rylee Sutton more intoxicating than the last. "She's not on social media. These photos are from Evan Phillips' personal computer. *All* of them. We're talking hundreds of pictures *just* of her."

Completely enraptured, Tomas couldn't look away from the screen, his gaze greedily feasting on her flawless features, the glossy shine of her brown hair, those sexy full lips, gleaming silver eyes, the healthy glow of her porcelain skin, and the curves of her exquisitely toned body in a glittery dress, a tiny swimsuit, obscenely short shorts—

Cole snapped the lid of the laptop closed, breaking the trance.

"Christ." Tomas cleared his throat, trying not to imagine her naked and failing miserably.

"That battered woman in your bedroom is undeniably attractive. But when she's healthy?" Cole made a whistling sound. "She's the kind of beautiful that makes a man do crazy, desperate shit."

No shit. The last time Tomas had such a gripping, ravenous reaction to a woman was…never.

And he wasn't the only one. Paul Kissinger should've used the last of his energy to find water and survive the desert. Instead, he'd circled back and forced himself on her. A stupid fucking move but at the same time, sickeningly understandable for a guy who'd been ogling her through his binoculars for six months.

"Maybe," Cole said, "we're dealing with something as simple as an infatuated lover. Could be the ex-husband or the neighbor or some random hookup who's feeling extra possessive of a beautiful woman."

That didn't sit well with him. He'd rather Rylee be a person to blame, not a victim. "Does the neighbor have pictures of other women?"

"No."

"Did you come across compromising photos of Rylee?"

"None. No sex tapes or anything that implies that Evan is creeping on her without her permission."

"He has a private photo collection of her." An uneasy sensation coiled in his stomach. "I don't like it."

"I agree. It looks suspicious." Cole turned to him, his gaze probing. "Maybe he loves her. Or maybe he just appreciates her beauty. I mean, if you were fucking a woman who looks like that, wouldn't you keep photos of her?"

No question, he would keep them. And stare at them. Hell, he was never going to fuck his hand again without a visual of her in his head.

"Collecting photos is one thing." He pinched the bridge of his nose, thinking. "But we're dealing with someone who hired a man to watch her. Someone who is obsessed with every detail of her life. *What she eats, where she goes, who she talks to, and most of all, who she's banging.* Those were Paul's exact words."

"Sounds like a domestic issue. I should be able to determine who hired Paul within the next few days. Once we know that, we'll know if it's connected to us." Cole drummed his fingers on his knee. "Best case, she has a creepy admirer and hasn't told anyone about your emails."

"Then we clean up and go home."

"Yep."

He wanted to spank the ever-loving shit out of her and leave a permanent reminder on her ass. But a few threatening words against her loved ones would be sufficient in keeping her quiet when he vanished from her life.

"The worst-case scenario…" Cole rolled that small plastic disk between his fingers again. "She's planning to do something with the evidence she has against us, and she's not working alone."

"She didn't know Paul Kissinger."

"No, but she's somehow connected to whoever hired him. Think about it. We send our people on missions all the time with tracking devices. We bug their cars, their clothes, their bodies." Cole's lips twitched. "I heard Camila once wore a GPS chip in her tooth."

"Yeah." He grinned. "She's fucking crazy."

He missed her. He missed his whole damn team and longed to return to them.

If Rylee was working with someone, it made sense that they wanted to track her whereabouts and jump in when needed. That would explain Paul. She disappeared in the desert, and he showed up to find out what happened.

The device on her truck was the only one Tomas found. He'd scoured her belongings but… "I didn't check her body for chips."

"I have a reliable detector." Cole nodded at his bag on the table. "She's clean."

"And you verified her occupation."

"Yes, but it could be a front. Especially if a three-letter agency is involved." The disk in Cole's hand stopped moving. He looked up and tossed it to Tomas.

He caught it and turned the plastic coin-shaped object this way and that, baffled. "What is this?"

"A high-tech GSM bug. I pulled it from her house and disabled it. There are dozens more there."

"Shit." He inspected it more closely. "I've never seen anything like this."

"Brand new technology. Insanely long battery life. High-speed transmissions. You can't even buy that on the black market. It's impossible to obtain unless you're tied in with NSA or black ops."

A chill trickled down his spine. "You think she could be involved with a government agency?"

"An agency or an agency rogue." A dark look clouded Cole's expression, and he ran a hand down his face. "She could be working for someone. Running from someone. Or she has a lusty-minded stalker with access to cutting-edge espionage tech."

"Fuck." Tomas dropped the bug on the coffee table and slumped back on the couch. "So in summary, she knows everything about us. We know very little about her, and at this point, anything is plausible."

"Pretty much."

TEN

Tomas scraped a hand over his head, impatient to be back in Colombia with his friends and eager to leave the desert memories behind. Ghosts lived in these walls, in the dust, in the arid sand.

He didn't want to be here.

Cole pushed off the couch and ambled to the kitchen. A moment later, he returned with two Bud Lights.

"Thanks." Tomas accepted the cold beer and reluctantly said, "Thanks for coming."

"Yep."

Cole would scour Rylee's life from end to end until he flushed out the truth. In the meantime, Tomas needed to bury a body and babysit the meddling woman.

She wasn't going to be cooperative. By the time she woke, she should have enough strength to bathe herself. And fight him tooth and nail. After the hell he put her through, escape would be her priority.

Her health, however, wouldn't be one-hundred-percent. She hadn't eaten in three days. He could starve her for up to three weeks. That had been his plan—keep her weak and hungry, wear her down, and offer her food in exchange for information.

He'd put the rule of threes in play to fuck with her head and prove his ruthlessness. No air for three minutes. No water for three days. She knew what came next.

He drained the beer. "I'm going to starve her."

"What?"

"You heard me." Resting his elbows on his knees, he met Cole's eyes.

He didn't need to explain himself to anyone, but there was no reason to be a dick. So he told Cole why he'd put her in the desert and what he planned to do with her next.

"Jesus." Cole blew out a breath. "What if she knows nothing, and her only crime is reading your emails?"

"If you tell me you never tortured an innocent suspect during your *unofficial* government career, I'll eat my shoe."

"I can't tell you that. But I will say this. It fucks with you, Tomas. Doesn't matter what cause you're fighting for. When you hurt someone who doesn't deserve to be hurt, that shit leaves scars. Nightmare-inducing scars that keep you awake at night. The guilt festers and changes the makeup of your character."

"Which government agency did that to you?"

"Can't say."

"Are you still working for them?"

"I work for myself."

"What happened?" He directed his eyes at the

tattooed silhouette on Cole's arm.

From wrist to elbow, black ink filled in the figure of a woman on a dance pole. Last year, she was the only tattoo on that arm. Now a tapestry of drawings crowded in around her as if he were slowly working his way toward fading her out.

There was so much chaos in the illustrations it was hard to guess if each piece had been a spontaneous addition or somehow part of a premeditated vision. Spider webs, fire, chains, plants, various depictions of the sun, and random unknown symbols—all of it overlapped and blended together, sleeving both arms and one entire pec.

He returned his attention to the inked dancer. "Is she the one you hurt?"

"One of many." Cole stared at his beer. "The only one who mattered."

"How long ago?"

"Years. A lifetime ago."

He'd never seen Cole with a woman. Couldn't even imagine it. At the headquarters in Colombia where they lived, there was no shortage of willing pussy. The cartel loved their girls. But not Cole. Whenever one of the ladies approached him, she was met with a sneer of disgust.

"When was the last time you got laid?"

"None of your goddamn business." Cole stood and strode back to the kitchen, grabbing two more beers.

"That's a bullshit answer. For the past year, I've spent damn near every day with you, a lot of that time on the mats, letting you pound in my face and pick apart my weaknesses. I trusted you with my training. I trust you with this job. But beyond that? I don't know, Cole.

Because I don't fucking know you."

Cole handed him another Bud Light, sat in the chair across from him, and took a long draw from his bottle. Then he stared at him. Drank again. More staring.

At last, he leaned back and closed his eyes. "I fell in love many years ago."

"With a stripper?"

"A belly dancer. She floated up to me on the street like a damn angel emerging from a mist. Her smile... Fuck, it was so blinding it stopped me on my motorcycle and leveled my entire world." His leg bounced. Then stilled. "I asked her to marry me. Then I chose my job over her."

"The secret agent job?"

"Don't call it that." He cracked his eyes open, glaring through the slits. "I was sent out in the field for a while. Mistakes were made, and I was forced to fake my death to protect her. By the time I cleaned up the mess, quit the job, and returned home to her, she'd fallen in love with my best friend."

"Ouch."

"She's happy. That's all I ever wanted."

"I don't believe that. I've seen the wedding ring you wear on the chain under your shirt. A woman's ring. She's inked on your arm, and unless you're hiding a health problem, your dick still works. You're still a man. But I'm guessing you haven't had sex with anyone since her."

"There isn't a woman out there who comes close to the one I had."

"Trust me, Cole. You have to let go and move on. If you're afraid of falling in love again—"

"I will always love *her*. End of." Cole steadily met

his eyes. No defensive anger. No emotion at all. "My refusal to bed random women has nothing to do with fear and everything to do with self-control."

"I get it. I fucking *lived* it." He softened his voice, recalling his own pain and the celibacy that accompanied it. "Caroline was only fourteen when she died. As innocent as it sounds, I saved myself for her. Then Van happened. A fucking traumatizing way to lose your virginity. He and Liv forced me to perform sexual acts, but I didn't willingly touch a woman for the first time until much later. Those were some dark years."

"What changed?"

"I was so goddamn lonely that I went out one night and got laid. Just like that. I don't even remember her face. Doesn't matter. It was the intimacy that I needed. It pushed me out of the dark." He met Cole's eyes. "You're making a regrettable mistake if you condemn yourself to loneliness for the rest of your life."

Cole's gaze slid toward the back bedroom and locked on something out of view.

Tomas couldn't see around the corner, but he knew she was there. His neck stiffened. "Eavesdropping again, Rylee?"

"Leave Cole alone." She shuffled into the room, looking ragged and filthy and breathtakingly gorgeous. "He's not like you."

Cole winged up an eyebrow.

Tomas tensed as she looked at the front door, scoped out the kitchen, and returned to the door. She reeked of desperation. To find food. To run for her life. Neither was an option until she spilled her secrets.

"Go take a shower." He guzzled down the second beer.

"I want to hear what the psychologist has to say about our conversation." Cole nodded at her. "Go ahead, Rylee."

"I didn't hear all of it." She rubbed her arm where she'd removed the IV and stole another glance at the kitchen. "I'm hungry."

Cole wasn't on board with Tomas' plan, but he didn't twitch a muscle to interfere. At least, not yet. He simply observed her, waiting.

When no one spoke, she stepped farther into the room, positioning herself closer to the front door.

Would she run? Tomas counted on it. What he hadn't expected was her blatant disregard of his presence. Surely, she felt him glaring at her, daring her to look at him.

After a moment of deliberation, she lowered her head.

"Everyone handles a broken heart differently." Her shoulders twitched, her eyes shifty and tired. "Some people only love once, and if they lose that love, they never look for it again. They find other things in life that stir their passions. Like their work. Their hobbies. Or throwing themselves behind an important cause." She peered at Cole through her lashes. "You don't waste your time with hookups because you don't do casual relationships. You had the real thing, and there's no replacement. You're a one and done kind of guy. But a word of warning, Cole. Fate might not be done with you."

"I fucked fate to hell, darlin'." Cole traced a finger along his bottom lip, his voice taking on a menacing edge. "Believe me. That train crashed and burned."

"Okay, but if you're wrong, if love comes for you

again, it's going to blindside you and knock you on your ass. You'll deny it. You'll fight it with every breath in your body. But having already experienced it once, you know it's a fight you can't win. So maybe, if and when it happens, give yourself a break. Don't fight so hard."

"Is that your professional opinion? Or personal experience?"

"Professional." Her brows furrowed. "Or personal. Both, I guess." She lifted her gaze, struggling in the effort to drag it across the room, pushing it toward Tomas, and finally, *finally*, she met his eyes. "You told him my husband cheated on me?"

He stared right back, giving her nothing, even as his blood flew through his veins. It wasn't her words that affected him. It was everything she didn't say.

Censure blazed in her glare, fury so hot he felt it flare against his chest. She abhorred him, scorned him, and found him severely lacking. Perhaps that was what struck him the most. Her burning disappointment.

As if she'd come here expecting to find something dramatically different. She must've read something into his emails that wasn't there. Maybe she thought if a man was stupid enough to write the details of his criminal life to a dead girl, he was stupid enough to fall in line with her agenda.

Well, she could shove her disappointment up her ass, because he wasn't that guy.

"Some people have more aggressive ways of dealing with a broken heart." She addressed Cole, but her eyes were all for Tomas. "Like standing on the edge of a bridge and welcoming death. Or writing emails and pouring out their regrets. Or hate-fucking every willing body they come in contact with."

Hate-fucking? That was what she thought he did? Or was she projecting her own issues? That would explain a lot.

"Are you having hate-sex with your neighbor?" He leaned forward, his posture rigid.

"God no."

"How many have come before Evan Phillips?"

"Not nearly as many as you parade in and out of your bed."

"Give me a number."

"Rot in hell."

"You know mine. In fact, you know every detail of my sexual history. I want yours."

"I'm not giving you shit." She backed toward the door, clumsy and nervous. She wouldn't get far.

"You want to eat? Give me the names of your lovers. Timelines. Descriptions. You're going to tell me who you're fucking, everyone you're connected with, and what they know about my friends and me."

"This again?" She took another backward step. "You already know about Mason and Evan. You know my occupation and where I live. Whoever that Paul guy was, I don't know him. He's connected to *you*."

"Then why was the tracker on *your* truck? Why was he watching *you* for six months?"

"I guess you should've asked him instead of dumping him in the desert with me. I told you everything I know about that, and I hope you figure it out. But I can't help you."

She reached for the door, but he was already moving.

"Don't do this!" She fumbled with the handle, breathing heavily and whimpering in her struggle to escape.

He pressed a hand on the door above her head, forcing it shut. "Get in the shower. You stink."

"No! I'm leaving!"

"Have it your way." With little effort, he flung her small body over his shoulder and carried her toward the bathroom.

Her little fists bounced off his back, the rest of her bucking ineffectively as he crossed the short distance. As his gaze intersected Cole's, they shared a look, but he didn't know what it meant.

Disapproval? Indifference? Definitely not encouragement. It didn't matter so long as the man didn't interfere.

In the bathroom, he turned on the shower and dropped her beneath the cold spray, clothes and all.

She yelped and clawed at the shower curtain.

He caught it before she tore it down and shoved her back into the tub. "Do that again, and you'll be showering with no privacy."

"Fuck you." She spluttered in the downpour of water, slipped on her socked feet, and scrambled up again, pressing her back against the shower wall.

Wet cotton and denim clung to her stunning figure. Strings of dark hair stuck to her face, and her silver eyes glinted with ferocity, sharp as honed steel and enthralling beyond reason.

Rylee Sutton was devastatingly sexy when she was mad.

"The soap is behind you." He leaned against the vanity, his jeans too painfully tight to contain his reaction to her. "Use it."

With a feral smile, she snatched the bar of soap and

hurled it at him.

ELEVEN

The soap bounced off Tommy's chest and fell to the floor with a dull, anti-climatic *plonk*.

Rylee stared at it, her heart pounding in her throat. "That would've hit harder if I weren't starving to death."

"Then I should feed you." His tone scraped, stinging her nerves. "Just to ensure that the next thing you throw leaves a mark."

"Why are you such a jerk?" She shivered even as the spraying water started to heat and form a cloud of steam between them.

He blocked the exit with his sheer size, wearing a hateful scowl, dark jeans, and a black muscle-hugging shirt. Mist collected on the fabric in a blurry shine, making him look otherworldly, like an angry, avenging warlord.

If he expected her to take a shower while he watched, he could fuck right off.

"Move." She stepped over the bathtub ledge only to be shoved back in.

Indignation warred with fatigue, and the latter won out as she staggered and fell on her butt.

"Goddammit!" She staggered back to her feet and swayed. "Let me out!"

The hollows and slashes of his sculpted cheeks, the twisted sneer of his mouth, all of it carved a cruel expression in his unbearably handsome face. But his looks were overshadowed by the dispassion in his steady, golden eyes. Didn't matter what she said. He had a plan for her, and it wouldn't be merciful.

His gaze took a tour along her soaked clothes as he drifted closer, so close she detected fumes of beer on his breath. The piney, masculine aroma agitated her hunger and stirred other things she refused to acknowledge.

She met his eyes. "I'm not stripping in front of you, motherfucker."

His lip curled, and he leaned back. "You're old enough to be my mother, and that's a hard pass." He tossed the soap into the tub and yanked the shower curtain closed between them. "You have five minutes to undress and clean off the blood."

His nastiness penetrated, leaving a toxic, coiling pain in the deepest chambers of her heart.

"If I don't?" she asked.

"I'll do it myself, and neither of us will enjoy it."

So he'd rather insult her than see her naked. Fine. That was preferable. She could handle spiteful words, even if they hurt.

It was time she stopped thinking of him as the boy she'd connected with ten years ago. That kid was gone, and this man was beyond saving.

She only needed to save herself.

Lightheaded and famished, she shook from head to

toe, her fingers uncooperative and trembling as she pulled off the soggy clothes and washed her hair.

If he remained on the other side of the curtain, she couldn't hear him. No amount of curiosity would compel her to steal a peek. Besides, he wouldn't go far.

Even if he thought she was old enough to be his mother.

Over the past few years, she found that maturity in women warded off shallow, insecure assholes — the same way aposematism warned off predators. If he was repelled by her age, it was working.

But his jab still burned her up. She was only forty-one. Fourteen years older than him. Maybe it was biologically possible to birth a child at that age, but she didn't know any fourteen-year-old mothers.

Why was she still thinking about this? Fuck him.

She needed the keys to her truck and an escape plan.

She needed food.

Finishing the shower in a rush, she shut off the water and grabbed the curtain. Then she slowly peered around the edge.

The bathroom was empty, the door cracked. No sound drifted in, but she knew he was out there, waiting with animosity in his eyes.

When she drove here three days ago, she saw this playing out so differently. If that rapist piece of shit, Paul, hadn't shown up, maybe Tommy would've despised her less and listened more.

Or maybe he'd just sounded nicer in email, and she didn't really know him at all.

A towel sat on the vanity, along with a clean pair of her pajama pants and an unfamiliar t-shirt. She hurried through drying, dressing, and using the toilet, left her ruined clothes in the bathtub, and stepped into the narrow hall.

Glancing toward the bedroom, she noticed the bed had already been stripped and replaced with clean bedding. Meticulous as ever, he would undoubtedly have all traces of Paul's blood gone from his property by nightfall.

How strange to be inside this house after hearing about it for ten years. It was exactly as he'd described—dark, cramped, cozy. And *quiet*.

The scent of food invaded her nose. She'd guzzled water and apple juice when she woke, but the gnawing emptiness in her stomach screamed for substance.

Her pulse quickened as she entered the front room.

Tommy sprawled on the couch, a sun-browned hand hanging casually over the armrest. Steam rose from a bowl that sat on the table before him, the aroma of delicious spices pervading the air.

Chili. Out of a box, a can, wherever it came from, she didn't care. Saliva pooled in her mouth, and her belly churned with ravenous need.

"Where's Cole?" She tugged on the oversize shirt, fighting the impulse to attack the food.

"Out." His gaze followed the action then lifted to hers, hard as polished gold. "Sit."

The front door beckoned, but the chili promised instant relief.

She crossed the room and sat across from him, her eyes on the bowl.

He straightened, leaning toward the table, and grabbed the spoon.

"Let's start with your bed partners." Scooping a

huge helping of beans and meat, he held it between them and wet his lips. "How many men have you fucked since you started reading my emails?"

For a bite of that food, she could give him an estimate. A staggering number, to be honest, especially for a woman who thought she'd married her one and only. She wasn't ashamed of her sexual history or her voracious libido, but none of it concerned Tommy. If she told him about her past hookups, it would turn them into suspects and put them in his crosshairs.

"I've had one lover in the past year." She didn't want to look desperate, but her gaze kept drifting to the spoon, pulling like a magnet. "Evan isn't a criminal. He knows nothing about you. There isn't a chance in hell he's involved in this."

"Who came before him?"

She shook her head rapidly, frenzied in her hunger. "Tommy, please. I'm starving."

He veered the scoop toward his mouth and wrapped his mean lips around the entire bite, humming as he chewed.

There were a million words in the English language, but not one could adequately express how badly she wanted to stab him with that goddamn spoon.

She could try to take the bowl from him, but she was operating at a fraction of his strength and speed. If she behaved, maybe she wouldn't have to fight him at all. Maybe he intended to share with her.

He shoveled a second helping of chili and hovered it before her. "Give me names."

"Douchebag. Fuckface. Jackass. Mouth breather."

The spoon slid between his lips, another bite stolen.

She saw red. "You want to know why Paul followed me here? Look at your own history, the people you've murdered, the women you've fucked, and the ruthless company you keep. *That's* where you'll find your answer."

"I'm looking at all connections, but the most glaring one is you. The more you cooperate, the quicker this ends." He ate another spoonful, twisting pain through her stomach.

"Who I've slept with has no bearing on this."

"You have no family or friends. It seems the only people who come into your life are the ones who come between your legs."

"That's not true." A hot ember flared at the base of her throat.

"Then tell me, Rylee." He spooned more chili, eating it cruelly in front of her and talking with his mouth full. "Among your acquaintances, who hasn't been in your pants?"

"God, you're such a prick."

He continued eating, watching her with callous indifference as the bowl slowly emptied before her eyes. She could almost taste the hearty beans as they disappeared in his mouth.

"My colleagues." A prickly burn swarmed the edges of her eyes. "I don't sleep with them, and they're my friends."

"Colleagues," he echoed in an acidic tone and wiped the back of his hand across his lips. "Define your relationship with them."

"What do you mean?"

"Have any of them been to your house? Or called you on the phone just to shoot the shit? Or invited you to hang out or grab a beer after work?"

"No." *Not once.* "I don't make friends like that easily. I'm shy. Reserved."

"A shy woman doesn't show up at a known criminal's house by herself. But you're not alone, are you? Whoever you're working with sent Paul to check on you, and when he doesn't return, they'll send someone else."

"Jesus, you're all over the place with your theories. Which is it? Am I being tracked by an enemy, a lover, or some cohort who is helping me plot your demise?"

"You tell me."

"None of the above. I'm so damn shy and guarded it took me ten years to work up the nerve to talk to you. Luring you here to meet you in person is so far out of my comfort zone. I told no one about you or where I was going. I just…I thought you were in danger with the cartel, and I panicked when you said goodbye in your last email. I don't have friends like you do. I'm not good at letting people in."

"You don't have friends because you're a lying, deceitful—"

"I'm afraid of being hurt again." The confession blurted on a rush of anger.

He stared at her like she was the village idiot. Maybe she was. She'd made a terrible mistake coming here. Too late to take it back. But she was educated. Trained to listen to criminals and understand their motivations, views, thoughts, and actions.

If he didn't view her as a person, he would continue to hurt her. She needed to remind him she was human.

"I pretend I don't need anyone." She swallowed,

her vision blurring with tears. "I keep everyone at a distance. But deep down, I still dream of finding a life partner, someone who loves me enough to be loyal. *Faithful*."

"Is that why you're fucking Evan? You want him to love you?"

"No." She wiped at her wet cheeks and looked away. "He's charming and nice and…"

Too perfect. Too doting. Too much like Mason. That scared the crap out of her.

"Women love him," she said. "I'm not his only lover. I mean, we don't have that kind of relationship. We're just neighbors."

"With benefits." His judgmental tone added insult to his narrowed glare.

"You're not in a position to look at me like that. You fuck whomever you want and make those women hurt. *Your* words. Don't you dare shame me for having a sex life."

With a grunt, he turned his attention back to the chili and ate another spoonful.

There was only one bite left.

She balled her hands so tightly her nails dug into her palms. "You're not going to let me eat?"

"Give me the names of your sexual partners, and I'll feed you."

"I don't know their names."

"You don't know who you're fucking? How did you meet them?"

Her hunger outweighed her pride, making it easy to answer. "Dating sites and hookup apps. Their usernames were probably not their real names, and I don't remember any of them anyway."

"Where's your phone?"

He already knew her identity. There was nothing in that duffel bag worth hiding.

"Buried in the ruins of the Milton house," she said. "Southwest corner."

He shoved the bowl toward her.

She fell upon it like a rabid dog, sucking the last bite off the spoon until it gleamed. Heavenly flavors exploded on her tongue as she dropped the utensil and dragged her fingers along the bottom of the empty bowl, frantically scraping out every drop.

"Where are you?" He stood with his phone to his ear. "Okay. Swing by Caroline's house on your way back."

As he recapped the conversation about her duffel bag, she cleaned every speck of chili from the bowl with her fingers and tongue. It didn't come close to putting a dent in her hunger.

He ended the call and turned toward her. "Are the dating apps still on your phone?"

"Yes, but I swear, Tommy, I never told anyone about you. Don't hurt those guys. They were just one-night stands."

"Let's go." He gripped her arm and wrenched her from the chair.

"Go where?" She tried and failed to escape his grip as he dragged her toward the bedroom. "Wait! I'm still hungry."

"Not hungry enough."

"What do you mean?" She dug in her feet and stumbled with the force of his forward motion. "I answered your questions."

As he hauled her away from the kitchen, it became

horribly apparent that one bite of chili was all he would give her.

Eating was imperative. But more than that, she felt the overpowering instinct to run.

She went wild, thrashing, punching, biting, kicking, and somehow, she broke free. Her thoughts spun into chaotic indecision, but her body took the reins, bolting through the house and toward the front door.

Blood pounded in her ears, her pulse spastic and breaths bursting.

Running into the desert would be suicide. She needed her keys and scoured every surface as she flew past the front room. *Nothing.* But she didn't slow.

Outside, she slammed into a wall of hot air, the sky pitch black and her truck nowhere in sight.

Oh fuck, oh fuck, oh fuck.

She darted around the side of the house, searching for anything that might help her escape this miserable wasteland. Where was her fucking truck?

If she sprinted in the direction of the Milton house, could she find her way in the dark? Did she have the strength to travel two miles on foot? Then what? She'd dig up her phone, but it didn't have a signal. And she needed the map in her truck to find the closest town.

Fuck!

"You'll die out there." His chilling voice fell against her back, terrifyingly close.

She spun, backing away from his towering silhouette. "Where's my truck?"

Only a few feet separated them, and he stayed with her, prowling forward as she reeled backward.

Twilight threw the hollows of his cheekbones into shadow and accentuated the handsome planes of his face.

He was a vigilante criminal, a lawless punisher, with righteous murder pumping through his veins.

His dangerous lifestyle was echoed in the strength of his hands, the cruelty from his lips, and the sheer power of his body as he trapped her like the sun in the barren desert. Inescapable heat, nowhere to run, and she was starving, the looming threat of another day here as brutal and unforgiving as the man himself.

"Let me go, Tommy." Her heart hammered, and she retreated another step, trembling. "I know you think I'm a loose end, and you're meticulously good at your job, always finishing every task set upon you, even the ones that are bothersome and undesirable. But I'm not a job. You're starving an innocent woman and holding her captive. That violates everything you and your friends are doing. If there's someone truly after me, you should be protecting me not hurting me."

He stepped forward, slow and menacing.

Revenge was his life, in his blood, and he intended to punish her in payment for a wrong that had been done. He was beyond listening.

She turned and ran.

TWELVE

Rocky sand bit into Rylee's bare feet as she sprinted through the dark. In normal circumstances, she would've been terrified of stepping on a scorpion. But there was a deadlier threat on her heels, breathing down her neck, closing in—

His fist caught her throat, his other twisting in her hair. The punishing grip wrenched her off her feet, dragging her knees and scraping her hands along the ground as he hauled her back into the house by her hair.

No amount of fighting or screaming slowed him down. By the time he wrestled her into the bedroom, she was out of strength, out of breath, and he hadn't broken a sweat.

He tossed her onto the bed like a rag doll and followed her down, straddling her legs and pinning her arms above her head.

"You fucking psycho!" She wheezed, trying to catch her breath. "This is wrong. This isn't you. Please, Tommy. Stop this madness!"

The sound of metal clanked above her. She twisted her neck and glimpsed handcuffs in his grasp.

"No!" She renewed her fight, but it was a wasted effort. "Get away from me!"

Within seconds, he shackled her arms to the wrought iron headboard. His thigh pushed between hers. His hand covered her mouth. Then he gave her his weight. All of it.

Fucking God, he was muscle-heavy. Hard. Dense. Utterly immovable. His heat, his strength, every inch of him pressed her into the mattress, making her whimper against his palm. And his eyes. Damn those eyes. They were so shockingly, brilliantly gold. Gorgeous. Mesmerizing. *Vicious.*

He radiated rebellious, bad-boy intimidation coupled with a virility so potent it made every warmblooded woman's head turn and mouth water.

This was the closest she'd ever physically been to him, and while she loathed him for hurting her, it wasn't enough to dampen her reaction to his masculinity.

A sharp, carnal tug pulled inside her, dirty and wanton. There was a wicked wildness about him that called to her filthiest desires. After accusing him of hate-fucking women, she couldn't stop herself from imagining him doing that to her. Didn't mean she wanted it. No way in hell. But the naked possibility of such a thought messed with her head.

His hand moved from her mouth to wedge beneath her nape, tightening at the base of her skull and yanking her toward his sinful lips. Not to kiss her. He just held her mouth against his, breathing, seducing, making her squirm between want and repulsion.

He'd written in detail about his captivity in Van's

attic. Eight weeks of brutal sexual instruction. Van had whipped him and taken his virginity. Liv had taught him how to kiss and suck a cock, but she never fucked him. He didn't have intercourse with a woman for the first time until years later.

The intimate position made it impossible not to think about everything he'd endured. Everything he'd *learned*. He was trained in sexual pleasure and knew how to use it to lure and torture. He was tormenting her with it now, arousing her, confusing her. Just to be a dick.

"I know what you're doing." She jerked her face away.

He gripped her jaw and yanked it back.

She drank in the youthful texture of his skin, his symmetrical, rough-hewn features, the flavor of his breath, the faintness of beer, spicy meat, and all man. The delectable, warm scent of him enveloped her like a fantasy.

While she reeled from his overbearing proximity, she wasn't the only one affected. Electricity writhed between them, twisting the dynamic of their tumultuous relationship and weaving layers of toxic complexity.

They had no business staring at each other like this. There was too much animosity and resentment in the air. But neither of them looked away, their breaths melding into shimmers of hot, poisonous attraction. It punched through her, almost causing the last of her senses to desert her. Christ, she was shaking.

He responded to it by sliding his touch along her jaw, studying her with his fingertips, feathering them along her cheekbones, her nose, her lips. Then his touch grew heavier, harder, pressing against her skin until his entire hand was squeezing her face.

Anger. His reaction to her was pissing him off. Or maybe this was what he'd meant in his emails. When he was intimate with women, he always hurt them.

"Tommy." She shook her head, gasping and trying to break his cruel grip. "You're hurting me."

He was all biceps, abs, and rock-hard thighs, bearing down on her like a brick wall. He must have felt her shifting beneath him because he removed his hand from her face. Then he stared at her mouth, watching her gulp for air under his heavy body.

Lifting slightly, he transferred some of his weight onto his elbow and leg. It was such a small thing, a tiny glimpse of thoughtfulness.

He wanted to make her pay, but that wasn't how his mother raised him to treat a woman. Nor was it the first time he'd shown a trace of compassion.

"I know you put sunscreen on me before leaving me in the desert." She peered into his eyes from inches away. "Why?"

"Your skin is flawless. I've never seen anything like it." His gaze traveled along her throat, the neckline of the shirt, and returned to her eyes. "It would be a shame to ruin something so beautiful."

That was the nicest thing he'd said to her, but she needed a lot more than a compliment from him.

"Keep starving me, and there won't be any flesh left on my bones."

"Starvation is a very slow, agonizing death."

"Three weeks."

"This will end before then."

"How will it end? I know you've killed horrible men, but do you have it in you to kill me?"

"I guess we'll find out."

She drew in his threat on a sharp inhale. "This is why I filed a protective order against my ex-husband."

He glanced at her arms. "Because he handcuffed you?"

"No. He forced his way into my house. Then he forced himself on *me*."

The heat, the intimacy, and the weight of his body vanished, leaving nothing but cold vulnerability in its wake.

She should've been relieved to gain the space. But she was still restrained to the bed and knew that when he left the room, she would be stuck here with nothing to distract her from the hunger pangs.

"He raped you?" He stood beside the bed, his expression unreadable.

"No. He got aggressive and handsy and wouldn't leave. It scared me enough to call the cops and file a restraining order."

"This happened last year. Yet you divorced him a decade ago."

"He never wanted the divorce and has been trying to get me back ever since. He's a relentless pest, but that's *all* he is. He shows up at my house, at my work, calls and texts and sends gifts. But it's all harmless. He's not a threat."

"Until he forced himself on you. Why are you defending him?"

"I'm not. It's just...I know him. He wouldn't hire someone to watch me."

"What about Evan Phillips?"

"No way. He doesn't have the money to throw around on shit like that. Besides, we're together all the time. He lives right next door. There's no reason for him to hire someone to watch me."

"You'd be surprised what a desperate man would do. He has hundreds of photos of you on his personal computer."

"What?" A chill zinged along her scalp. She didn't know what bothered her more — his announcement or the fact that he had access to Evan's computer. "Hundreds?"

"Yes."

"Wow, okay. I mean, I know he takes pictures of me with his phone sometimes. I didn't know he saved them. But he's with a lot of women and probably has photos of them, too."

"Nope. Just you."

That's fucked up.

But was it really? Evan repeatedly pressed her to take their relationship further. Maybe he liked her more than she thought?

"Just because he has photos of me," she said. "That doesn't mean he hired Paul to watch me."

He stared at her for an eternity, his face unfairly gorgeous. And blank. She would give anything to read his mind.

Growing antsy, she twisted her wrists in the handcuffs and pulled. He'd secured them correctly, ensuring she couldn't escape and while keeping them loose enough not to cause discomfort. She could flip over but would have to sleep with her hands above her head.

Turning away, he grabbed a bottled water from the stash on the small desk and sat beside her hip.

"This is your childhood room," she said. "You were in here when you started emailing Caroline."

His jaw hardened as he lifted her head and helped her drink.

She knew he'd burned all the furniture and everything else that had once been in this house.

"I cried for you that day." She drank another long gulp, draining the rest of the water. "The day you burnt your belongings. I know it was hard for you. But it was also cathartic."

His neck stiffened, and he tossed the empty bottle in the direction of the desk.

"I want to know…" He leaned over her, his eyes ablaze with accusation. "How far did you let your ex-husband go before you told him *no*."

"What?"

"You loved him enough to nearly kill yourself when he cheated." He lowered his head, hovering his lips a hairbreadth away from hers. "When he put his mouth on you, did you open for him? Did you draw him in?"

Her mouth opened now on a shocked gasp. "No, I—"

His tongue swept in, lashing and licking at the stunned flesh of hers. She didn't kiss him back, for this wasn't a kiss at all. It was anger and violence. He grabbed her face and mauled her with his mouth, biting, sucking, and decimating her defenses.

Before she thought to bite him back, it ended. He stared down at her, his breaths fast and hot against her face, his lips swollen and glistening.

"Why did you do that?" she asked, furious.

"To test your reaction."

She ground her teeth. "What did you learn?"

He touched a finger to her mouth and trailed it down her chin, her neck, her breastbone. His eyes followed the movement, his intention clear a half-second before he pinched her nipple through the shirt.

"Stop!" She wasn't wearing a bra and had no protection against the assault. "Don't touch me!"

"Is that what you told him?" He squeezed harder, shooting pain through her breast and stinging her eyes with tears.

"Yes!"

"You told him *yes*?"

"No!" She kicked her legs, aiming a knee toward his back. But she couldn't reach him. She didn't have the strength. "I told him *no. A* million times *no*."

"But he couldn't keep his hands off your hot little responsive body." He cupped her breast in a ruthless vise, adding ungodly pressure as his thumb rolled over the pebbled peak. "Your nipples were hard before I even touched them. My God, you're hungry."

"You sound like a rapist."

He clicked his tongue. "Are you wet?"

"Are you hard?"

He twisted, slid a leg over the top of hers and pressed the hardest, *largest* erection she'd ever felt against her hip.

Her pulse quickened. Her body shuddered, and her mouth went desert-dry.

That couldn't be real. No goddamn way.

His cock jerked against her, and swear to God, it felt like a baseball bat was stretching the threads of his jeans from groin to knee.

Instinct bellowed at her to retreat, but she refused to wither beneath him.

"I know you get off on hurting women, but I'm a *hard pass,* remember?" She lifted her pelvis and pushed into the threat, challenging his execution. "Go fuck someone your own age."

"I don't want to fuck you, Rylee. I'm only interested in hurting you."

He flipped her to her stomach and shoved the hem of the shirt up her back.

"What are you doing?" She jerked on the restraints and bucked beneath his ruthless hands.

He yanked down her pajama pants and exposed her bare backside.

Her breath left her.

His palm came down with a shocking, fiery *smack*. She gulped, stunned, and opened her mouth on a silent scream.

Another strike. And another. He wailed on her ass with all the fury of a punishing god. She could only lie there and take it like a shameful child. But she wasn't ashamed. She was burning, panting, sinking into his blistering attention in the most sickening way.

It wasn't just the bite of his hot palm or the delicious chill that followed each blow. It was the crescendo of his breaths, the guttural growls from his throat, and the blustering pulse in her ears, in her pussy — all of it echoing in an erotic symphony and growing faster, faster, until there was no pause between the primal beats.

Then he was on her. His hands, his teeth, tearing into her welted flesh, sinking into burning muscle, piercing skin, slapping, biting, and groaning with sexual savagery.

He spread her cheeks and took his mouth to her anus, teasing and tormenting the ring of nerves. His tongue prodded and lapped up and down her crack, delving deep. So deep. Oh, God, he knew what he was doing. If this was him when he lost his temper, she couldn't fathom what he could do to a woman when he was in full control.

It felt too good. Too atrociously depraved and shocking. She'd wanted this level of rough, raw lust for as long as she could remember, to burn beneath the intensity of male heat, to explore the dark, uncharted corners of her imagination, but she'd never found a man who could take her there.

So instead of fighting, she lifted her ass and writhed against him to heighten the sensation.

"You fucking slut." He spanked her again, harder, meaner. "I don't hear you saying *no*. You tease men with this perfect, round ass. You fuck them and forget them and wonder why you have a stalker."

The heat of his mouth replaced his hand, his tongue stabbing between her buttocks, and lower, lower, reaching for her pussy.

Nonsensical sounds bubbled in her throat as she jerked like a mindless thing, trembling, gasping. The throbbing between her legs came at intervals until those intervals blurred into one blinding pulse. It overtook her.

She was going to come.

He tore his mouth away and climbed off the bed.

Her stomach seized and plummeted.

Without warning, he plunged two fingers between her legs, gliding the tips along her soaked slit. She squeezed her thighs together, but he got what he wanted, proving it as he brought his wet hand to her face and smeared her arousal across her lips.

If she felt shame, it was diluted by an inglorious blast of rage. Rage at herself for falling into his trap.

His other hand caught her hair and wrenched her head back at a painful angle. Then he kissed her fully, brutally, with such appalling intensity and hostility that it shriveled her insides.

Shoving her away, he strode toward the door.

True to his word, he didn't fuck her.

He'd hurt her.

"Tommy." She seethed with contempt and panic. "Let me go!"

He shut off the light and left her quivering in the dark by calculated intent.

THIRTEEN

Rylee lay in the dark, listening to male voices drift in from the front room. Cole had returned, and no one had come to check on her. Hunger only scratched the surface of her misery.

The welts on her backside throbbed. The restraints on her arms prevented her from pulling up her pajama pants and cleaning away the damp reminder of her arousal. Tommy had deliberately left her in this position, knowing she would squirm in discomfort and despise herself as much as she despised him.

What sane woman craved the touch of a cruel man? She couldn't even claim Stockholm syndrome because she'd known him for ten years, had willingly put herself in this situation, and felt absolutely no positive feelings toward him.

Except for this sick, sexual attraction.

She needed to get far, far away from him before she lost her damn mind.

He and Cole spoke in low murmurs, too muted for

her ears. They were probably going through her duffel bag and dissecting all the messages, apps, and private activity on her phone.

Hopefully, their intrusive investigation would prove she wasn't connected to Paul Kissinger.

How had she not known she was being followed for six months? As frightening as that was, if the person who'd hired Paul wanted to kill her, she would already be dead.

Ironically, this had all began on the one night she'd actually wished for death. Tommy had inadvertently saved her life on that bridge, and now, a decade later, he was intent on destroying it.

Too bad she didn't have the training to negotiate her way out of this. But criminal psychologists were not effective as negotiators.

First off, if she attempted to counsel him, no matter how subtle her technique, he would know what she was doing and rage against the implication that he was crazy.

Secondly, therapy was *not* the same as negotiation. Therapeutic intervention took months or years to achieve positive growth and relief from suffering. She was no longer interested in helping him grow past his trauma. Her only goal now was escaping as quickly as possible.

Thirdly, he wasn't mentally ill. He didn't have bipolar disorder or schizophrenia. He was a sane man, a ruthless vigilante, who knew no bounds and harbored a blatant disregard for laws and authority.

Hours must've passed, and at some point, she fell asleep.

When she woke, Tommy was in bed with her.

Morning light filtered into the bedroom through the open doorway, illuminating the hard, sinewy arm that rested on her hip like an iron bar.

Her pants had been put back in place, and even more surprising, her hands were free.

She lay on her side, turned into him for some reason. All she could see was a flat nipple and taut, tanned skin stretched over the ridges of a chiseled chest.

Her pulse accelerated, her joints frozen. Had he slept here all night? Was he sleeping now?

His hand moved, fingers ghosting along her back. She stiffened.

Swallowing past the resentment in her throat, she tilted back her head and locked onto alert, golden eyes.

"Why did you sleep in here?" she asked, suspicious.

"The other bed was taken."

"So was this one."

"While I despise the sight of you, I'd rather sleep beside you than the sweaty, bearded bastard in the other room." He lowered his hand to her backside and squeezed the abused muscle. "How's your ass feel this morning?"

"Fine." She resisted the impulse to jerk away and give him the satisfaction of a reaction.

"Liar." He gave her a light smack on the butt and rose from the bed. "Go take a shower."

He strode out of the room, wearing workout shorts that hung so low on his hips she could see two deep dimples near the crease of his firm butt.

No one should look that sexy after just waking up. Especially not the motherfucker who was responsible for the stitching pain in her stomach.

How many days had it been since she'd eaten? Four? It felt like forty, and her strength was paying for it.

Any escape attempt right now would be laughable. Hence the reason he'd removed the handcuffs.

The room spun as she wobbled toward the bathroom. The only reason she wanted another shower was to wash off the remnants of last night's arousal. She couldn't let that happen again.

Today, she would find a way to leave.

Fresh clothes—taken from her truck—waited for her on the vanity. No undergarments, but there was a tube of ointment. She glanced at the label, realizing it was meant for her welts.

Was that what Tommy did for all the women he fucked? Blistered their asses then tossed them a tube of aftercare?

Her blood boiled, and she snatched the ointment, hurling it across the bathroom.

She made it through a quick shower without passing out, all the while imagining driving her fist into his handsome face repeatedly. As she dried herself off, she caught her reflection in the mirror.

Four days of stress and starvation had already taken its toll. Her cheekbones sharpened under the dark circles bruising her eyes. Her shoulders and ribs were more pronounced, pressing starkly through the pallor of her skin. She looked gaunt. Almost cadaverous. She felt sick.

Reluctantly, she located the ointment and smeared it on her welted backside. That done, she dressed in jeans and a white tank-top, cleaned her teeth, and left her hair dripping down her back.

Then she opened the door to the overwhelming fragrance of pork grease and coffee. The aroma buckled her knees. Staggering, she followed the scented trail into the kitchen.

Tommy sat at the table, a mug in his hand and his eyes drilling into hers. Shirtless and sprawled with his legs spread, he took up too much room, too much air. He knew it, too, with his brown hair all tousled from sleep and his lips twitching with arrogance.

He knew exactly how women looked at him, including the one he starved.

She tore her gaze away and found Cole standing at the stove, frying eggs and bacon. A basket of colorful fruit sat on the counter, along with cheese, bakery sweets, and milk. He must've gone to the store while he was out yesterday.

Salivating and dizzy with hunger, she couldn't endure this. It was cruel enough to starve her. But to torment her with a goddamn breakfast buffet right under her nose was beyond brutal. It was coldblooded and diabolically evil.

Tommy stood, put his empty plate and mug in the dishwasher, and strode past her without a glance or a word. A second later, the bathroom door shut, and the shower turned on.

"Sit." Cole pointed a spatula at the table and turned back to the stove.

If she didn't sit, she would collapse. So she obeyed.

He joined her, holding a heaping plate of food.

Her eyes watered, overflowing with despair. "Would you kill me if I fought you for a bite?"

"No need." He slid the plate toward her and wrapped her trembling hand around a fork. "Hurry up. You only have about five minutes."

Shocked elation jolted through her, but she didn't hesitate. Eggs, bacon, pineapple, glazed donuts — she shoveled it all in, groaning, whimpering, and casting off her manners in lieu of stuffing her face. "He doesn't know you're feeding me?"

"No, and if you tell him, this will be the last time I interfere on your behalf."

Focused on devouring every bite, she didn't come up for air until she'd licked the plate clean.

Cole held out a glass of water, regarding her too closely.

She drank deeply, washing down barely chewed food. "I'm not complaining, but what are you playing at? Good cop, bad cop?"

"If you think I'm the good one, you're terrible at your job."

The bathroom door opened.

Cole reached out and swiped a thumb across her lips, clearing away crumbs. Then he moved the empty plate, setting it in front of him.

Her blood-sugar levels were already rising, surging energy through her system and chasing away the trembling effects of hunger. She was far from feeling like her normal self, but the meal had quickly taken the edge off.

She met Cole's eyes, and maybe he saw the gratitude in hers. But she wouldn't thank him. He was an accomplice in her suffering, and she owed him nothing.

With a smirk, he reclined in the chair and ran a finger along his beard.

He wanted her to think he wasn't a good guy. He could mostly pull it off with that unnerving smirk on his rugged face and the sheer number of tattoos that competed for space on his strapping arms. And maybe his heart was a little jaded and a lot broken. But those bloody, beating scraps still had the capacity for compassion.

As Tommy walked from the bathroom to the bedroom and back to the hall, she pinched the neckline of her tank-top and scrubbed the inside of the material over the surface of her teeth, trying to remove any evidence of that satisfying meal.

Cole arched an eyebrow.

She tipped up hers in return. She'd meant what she told Tommy that first night in the desert. Keeping secrets was a weakness of hers. She did it too well and often lied to protect someone's feelings.

Tommy emerged, wearing a cowboy hat, black t-shirt, faded denim, and dusty boots. His gaze went to her, the empty plate in front of Cole, and made a pass through the kitchen, taking in every detail.

"We're going for a ride." He prowled toward her, reaching into his back pocket.

She stood. "Where—?"

He slapped a handcuff on her wrist and looked at Cole. "I'll be out of signal range for a few hours."

"Where are you taking me?" She kept her movements slow and her stance weak, feigning starvation, even as every muscle in her body burned to fight the restraints.

"I'm heading out, too." Cole pushed from the table, ignoring her as efficiently as Tommy. "I'll be back tonight."

"Don't go after Evan or Mason." Panic shook her voice. "I swear to you, Cole, they're not involved."

"Come on." Tommy pulled her along by the handcuffs, hauling her out the door and into the morning heat.

She shaded her eyes with her free hand, faltering at the sight of a 1980's doorless, topless Jeep Wrangler.

"Where's my truck?" She turned, searching the property, and spotted a black Harley-Davidson motorcycle. "Please, tell me you didn't get rid of my truck. It took me years to pay that off!"

He lifted her, dropped her in the Jeep's passenger seat, and made quick work of shackling both of her hands to the handle on the dash.

As he walked around the front, she took an inventory of the cargo. A shovel, pickax, large plastic containers filled with water, other containers with unknown contents. Her attention returned to the shovel.

"You're going to bury Paul Kissinger?" Her heart shivered.

He climbed in, buckled her seat belt, did his own, and started the engine. Then he shoved the Jeep into gear and took off.

Speeding over ruts and prickly shrubs, he worked the clutch and the gear shift and... *Fucking fuck fuck fuck!*

Even if she managed to escape the cuffs and knock him out, she wouldn't be able to drive out of the desert. Because she didn't know how to drive a goddamn manual transmission.

She dropped her head back on the seat and groaned.

Endless miles stretched in every direction — an expanse of searing, white-hot hopelessness. Gusts of dusty air blasted in through the open top, whipping her hair around her face and stinging her eyes. If she died and went to Hell, it would probably just be more of this.

"I have a newfound aversion to the desert," she said aloud.

"Tell me about it."

The fact that he responded at all surprised her, but it was his words that drew her gaze.

"What?" He glanced at her from beneath the brim of his hat. "I hate this fucking place and never planned on returning."

That was her fault. She'd given him no choice.

"I'm sorry." And she was. "I demanded you to come here because you were in over your head in that undercover job. What happened with Luke? Did he make it out?"

His hand clenched on the steering wheel, his mouth a slash of grim silence. The silence continued for the remainder of the drive through the desert.

He didn't use a map or GPS to find his way. He knew this land better than anyone.

An hour later, he slowed the Jeep, approaching a butte on the horizon. It looked like all the others in this region, but the flock of vultures circling overhead told her that this butte had a narrow cave at the base. And a dead body.

When the corpse of Paul Kissinger came into view, she wanted to close her eyes and hold her breath. She wanted to turn back.

Tommy parked the Jeep far enough away not to smell the rot. Large black birds of prey darted and swarmed in her periphery. She couldn't look. If she did, she would lose her breakfast.

He shut off the engine and unlocked her handcuffs.

She rubbed her wrists, her senses on high-alert. If she ran, he would catch her. If she stole the Jeep keys, she wouldn't know how to operate the clutch. She was free of the restraints, but not free at all.

"Luke is safe." He turned his neck, blinding her with the golden depths of his eyes. "I talked to him last night." The corner of his mouth bounced. "He fell in love with her."

"With the target? Vera?"

"Yeah." He unbuckled his seat belt and stared out at the desert through the windshield. "If I hadn't left the cartel compound when I did, things would've gone differently. Probably worse. Maybe my departure saved lives. Maybe Luke, Vera, and I would've survived either way." He turned his harsh glare on her. "But you had no business interfering. I don't give a fuck if you're telling the truth about your motivation or lying through your teeth. You're a stranger to me. You had no right reading my emails and making demands."

She swallowed down her objections and considered his words. "You're right. I shouldn't have invaded your privacy. I've made a lot of mistakes when it comes to you. But the punishment you're doling doesn't fit the crime."

"That is yet to be determined." He reached toward the back and tossed a bottle of sunscreen on her lap. "Lather up. We're going to be out here a while."

FOURTEEN

The miasma of death overpowered the desert air, making every inhale a poisonous, stomach-turning affliction. Rylee bent at the waist and gagged, her insides burning in misery.

Tommy stood in a shallow grave, seemingly unaffected by the stench as he swung the pickax over and over. He'd been digging forever, making excruciatingly slow progress in the hard, dry earth.

Since tampering with evidence and hiding a human body were crimes, she refused to help. But it was also a crime to fail to report a death and to fail to report the disposal of the body. Neither of which she intended to do.

She would take the secret of Paul's murder to her own grave. Not because she forgave Tommy for his heinous treatment of her, but because she was indebted to him for this murder. The only reason he killed this man was to stop him from raping her.

The desert sizzled with dry heat as far as she could

see. She wasn't even tempted to run. Paul hadn't been able to escape this place, and the grisly aftermath of his failure lay in a pile of vulture scraps. It would be a long while before anyone stumbled upon his grave, if ever.

Even if law enforcement was tipped off to search the area, it would be a race against time and the elements, as the scorching temperatures ensured the remains would quickly decompose. The evidence of homicide would soon dry up with the corpse.

Gruesome thoughts. But comforting. She was so certain the crime scene would never be discovered that Tommy probably didn't even need to bury the body. But he was scrupulous in every job he undertook. He wouldn't leave here until every trace of foul play was gone.

The sounds of scraping and hammering rent the air. He threw the pickax with brutal strength, breaking up rocks and chipping away at the sandy soil.

Muscles and stamina. He had an abundance of both, flexing through each swing, his lips set in a severe line, his physique as rigid and uncompromising as stone.

She would have to be stupid or blind not to notice his honed, sun-splashed body, his shirtless chest glistening with sweat, and his face overheated and red as Lucifer's was by nature.

The handsome devil paused, tossed off the cowboy hat, and raked damp hair away from his forehead. It was cropped on the sides and back and darker at the roots. The longer strands on top were straight and sun-bleached to a lighter shade of brown. If left untouched by his combing fingers, his rebellious bangs hung to his eyebrows.

It was a youthful hairstyle, one he could pull off

without a receding hairline like many men her age had. A reminder that too many years separated them.

He resumed digging, angling away and slamming the ax into the ground. Her gaze followed the action, her lips parted in admiration.

His jeans hung low, molding to his contoured backside and exposing the carved indentations at his hips. His boots bore a thick layer of dust, and all those twitching back muscles streaked with dirt and sweat.

Lethally gorgeous.

Impossible to look away.

He was violence and sex and salvation. Salvation for trafficked women, not for her.

For her, he was corruption.

Damnation.

Death wasn't off the table.

That was the real reason she refused to help him dig. If she stepped into that grave, he might not let her leave it.

But as the day grew hotter and the stench of rot grew riper, she just wanted to get this over with.

With a sigh, she grabbed the shovel and forced her feet toward his sculpted back.

He stilled at the sound of her approach and glanced over his shoulder, his eyes as hot and golden as the blistering sun.

"I'll help." She shrugged. "But it better not be *my* grave I'm digging."

He cocked his tousled head, and a mischievous grin touched his lips.

An honest-to-God smile.

She couldn't have imagined such a thing on his stern face, but now that she witnessed it, she didn't want it to fade. It matched the glint in his eyes and made him look boyish, less threatening, and unreasonably, heartbreakingly stunning.

She was thunderstruck.

He turned back to his task, breaking the spell.

For the next two hours, they dug in silence, taking water breaks in the shade every fifteen minutes.

When he finally deemed the grave deep enough, she crawled out and stood by while he pulled on work gloves and dragged the half-eaten body into the hole.

She gagged and fought surging nausea as they covered the remains with sand and rock. The stench was eye-watering, the sight of squirming maggots and mangled flesh forever branded in her mind.

When the last scoop of dirt dropped on the grave, she charged toward the Jeep, breathing through her mouth and swallowing down bile.

Please, don't puke. Please, don't puke.

She chugged a bottle of water, sweating, shaking, desperate to leave this place and never return.

Footsteps approached from behind. He tossed his dirty gloves and grabbed a water, guzzling it in one long drink.

Dropping her brow against the side of the Jeep, she gagged again. It was all she could do to keep her stomach from emptying precious nutrients.

He moved in behind her and spoke at her ear. "A cock in the ass stops the gag reflex."

Her heart sputtered. "Are you offering?"

"It's a helpful tip."

"So you're offering just the tip?"

"For you, I'll bury it to the root." His breath heated her nape, his body heavy and damp against her back.

Her skin tingled in response, in memory, and she hated herself for it. "Get off me."

"I read the messages on your hookup apps and know for a fact that anal isn't just a notion in your lexicon of filthy thoughts. It's a must-have for your one-night stands."

If he was trying to insult her, he needed a different approach.

"That simply isn't true." She twisted to face him, smirking. "I enjoy all sorts of sex. I'm open-minded that way."

"If I knew that women your age were kinky, I would've bagged a horny old lady years ago."

That hit the mark.

The outrage this man inspired in her was fast and sticky, climbing through her limbs and burning her hand. She swung, slamming her palm across his face.

He didn't flinch or raise his hand. His chilling calmness was threatening all on its own. "You wouldn't have the strength to do that if Cole hadn't fed you."

Denial tangled in her throat and surged onto her tongue. "He didn't."

He strode toward the back of the Jeep, lifted a huge container of water, and poured it over his head. His wet, powerful physique defied the downpour, standing proud and mighty like an impregnable fortress.

Bronzed by the sun, his chiseled chest provided deep grooves for the rivulets of water to travel. It streamed down his well-thewed arms and darkened the denim at his hips. More trickled over the blunt angles of his face and along the thick column of his neck, racing between the hollows of his bulging chest muscles.

He lowered the container, and a fat, glistening

drop clung to the ridge of his brick-hard pec. Finally losing its slippery hold, it cascaded down his flat abdomen and into the thin line of hair that led an enticing path beneath the waistband of his jeans.

"I smelled the bacon on your breath." He stepped forward, his eyes ablaze with malice.

She backed up. "I stole a piece off Cole's plate when he wasn't looking."

In a blur, he dumped the rest of the water on her head. As she sputtered beneath the deluge, he gripped her tank-top and ripped the straps, the neckline, and the material straight down the front.

It fell to the ground in tatters, leaving her braless breasts exposed. She didn't bother covering herself in some pretense of being a shy virgin. They both knew she was anything but.

He watched the water run over her bare chest the same way she'd watched him. The appreciative gleam in his hooded eyes hardened her nipples and boiled her blood.

"You insult my age then ogle my tits?" She grabbed the shovel she'd left against the Jeep. "What kind of bastard are you?"

"A hungry one." He licked his lips, his voice smooth, deep, dangerously masculine. "Remove your jeans."

"Like hell I will." She raised the shovel with both hands.

"Make me hurt you, Rylee." He wrapped his mouth around the words, enunciating slowly. "Beg me."

She swung.

He seized the weapon with a vicious jerk, yanked it from her grip, and flung it out of reach. She slapped his face. Or tried. A fist caught her hair, whirling her off balance. She swung at him again, and he snared her wrist.

"You can't keep your greedy eyes off me." He forced her backward and sideways, crushing her between his body and the Jeep, his breaths coming so hard and angry against hers. "Because you like what you see."

"You have nice hair. Healthy bones. But your personality needs work. Far more than I'm willing to invest."

"Liar. You want me so badly it scares you." He leaned his weight against her, letting her feel the hard, impossibly thick, rigid length of him. "You like it rough and crave an aggressive, heartless man who will smack you around and fuck you like you just kicked his dog."

"You make me sick."

"You lied to me about breakfast, and you're lying now." He wrapped a hand around her throat. "But you're going to make it up to me by taking every inch of my cock."

She couldn't help it. She laughed, a loud, coarse, mocking guffaw that was cut off by his mouth as it slammed down over hers. He kissed her so cruelly and with such sublime devastation of heart and body that it only made her more furious, spurring her to kiss him back with equal venom.

He made a guttural sound deep in his chest as he assaulted her mouth, the thrusts of his tongue lashing against hers, punishing, seducing, making her need him and fear him until the past and present twisted together, doubts and certainty tangling so messily that one couldn't be distinguished from the other.

She arched into him, and he gave her his powerful

body, fucking her with his tongue, squeezing her breasts, choking her throat, and smothering her with the fury of their toxic need.

His kiss was born of darkness, in the horrors of an attic, where pleasure could be plucked from hell if one were demented enough to reach for it. And reach for it, she did, with her lips, her hands, her entire body rising to him. He grabbed her hips, trapping her against the Jeep, and devoured her mouth as if he were trying to suck the life from her soul.

He captured her breaths, swallowed her whimpers, and plunged her into a madness of lust and helplessness. His body was a weapon of enticement, his tongue the trigger. He held her hostage with his mouth, his dominance, and she only wanted to give more, more, more until nothing remained.

When he let her breathe at last, his grip still firm above her collarbones, she could do no better than stare.

He stared back, panting, seemingly dazed.

Christ, he was irresistible. Sexy as fuck. Gorgeous beyond human nature.

And mean as a snake.

She hated him. But she loved the feel of his assertive hands, the taste of his cruel lips, and the dark, deadly passion in his labored breaths. She wanted him to touch her. Her breasts ached for it. But she was scared.

Scared he was toying with her.

Scared he would reject her.

Terrified he wouldn't.

"You wrote in your emails that you can't have sex without inflicting pain. Yet you fight for a cause that saves women." She touched his hand at her throat, pulling on his immovable fingers. "I don't know what this is, if it's just two angry people lashing out at each other and using sex as an outlet, but I don't want any part of it. I won't willingly let you abuse me. If beating women gets you off—"

"Beating women?" He slammed a fist against the Jeep beside her head, making her jump. "Touch me, Rylee. Right now." His face twisted in rage, contorting the masterful planes of beauty as he roared, "Put your fucking hands on me!"

His thundering voice rang in her ears and shook her from head to toe. She swallowed, confused by the demand, and lowered her hands to his jeans.

He tensed as she touched the swollen outline of him beneath the zipper. Her fingers trembled as she followed the impressive bulge, down, down, down, still going…

Holy mother of God, what she'd felt last night hadn't been her imagination. He was enormous, thick, and so fucking long. Like porn-star long.

"Tommy?" Startled, she removed her touch.

Flattening his palms on the Jeep behind her, his arms supported his assertive lean and caged her in. He scrutinized her face, glaring, invading her space, and stealing her air with blatant intimidation.

"Pull me out." A deep, insistent command. Taunting.

This wasn't foreplay or seduction. He was being mean. But there was something else going on. Something straining beneath the antagonism.

Interest? Desire? He was hard as a rock, so yeah, he wanted to fuck, and she was the only female within a hundred miles. But he would never rape her. She'd miscalculated some things about him, but she was certain he would need a damn good reason to force a woman.

And that was what she'd detected beneath his growly, imperious command.

Uncertainty.

Vulnerability.

Was he anxious about her seeing him in the flesh and casting judgment? There was only one way to find out.

Her heart galloped as she unbuckled his belt and lowered the zipper. His breath hitched as she bent, wrestling the snug denim and briefs down his brawny thighs.

He didn't spring free or jut upward. His erection was too heavy, too inconceivably massive to do anything but hang. God help her, he was hung. In his fully aroused, undeniably hard state, he was easily ten inches.

Disbelief compelled her hands. She touched without hesitation, drawing a gasp from his lips. The skin was warm, circumcised, and oh-so silky beneath her trembling fingers, the engorged muscle beneath like bedrock. The hair at the base was dark brown and neatly trimmed, his huge, full testicles completely shaved.

He was beautifully formed, and at the same time, monstrous. A woman's body wasn't designed to take an invasion of this size. Not without horrible stretching and…

Pain.

He couldn't have sex without hurting women.

Realization sank into her stomach, stabbing her with guilt and dread.

"Now you know." He curled his fingers around hers, holding her grip to his shaft. "You invaded my privacy, read the personal journals of my life, and jumped to assumptions about my conduct with women." His hand tightened, crushing the bones in hers. "Your narrow-minded, judgmental idiocy led you into a sick, twisted fantasy world, where I star as some abusive, raging beast."

"You are abusive! Your treatment of me is deplorable."

"That's what *you* want." He grabbed her throat and slammed his body against hers, pinning her against the Jeep. "You came here in search of a sadist who breaks laws and fucks the shit out of women."

"No!" She shook her head rapidly, her neck locked in the cuff of his bruising hand.

Without releasing her, he toed off his boots and kicked away his jeans. Then he set his mouth against hers and fed her his infuriating demand. "Beg me."

"Never." She grabbed his thick neck, mirroring his choking grip.

"For a psychologist, you have a shitload of issues." He wrenched her closer and bit the skin beneath her ear. "I'm going to fuck all that pent-up anger out of you."

"Eat a dick." Fuming, she aimed a punch at his arrogant face.

"I have." He knocked her hand aside and hauled her back against the Jeep. "But you already know all about that because you're a creepy, spying little bitch."

"I was there for you!" She exploded, clawing at his cheeks and kicking him in the shins. "I cried for you. I hurt for you. You ungrateful prick!"

"Oh, Rylee." Laughing cruelly, he dodged her strikes and swatted away her fists. "You break my heart."

"You harden mine." She went after his throat again, trying to strangle him. "Men like you remind me why relationships fail."

"What the fuck does that mean?" He restrained her hands between her bare breasts, his eyes burning with aggression. "Men like me?"

"Playboys. Manwhores. The cheaters and manipulators who fuck their way through the female population without giving a damn about their feelings."

"Pot calling the kettle, baby." He flicked the button on her waistband. "You're the queen of fuck-'em and forget-'em."

He had her jeans open and down her legs before she even registered the sound of the zipper.

Her heart seized, and she dropped to a crouch, twisting out of his grip. Her clothes, now bunched around her legs, tangled up her attempt to run. She fell, spitting and shrieking and frantically crawling away.

He dove for her and grabbed her ankle. She kicked him in the face. He caught her other leg and wrangled off her shoes and clothes until she was as naked as him.

She screamed every curse she knew and scrambled over the rocky ground, scraping her hands and knees. He chased, his breaths hot on her bare ass.

The instant she left the shade of the Jeep, the sun-scorched sand fried her skin. She screamed and scrambled back.

And he was on her, flipping her over and dropping his huge, hard body between her legs.

The astounding sensation of all his hot skin against all of hers was more than she could bear. With his strength so close and his monstrous erection stabbing into her belly, she couldn't escape. Couldn't breathe. Couldn't look away from the furious hunger in his eyes.

He wrapped his hand around her hip and held her

firmly to him. She grabbed his hair and pulled with all her strength. He choked her. She yanked harder on his hair, jerking his head.

He glared at her. She glared at him.

Neither of them moved.

Deadlocked.

Seething.

Seconds from boiling over.

They just stared at each other, unblinking, exchanging a look of pure hatred.

Then suddenly, it was on.

They collided in a clash of mouths and teeth and grappling hands. Rolling, slapping, kissing, scratching, they ground their bodies together like horny, deranged teenagers. Each time they inched out of the shelter of the shade, he dragged her back into the Jeep's shadow and attacked her again.

His cock rammed against the juncture of her thighs, demanding entry. Her pussy throbbed in invitation, convulsing and opening in a flood of arousal. But no amount of wetness could prepare her for his size.

She didn't want him. She couldn't fucking stand him. But the burning, tightening demands of her body made it damn hard to resist his bold touch, ripped physique, and the fascinating yet terrifying equipment between his legs.

"You're despicable." She brandished elbows, knuckles, and knees, hammering her sharpest bones into any part of him she could hit.

He ducked his head, dodging her strikes, and veered his mouth downward to chase the curves of her body. He licked and sucked every inch of her from breasts to pussy. She kicked at him, bowed into him, and tore at his hair.

"I hate you!" She jerked her hips, rocking against his face. "Oh God, don't stop. Don't fucking stop, you son of a bitch."

He bit her clit, and she screeched, smacking his head and sinking her nails into his flesh.

"Fuck, woman!" Teeth bared, he shot up her body and grabbed her face.

Livid didn't begin to describe the fire in his eyes.

She yanked him close. He dragged her closer and took her lips, kissing her, fingering her, and grinding against her to the echoes of her own traitorous groans.

They reached for his cock at the same time, wriggling and lining up their bodies, wild and clumsy in their urgency. She knew he would stretch her, bruise her, possibly injure her, and she didn't even care.

She counted on it.

With the broad tip of him notched at her entrance, he wrapped a fist around the base of his shaft. A habit? To prevent himself from sinking in all the way?

Clenching his jaw, he held her gaze and pushed past her opening.

Sensations unfurled, exploding shimmers of pleasure around the stretching invasion. His entire body shook with the effort to control his thrust, and she trembled with him, moaning, squirming, needing more. More burning, more pressure, more *him*.

She slapped him across the head. "Hurt me, goddammit. I want to feel you."

He stopped breathing, eyes wide and frighteningly angry.

Then a nefarious smile lit his face.

He dropped his hand from his cock, removing that

barrier, and impaled her to the hilt with absolutely no mercy.

FIFTEEN

Rylee let out an ear-splitting scream of pain, and Tomas choked on a groan, shaking in the exquisite grip of her body. Christ, he was going to come.

From one thrust.

Holy fucking fuck.

He wasn't a sadist, but damn, this woman had begged for it so beautifully. Not just begged. She'd demanded it.

Hurt me, goddammit.

Yeah, he was hurting her, and she was taking it like a champ. Every inch of him. Each time he hit the back of her hot cunt, she wailed, cursed, and clutched his ass, pulling him tighter, harder against her.

She was tougher than he'd thought, and everything was so wet and warm around him, sucking him in, gripping him like a glove. The sweet smell of her skin, the intoxicating way she tasted, her sexy little cries of hunger and rage — these were things he would never forget. Fucking incredible. Hotter than hell.

That only enraged him more.

Why wasn't it like this with other women? He was so accustomed to the gasps of fear, awkwardness of penetration, and pleas for him to slow down and be gentle. He couldn't remember the last time he'd just let loose and plowed into a woman. Or when he'd actually had sex without holding a hand around his cock.

Never.

Rylee was unlike anyone he'd ever been with. Just his goddamn luck.

Only four days ago, he'd strangled the life out of her and contemplated leaving her for dead. And that was before he knew the infuriating depths of her stubbornness. The best thing to do now was just fuck her until she broke.

He grabbed her by the throat, growing painfully hard at the sight of her huge silver eyes, the gaping *O* of her swollen lips, and the jiggle of her perky, round tits as she tried to suck in air.

She was beyond gorgeous. Utterly perfect. He fucking despised her.

Driving viciously against the walls of her cunt, he rammed his tongue down her throat in the most aggressive kiss he'd ever taken.

When he finally let her breathe, she growled and ripped at his hair. But it didn't stop her from kissing him back. Their mouths fused, crashing and mauling like they were trying to dislocate each other's faces. It was violent and crude and emotionally unbridled, releasing an unfathomable flood of passion.

He pounded into her, biting her lips and licking the tears that drenched her face. Sand and grit clung to her hair, his hands, their arms and legs.

The heat was unbearable, the sun relentless. But the fever between them overpowered everything, flowing uncontrollably through their locked tongues, breaths, and hips. Nothing was stopping them.

With a surge of strength, she pushed him onto his back and started to ride him, clawing at his chest, trying to claw away his dominance.

Fuck that. He rose to his feet without disconnecting their bodies, continued to grind her on his cock, and crossed the distance to the cave.

He dumped her on the ground in the shade. She landed with a yelp, and he fell upon her, thrusting deep, power-fucking her into the rocky sand, dripping with sweat, and tearing her up like an animal. She choked him. He choked her right back, and within seconds, she was coming in a torrent of incensed screams.

"Fuck you, Tommy!" She sank her nails into his arms, panting and thrashing and gushing all over his cock. "Oh, Jesus, it hurts so good. So fucking good."

Impaled on the full length of him, she came and came, flailing wildly, unabashedly through the longest orgasm in history. Sweet God in hell, she was the most arousing, extraordinarily beautiful thing he'd ever seen. Such a sexy, uninhibited screamer, who liked it rough, got off on pain, and left shameless scratches all over his body. So fucking satisfying.

But he wasn't satisfied.

He didn't want her to enjoy it more than he was.

Pulling out, he flipped her over in the dirt and spanked her. She fought him belligerently while wriggling her ass for more.

"You're such a slut." He grabbed her hips and slammed into her from behind.

"If I'm a slut…" Panting, she pushed back and forced him deeper. "You're a depraved, twisted pervert. Give it to me, you sick fuck. Make me feel it."

His balls tightened. His skin caught fire, and the pressure in his cock exploded. He came violently, dizzyingly, groaning, jerking through the thrusts, unable to slow down as he fucked her like a dog.

He shouldn't have shot his load that quickly. Hell, he shouldn't have fucking come in her at all.

Irritated, he pushed her away, his cock still rigid and throbbing.

She fell onto her back, legs spread, pussy glistening, and eyes glimmering with filthy, forbidden temptation.

He wasn't done. Not even close.

In the next breath, he was inside her again, his tongue in her mouth, his furious thrusts stabbing between her thighs. He'd never been a gentle lover, but he was really going at it with her, slapping her tits, biting her throat, marking her flesh, leaving hickeys and bruises, and God only knew the damage he was inflicting on her cunt.

He wouldn't pretend it was the moral thing to do or that he was justified in any way, but what followed was the angriest, loudest, sweatiest, most passionate sex of his life.

Every time she climaxed, he spiraled with her, falling deeper, further into her corrupt, dishonest, deliciously tight clasp.

His recovery rate was unprecedented. He'd never been able to go multiple rounds without breaks in between. But with Rylee, he never wanted to stop.

He used her mercilessly — on the ground, against

the Jeep, and across the front seat with the air-conditioning blowing at full speed. It went on and on, orgasm after orgasm, in every position. Just when he thought he couldn't go another round, she did this seductive lip-biting thing with an evil glint in her eyes, and blood surged to his cock with a vengeance.

They ended up at the entrance of the cave again where the shade from the butte was the coolest. With his back to the rocky cliff, he held her on his lap, hands clenched on her waist, moving her up and down on his sore, ravenous erection.

Scratches and bite marks covered her gorgeous breasts in a tapestry of destruction and passion. Their bodies were soaked in layers of sweat and come, with sand creeping into places they would never get clean.

"Fuuuck!" She threw her head back, moaning. "I love your huge, gorgeous cock. Even if you are a heartless asshole."

"Shut the fuck up." He dragged her mouth to his, kissing her hungrily, furiously, trying to quench an unquenchable thirst.

It was impossible. This felt too amazing. She felt too perfect. It was as if he'd been waiting his entire life to experience this. To experience Rylee Sutton in all her lusty, untamed glory.

He separated their mouths and stared at her, enraptured. Then he captured her lips again, his hand falling to the small of her back and gently fitting her against him.

His hips were no longer moving, his body no longer racing toward release. He was still hard inside her, but he just wanted to touch her, enjoy the nearness of her beauty, for no other reason than because he could.

He moved his lips to her throat, licking gently, savoring her salty-sweet taste.

"What are you doing?" She touched his jaw, pushing away his mouth.

With a hand framing her angelic face, he leaned in to kiss her.

She pulled back and wriggled on his cock. "Why did you stop?"

"I'm spent."

"Bullshit." She scoffed with disdain. "You dominate women in your sleep."

As conflicted and angry as he was with this crazy woman, he wasn't so far out of his mind to not recognize she had severe intimacy issues.

Her eyes hardened as if she could read his thoughts. Shoving off his lap, she gave him the finger and strode toward the Jeep.

No, she limped, nursing each step. He'd done that. He'd fucked her so brutally she could barely walk.

He smiled, feeling a sick amount of satisfaction in that.

Until she spoke.

"I thought a guy your age could go for days." She flashed a venomous glare over her shoulder. "Evan might be twenty years older than you, but he knows how to fuck me properly. He *loves* my ass."

Yeah, he knew all about Evan's ass-fucking, but it was difficult to hear.

What was this burning pit in his stomach? The sudden difficulty in swallowing. The loss of vision due to a blinding need to gut her neighbor from neck to balls.

Was it jealousy?

That was new.

So was her insult. He'd been with women who cowered and grimaced and sometimes cried in pain, but they never outright criticized his performance.

She was baiting him. He knew it, but he couldn't stop himself from moving. He just…lost it.

He caught her at the Jeep, bent her over the bumper, and fucked her pussy so hard that her head hit against the scorching metal hood.

Everything was so drenched down there he pulled out and slammed right into her ass. No barriers. No mercy. He put his back into it and went to town, giving her every inch of his cock and soaking up her screams.

Fuck yeah, she screamed, calling him every despicable name she could muster. But her verbal abuse only made him hotter. He loved how her tongue slurred over the vowels, her lilting voice and moaning cries rising up and down like notes on a musical scale.

If he thought she'd made him hard before, it was nothing compared to the excruciating grip of her tight little hole. She kept trying to finger herself, but he wouldn't allow it. He slapped her hand away. She hit him back and ended up coming without the stimulation.

She climaxed just from the stretch of his cock in her ass, soaking his balls, his legs. He shoved a hand between her thighs. Holy fuck, she was a squirter.

Another first for him.

His orgasm crashed into him, and he exploded like a goddamn fire hose, filling her with more come than he'd ever shot before and with such ferocity that he collapsed on the ground in a pile of exhaustion and astonishment.

Straightening, she stretched her arms overhead and rolled her neck. Thick globs of milky white slithered down her inner thighs, her perfect ass welted from his hands and coated in sand.

She wasn't embarrassed by any of it as she turned to face him. Her posture radiated pleasure and contentment.

The image of every man's wildest fantasy.

He'd wasted a lot of goddamn years fucking only young women.

Rylee was so far past modesty, bashful awkwardness, and indecisive teetering. Whether she was confident in her skin or mature enough not to give a fuck, she stood before him, gloriously naked, covered in savage bites, and *smiled*.

It was the first time she genuinely smiled at him.

Christ, he felt it.

Everywhere.

"I have a newfound appreciation for the desert. Best sex of my life." She walked away, wobbly on her legs and sexier than ever.

What they just did, it was destructive. But the twisted, fucked-up aspects of it had made it so much more passionate. They hated each other, and he might just kill her before this situation was resolved.

But he agreed with her. She was the best sex he'd ever had.

He joined her at the rear of the Jeep and lifted the second water container, pouring it over her as she washed her body. Then she held it over him while he did the same.

They didn't speak. Didn't smile. But their gazes touched and held, never shying away.

It wasn't awkward or normal or hopeful or angry.

It just...*was*.

When all the sand and body fluids were rinsed away, they pulled on their jeans. Her tank-top was ruined, so she stole his shirt.

He allowed it because seeing her in his clothes satisfied some weird, territorial instinct he refused to analyze. It was too soon.

They packed up the Jeep and drove back to the house in sated silence. He didn't shackle her. She didn't know how to drive a manual transmission — a prediction he'd guessed accurately when he'd put her in the vehicle this morning.

Yesterday, Cole hid her truck in a storage unit and bought this Jeep in a nearby town. They still didn't know who was watching her, if she was working with anyone, or if she was as clueless as she claimed to be.

Someone connected to NSA or black ops had put high-tech bugs in her house. That someone had an unnerving interest in who she was fucking. And now Tomas was on the list.

Was her ex-husband stalking her? Her neighbor? Or someone less obvious? Whether or not it was her intention, she'd led that someone directly to him and Cole.

That made him edgy, especially as he neared his property.

The house came into view, and he slowed, shading his eyes and scrutinizing every inch of the perimeter. Cole was still gone, as expected. Nothing appeared off-kilter.

"You're tense." She twisted in the seat, watching him. "Do you think we're in danger?"

"You led trouble to my front door."

"Yeah, you keep saying that, but I can't figure out

how or why anyone would be interested in me."

He was interested in her. Begrudgingly. Insanely. She'd sneaked beneath his skin, and if he wasn't careful, his attraction to her would become irreversible.

Parking the Jeep, he shut off the engine. As he stepped out, the distant purr of a motor reached his ears. He went still, his senses firing.

"What is it?" She followed his gaze to the horizon, shielding her eyes with a hand.

The engine grew closer, louder. Not throaty enough to be Cole's motorcycle.

"Get in the house." Pulse quickening, he lunged toward the glove box, unlocking it and removing a pistol.

She didn't move.

"Now." He slammed a palm against her butt, sending her in motion.

The sounds of her footsteps moved toward the door, and it slammed shut behind her. She better keep her nosy ass inside.

A black truck emerged on the horizon. Newer model. Expensive.

He concealed the gun in his boot and straightened his spine.

As the vehicle advanced, he saw only one occupant. A male driver. Texas tags on the truck. Not a local, though. The man was wearing a white collared shirt and black tie. No one around here owned a suit or drove a fancy truck.

The pistol sat heavily against his calf. If Rylee hadn't taken his shirt, he would've concealed the weapon in his waistband for easier access.

As the vehicle stopped a few yards away, Tomas leaned against the Jeep, arms folded across his clawed-up chest, and waited like a bored, rural redneck with nothing but time on his hands.

A mid-thirties man stepped out and directed his mirrored aviator sunglasses at him. Lean cheeks, clean-shaved jaw, aristocratically straight nose, ink-black hair worn high and tight—all of it lent him the air of official business.

He reeked of law enforcement. Probably a small-town detective, dressing for the job he wanted rather than the dead-end job he was stuck with.

Only one of two reasons would interest him enough to drive all the way out here. Paul Kissinger or Rylee Sutton. Both missing.

Except Rylee took a sabbatical from work and claimed she told no one she was coming here. The jury was still out on whether she was lying.

"Mr. Dine?" The man strode forward, flashing his shiny, self-important badge. "I'm Detective Hodge."

Tomas spat a wad of phlegm in the sand and glared.

"You're the owner of this property?" The detective paused a few feet away and peered at him over his lowered sunglasses. "Are you Tomas Dine?"

"Yep."

"I'm following up on a missing-persons report. Got a call that Rylee Sutton was spotted at your residence."

Spotted by whom? Paul Kissinger? The bastard must've notified someone that the tracker on her truck stopped here. That, or someone else was tracking her truck.

"If she was seen here," he drawled, playing the part of a moronic cowboy, "then she ain't missing, is she?"

Any moment, she was going to burst out the front door and run off her mouth about being beaten and held captive. Then he would have to shoot the detective and bury another body.

But he wasn't a cop killer. There had to be another way.

"I'm looking for Rylee Sutton." Detective Hodge cocked his head. "Age forty-one. Brown hair. Gray eyes. Tiny little thing. Absolutely gorgeous."

"Gorgeous? Is that in the official description, detective?"

"Well, it's the truth." The detective stood taller. "Have you seen her?"

The front door opened, and here she came. His hand twitched, the pistol burning in his boot.

"Dean?" Her footsteps approached. "What are you doing here?"

Oh, great. She fucking knew the guy. Probably worked with him. Another admirer?

He clenched his jaw.

She walked past Tomas, circling far out of his reach as if she weren't limping from the ramming of his cock. That was when he saw her duffel bag clutched tightly in her fist.

So she'd grabbed her shit and intended to leave with this douchebag. *Clever girl.*

Unless Detective Dean Hodge was compromised.

Tomas didn't know if she was in danger, but if she was, *everyone* was a suspect.

Tension flared beneath his skin, but he kept his expression relaxed and voice calm. "Who reported her missing?"

"Missing?" She turned to him, mouth open in

172

shock, and looked back to the detective. "I'm not missing, Dean. Who said I was?"

Now would've been the time for her to blurt the details of her captivity, but she didn't utter a word of it. Even stranger, she'd pulled on a jacket while in the house, hiding the abuse inflicted upon her body.

"Your ex-husband." Dean gave her a once-over, lingering on her mouth. *What the fuck?* "He said you disappeared four days ago."

"Try ten years ago. That's the beauty of divorce." She cocked her hip. "He doesn't get to know where I am or what I'm doing." She narrowed her eyes. "How did you find me?"

"We put out an alert two days ago. Got an anonymous call that you were spotted here."

Suspicion snaked through Tomas' veins. Either Dean was lying or someone was using him to get to Rylee, whether to deliver a message to her, pull her out of here, or something else entirely.

Everything about this felt off.

Her empty expression revealed nothing. Frozen, she stared at Dean's vehicle. What was she thinking? Escape, most likely.

"Rylee? Is everything okay?" Dean stepped toward her and touched her arm. "How do you know this man? Where's your truck?"

She could tell him everything, just lay out all the gory details right now. The detective would try to arrest him, and he would be forced to shoot or flee in the Jeep. He really didn't want to kill an innocent guy. But what if Dean knew more than he was letting on?

"Tomas is just a friend I met in town." She blew out a breath and hauled the duffel bag over her shoulder.

173

"My truck broke down. Mind if I catch a ride?"

SIXTEEN

Rylee's pulse sputtered frantically as she hobbled toward Dean's truck, sore and uncertain. She was making a decision that not only risked her life but that of her colleague.

Nothing was stopping Tommy from drawing that gun in his boot and shooting them both. But if she let this opportunity slip away, if she stayed here another day, he would continue to starve her and poison her mind.

She'd turned into something she didn't recognize today and grudge-fucked him in the desert. But that didn't make the grudge go away. No amount of sex — no matter how huge the cock — could erase the three days she spent in the heat without water.

Or the cruelty in his eyes as he ate that bowl of chili in front of her.

Or the dozens of other vicious acts he'd committed against her since she arrived.

She needed distance from him to think, figure out who was watching her, and talk to her nuisance of an ex-husband. Why in the hell would Mason report her missing?

Something didn't add up.

Dean followed her without comment, probably confused by her boldness in requesting a ride. She'd made a habit of avoiding all her male colleagues, coming across as a guarded, unapproachable bitch. She was there to work, not get laid.

Early on, she'd learned that something as innocent as eye contact often led to a wrong impression, which led to unwanted attention and harassment. So she kept her head down and avoided, avoided, avoided.

Which was why she had no friends.

As she reached the passenger door of his truck, the space between her shoulders itched.

She turned her neck. Their gazes locked. The desert held its breath.

They stared at each other with a familiarity, an intimacy that hadn't been there before. The voltage, the sparks, the unwanted chemistry that had been present from the beginning was there, too. But it hadn't grown into trust. Not even a little.

Someone knew she was here, and Tommy believed she was working with this person. She was under no delusions that sex had changed his opinion. If anything, he thought even less of her now.

She needed to get out of here.

Without looking away, she opened the passenger door.

His eyes narrowed to slits, his knees slowly bending as he reached to pluck the pistol from his boot.

Dean climbed into the truck, oblivious.

Panic spiked, and she subtly shook her head at

Tommy, begging him with her eyes.

Don't shoot him. He's an innocent man.

He went still, scowling at her. Even at this distance, she felt his murderous fury. It competed with the desert heat, blistering her skin and watering her eyes.

She forced her legs to move, stepping into the truck, her nerves on tenterhooks, shaking with the rush of her breaths.

He didn't move as she closed the door. Didn't draw his gun as Dean started the truck and drove away.

Angling her neck, she stared at the side mirror, expecting Tommy to chase or shoot. But he was nowhere in sight.

She held her breath until she could no longer see the house, until she was confident they were out of bullet range.

Then she dropped her head back and released a sigh of relief.

That had been too easy.

He'd let her go.

"You just met that guy?" Dean glanced at her and returned to the unpaved terrain.

"Yeah."

"Doesn't seem like it. I mean, the way he was looking at you…"

She didn't owe him an explanation. "Thanks for the ride."

His hand clenched on the steering wheel. "What's wrong with your truck?"

"Don't know." She cut her eyes at him. "Why was there an alert put out on me? Did you not ask around first? My neighbor would've told you where I was."

"Evan Phillips? Yeah, I talked to him. He said you

were acting strangely and left. Couldn't tell us your whereabouts. His statement didn't inject a lot of confidence in your safety."

"Ridiculous." She balled her hands on her lap. "I told him I was going to the desert for a much-needed vacation."

"A vacation with a man you just met?" His tone grated with judgment.

"You're crossing the line, Dean."

"All I'm saying is you should be more careful. That guy was putting off some serious hostile vibes, and I don't like the way he was looking at you."

"Like what?" she snapped impatiently. "How was he looking at me?"

"Like he couldn't decide if he wanted to hug you, fuck you, or throttle your neck. He definitely didn't want you to leave."

Perceptive man. He wouldn't be good at his job if he wasn't.

She pulled the collar of the jacket against her bruised throat.

"He was fun for a few nights," she said, at the risk of ruining her reputation. "But I need to get back to my truck."

She couldn't go home since Tommy knew where she lived.

When she'd spotted her duffel bag in his house, she'd only had seconds to go through it. Her ID, credit card, money, everything she needed was in there except her phone. Didn't matter. Since someone was tracking her, she would've left the device behind anyway.

On her way out, she'd ransacked the kitchen, searching for a weapon. A large butcher knife was the best she'd found. That went into the duffel bag, along with some of her spare clothes she found in the laundry room.

"Where's your truck?" Dean asked.

"May I?" She gestured at his phone, where it mounted on the dash, showing a map of their location and directions back to the nearest paved road. "I can't remember the name of the town."

She had no idea where to go. Somewhere with a motel, a cash machine, and food. Lots and lots of food.

At his nod, she zoomed out on the screen and started scrolling east, searching for the best place to lie low for a few days.

"Where's your phone?" He veered the truck around a deep ravine.

"Out of batteries." She paused the screen on a small town that showed a few restaurants, a gas station, and...*bingo.* A motel.

Pulling her attention away, she glanced at her surroundings. Sand, shrubs, more sand—all familiar but not recognizable. She didn't remember driving in this way, but she'd been watching her GPS map the entire time.

It seemed strange that Dean would travel three hours to follow up on an anonymous tip. If she were anyone else, he would've called in local law enforcement to check it out. But he knew her. They'd worked together for a couple of years. Maybe that explained it.

Maybe she shouldn't be trusting him.

"Is it slow at work?" She returned to the map, panning away from the town she'd decided on.

"Always."

"Is that why you're here? Nothing better to do?"

"I was worried, Rylee." He ran a hand over his head, his gaze straight ahead, avoiding hers. "I don't trust these local guys to do a thorough job, so I came to look for you myself."

It was the right answer, but something niggled.

If someone was after Tommy and they were tracking her to get to him, how deep could they go? Deep enough to involve Dean?

She was in the middle of the desert with a man who showed up at Tommy's house after Paul went missing. Dean could be on the same errand as Paul. He could be delivering her as a hostage to one of Tommy's enemy cartels. Or planning to kill her himself as part of some blackmail scheme.

Jesus, Rylee. Stop.

She was fucking paranoid. That was Tommy's fault. After reading about all the shit he and his team had been mixed up in over the past ten years, she'd developed a scary imagination.

Dean wasn't part of some criminal organization, but that didn't mean she could trust him with her whereabouts. If someone was monitoring his conversations, he could inadvertently mention where he dropped her off.

So she quickly scanned the map, searching for a different motel in the surrounding areas. A motel she wouldn't be staying at.

"Here it is." She announced the name of the desert town and set it as the destination on the map, rerouting the directions. "Thank you for coming for me."

"I'm happy to do it." He paused, eyes on the terrain, and dropped his voice. "What happened?"

"What do you mean?"

"I saw his chest. The scratches and… I don't know. Sure looked like bite marks. *Human* bites."

Heat rose to her cheeks. "We're adults. It was consensual."

And hateful and angry and so fucking hot she would never, ever experience anything as amazing or pleasureful again.

"He's a little young for you."

"Excuse me?" Her neck went taut.

"Hey, don't get mad. I'm just making an observation."

"That was an ageist insult, not an observation. If you have any more of those, keep them to yourself."

Awkward tension filled the cab, producing a bitter taste on her tongue.

For the next thirty minutes, they drove in silence. She should've been thinking about what she was going to do without a car and a phone, but her focus kept pulling back to Tommy, to the fervent way he'd kissed her, touched her, and claimed every inch of her body. He hadn't just physically branded her. He'd indelibly seared himself onto her soul.

His cruelty was unforgivable, but the sex was unforgettable. He was no longer in her sight, but she doubted he would ever leave her mind.

"I'm sorry." Dean turned onto the main road, following the directions on the map. "I shouldn't have said what I did."

Sand turned into pavement, but the desolate surroundings remained unchanged.

She stared out the window at the vista of buttes. "How's the Wagner case coming along?"

"We got a lead on the location of a meth lab."

For the remainder of the drive, they talked about work. A neutral subject. Familiar ground.

When he pulled up to the motel, she looked around and panicked. There was nothing around. Not a car or a restaurant or another building in sight.

She didn't intend to stay here. Not where Dean knew her location. She needed to get to the next town over, where she had options and could hide out for a few days.

He turned off the engine. "Are you sure this is where you left your truck?"

"It's the closest motel to the mechanic." She grabbed her bag and opened the door. "Thank you for the ride."

"I'll come in with you."

"No need." She stepped into the wretched heat.

He reached across the seat and caught her elbow, stopping her. "Let me take you to dinner. There's nothing here—"

"No." She wrenched her arm away. "I'll see you in a month, Dean. Drive safe."

She shut the door on his response and strode toward the motel office.

Inside, the scent of tobacco smoke attacked her nose. A young blonde woman sat behind the desk, flicking ash from a cigarette, her gaze glued to her phone.

Rylee turned toward the window and watched Dean pull out of the lot. She didn't move until his truck vanished beyond the horizon.

"Need a room?" the girl asked.

"I need transportation to the next town."

"Can't help you there, babe."

"You can't call me a cab? Or a vehicle for hire?"

"Nothing like that comes out here." The girl snorted without looking up from her phone. "You'll have better luck using your thumb out on that road."

Rylee glanced at the highway, which hadn't seen another car since she'd arrived.

Shit.

Desperate, she grappled for options. "When do you get off work?"

"In six hours."

Double shit.

She couldn't wait that long. She needed food, a shower, a bed, and a million other things to formulate a plan, and she needed to do all of it in a place where no one could find her.

Tommy might've let her go because he didn't want to shoot Dean. But he would come for her now that the detective was out of the way.

The girl lowered her phone and toyed with one of her short blonde ringlets. "I have a one-hour lunch break."

"When?"

"Right now."

Exhilaration coursed through her as she dug through her duffel bag and removed a wad of cash. "I'll pay you two-hundred dollars to drive me to the next town."

"Okay." The girl shrugged a shoulder. "Sure."

Yes! Mind spinning, she turned toward the cash machine in the corner. "Does that work?"

"Last I checked."

Perfect. She would withdraw enough cash to get her by for a few days and destroy her credit card. "Do you have a trash bag?"

"Umm…" The blonde's eyebrows knitted. "Yes?"

"I need that, too."

The duffel bag would stay here, and only the things she needed would go in the plastic bag. Things that couldn't have been bugged.

If Tommy or anyone else was tracking her, she was going to make it as hard as possible.

SEVENTEEN

For the next three days, Rylee holed up in the shittiest motel room in Texas. Restless, overstrung, and nearing her wit's end, she paced the stained carpet and chewed her nails down to nubs.

When she'd paid for the ride here, she had the girl drop her at a corner store a mile down the road. There, Rylee had bought a range of everyday items, including a cheap, prepaid smart phone. After paying in cash, she carried it all on foot to this smelly, dilapidated, out-of-the-way motel.

By the time she'd checked in, her body throbbed everywhere, a reminder of the beating she'd taken in the desert. Her immediate concern had been taking care of her basic needs—shelter, water, food, hygiene, pain-killers, sleep.

So much sleep.

God, she'd needed that rest. After asphyxiation, extreme thirst, starvation, and unthinkable stress over the past week, she slept through most of the first two days.

She never wanted to wake up.

But she couldn't hide forever.

The prepaid phone burned in her hand as she paced the room. She hadn't stepped outside once since arriving. Hadn't called Mason or Evan or any of her colleagues. Hadn't logged into her email at home or the systems at work.

The television stations reported no major news. A web search on Paul Kissinger turned up exactly nothing. As if he didn't exist. She didn't know who had hired him or why. She didn't have names, physical descriptions, eye-witness reports, behavioral habits, a motivation… Absolutely nothing to profile.

She had no plan. No solution. Not a single goddamn thing to go on.

Desperate, she'd pulled up an internet browser and typed random search strings.

How do I identify who's stalking me?

What types of devices are used to track cars?

Can bugs be hidden on a person?

If I'm being followed, what should I do?

Every answer led to the obvious course of action. *Call the cops.* Ironic, considering her occupation. She wanted to call her colleagues but didn't know who to trust. Dean had already helped her, so contacting him was the most logical option.

She wasn't ready to do that. Maybe paranoia was getting the best of her, but something about their interaction in his truck made her scalp tingle.

If only she had family or a close girlfriend to call, someone she could ask for help.

She had no one.

She was utterly, completely alone.

What was happening outside her little bubble? Was Mason looking for her? Was Evan still collecting her mail? She knew in her bones that Tommy was out there somewhere, hunting her right now.

She'd worked herself into a corner with nowhere to go. Her cash was dwindling. Her panic was rising. She was running out of time.

The only thing she'd achieved by coming here was healing her body back to full health. But if Tommy found her, *when* he found her, he would hurt her all over again.

It was horrifying that someone had monitored her for six months. But even more frightening was the thought of Tommy crashing through that door.

The fear he instilled in her was crippling, and she fucking loathed him for that.

Stepping to the covered window, she inched the curtain aside, just a sliver, and scrutinized the empty parking lot. The setting sun created shadows across the cracked pavement and arid wasteland surrounding it.

Nothing in sight for miles. No looming danger. The world went on without her.

As if the past week had never happened.

Maybe she was delusional. Overacting. Wasting her time here. Hiding for no reason.

She released the curtain and yanked down the neckline of her shirt. Stroking her thumb over the curve of her breast, she traced one of the dozens of bite marks that covered her body.

Tommy had positively happened. He was real. His rage, passion, and intensity had been as authentic as hers, and if she didn't do something soon, he would show up here more furious than ever.

Mason still lived in El Paso, a three-hour drive

away. She could call him, and if she detected anything suspicious in his voice, she would have time to ditch the phone and put distance between herself and this town. She would steal a damn car if needed.

But was it worth the risk?

Just to ask why he'd reported her missing?

She really needed to know.

Moving to the bed, she sat on the edge and dialed his number from memory.

He answered on the first ring. "Hello?"

"Why did you file a missing-persons report on me?"

"Rylee." The relief in his sigh chafed her nerves. "Thank God. I've been worried sick. Where are you?"

"Answer the question, Mason."

"Tell me where you are. If you're in trouble—"

"I'm on vacation. So imagine my surprise when Dean Hodge showed up, looking for me."

"Why did they send *him?* I hate that sleazy creep. He has a hard-on a mile long for you."

"You know what's creepy? The fact that you know everyone I work with, even though we've been divorced for ten years, *and* I have a restraining order against you."

"The restraining order expired."

"I'll file another one."

"On what grounds? I love you, Rylee. My life is a goddamn meaningless pit without you. How long are you going to make me pay for a mistake I made when I was a kid?"

"You were thirty-one when you cheated on me, and as you already know, my grudges last forever. Why did you call my place of employment and report me missing?"

The sounds of his breaths rasped through the phone for several seconds. "Your neighbor contacted me."

Shock chilled her spine as she lurched to her feet, heart racing. "My neighbor?"

"Evan Phillips. He said you were acting scared and disappeared."

"That's not at all what happened." Her lungs crashed together as she raced to the window, obsessively checking the parking lot. "If he was so concerned about my whereabouts, why didn't he call the police himself? Why would he call you?"

"You'll have to ask him that question."

"It doesn't make sense. He's collecting my mail. I told him I was leaving and where I was going."

"Because you're fucking him."

"What?" Outrage whooshed through her veins and rang in her ears. "Are you watching me, Mason?"

"I keep tabs on you. Always have. I can't let go, Rylee. I refuse to give you up."

She waited for an itch, a tingle of sentiment, and felt nothing.

Should she ask him about Paul Kissinger? If he didn't hire the man, the question would raise flags and needlessly involve him. If he were already involved, he would lie.

Because he was a dishonest, dirtbag cheater.

She had a remarkable gift for attracting the worst of the worst men.

"Tell me why you think I'm sleeping with Evan." Her voice rose several octaves, all patience gone. "Tell me right fucking now!"

"When he called me, I asked him outright, and he

189

confirmed it."

Was Mason lying about that? Was he jealous enough, obsessed enough, to hire a man to watch her fuck her neighbor?

"I hate it." His voice took on a bitter edge. "I hate every second you spend with other men because it's another second you're not with me. I hate that I had the entire world in my arms, in my bed, and I lost it all. I only have myself to blame. I lost you because I'm an idiot. You were the only woman I'd ever been with, and at the time, I thought..."

"You needed to play the field? How was the grass on the other side? Was it greener?"

"No. God, Rylee. No one compares to you. You're stunning beyond words, and every year that you age, you only look younger and more gorgeous. You're hard-working. Intelligent. Compassionate." His tone deepened. "A hellion in bed. But most of all, you were a devoted and faithful wife. You gave me one-hundred percent of your love, and I squandered it like a fool."

She'd never told him about the bridge. They'd never discussed the affair or anything that happened after. This was the longest conversation she'd allowed him to have with her since the divorce.

"Where are you?" he asked.

"I'm wherever you're not, and it's going to remain that way. If I see you again, I'll file another restraining order."

She hung up and tossed the phone.

A tremor started at the base of her skull and worked its way down her spine. Within seconds, she was shaking. Fighting tears. Shivering in a cold sweat.

"Fuck you, Mason." She swatted at the moisture

that leaked from her eyes, her voice soft, deadened. "Fuck you."

Outside, nightfall descended. She sat on the bed until the room went dark. She didn't turn on the lights, didn't want to draw attention to the room from anyone who might drive by.

She couldn't go home.

Maybe Mason had lied about Evan's phone call. Maybe he was telling the truth, and Evan was…what? Stalking her? Trying to control her life? She was a criminal psychologist, for fuck's sake. Her entire job was examining criminal behavior and diagnosing mental health conditions. How could she not detect red flags with the man she'd been sleeping with for the past year?

She just couldn't. It didn't fit Evan's personality.

He has hundreds of photos of you on his personal computer.

Was that a criminal offense? No, but it made him a suspect. If he was capable of involving Paul Kissinger, Dean Hodge, and her ex-husband in some unknown scheme, he was capable of tracking her phone if she called him.

Contacting Evan was out of the question. Not until she had more information.

And she couldn't rule out the most threatening possibility.

Tommy had a nefarious history with a list of enemies that stretched from Canada to South America. Her connection to him was the emails. How someone could discover that she was reading them was beyond her technical understanding. She'd had access to the *Tommysgirl* account for ten years, yet Paul had only been watching her for six months.

All of this buzzed through her mind as she lay in the dark. Every creak and bump made her jump. Even the silence rose the hairs on her arms.

After failing her marriage, she'd given up her reliance on people. She stopped depending on and trusting in all men. Avoiding relationships protected her from repeating the unspeakable pain she'd experienced on the bridge. Being alone had kept her safe for ten years.

But she didn't feel safe right now.

And she'd never felt so alone.

That night, she didn't sleep well. The next day brought more of the same—eating, napping, and chasing her thoughts in circles. Her supplies were running out, and the room was only paid for through one more night.

She would have to check-out tomorrow and call Dean.

Or hitchhike to another country. A far more appealing option.

Hours after dusk on the fourth night, she turned on the shower and set out clean clothes. While the water warmed up, she stepped out of the bathroom and into the dark room. From the nightstand, she grabbed the butcher knife she'd taken from Tommy's house.

Keeping the lights off gave her a false sense of comfort. If someone wanted to find her badly enough, a dark motel room wouldn't deter them. But she refused to cast a moving shadow on the curtains and make herself an easy target.

Showering in a motel room conjured the most terrifying murder scenes put on film. *Psycho, Evil Dead, Friday the 13th, A Nightmare On Elm Street.* She tightened her hand on the knife handle, working herself into a stupid panic.

A demented serial killer wasn't going to sneak in and slash her in the shower.

Steam drifted out of the bathroom, and her feet remained rooted to the floor. She couldn't bring herself to undress.

Come on, Rylee.

With a calming breath, she crept toward the external door, checked the flimsy lock, and reseated the swing bar latch. Both were secured. But she didn't feel secure.

She shifted to the window and peered through the crack between the curtains. Expecting to find the parking lot empty as usual, she jerked at the sight of a car.

Parked next to the office, it sat empty. A middle-aged man stood inside at the front desk, wearing a suit that looked wildly out of place.

Her blood pressure skyrocketed.

He wasn't a local detective. Not in a full suit. He didn't belong here.

She couldn't breathe.

The clerk stood, bending over the desk, and pointed at Rylee's room.

Trembling, reeling into gasping hysterics, she stumbled away from the window.

He was coming for her.

She spun and raced toward the bathroom, operating on impulse. A hot mist fogged the mirror and hung in the air as she yanked the shower curtain closed. Keeping the water running, she backed out of the bathroom and shut the door.

The gap beneath the king-sized bed allowed just enough space for her to fit. She squeezed herself into the hiding spot, her cheek against the carpet, which reeked of maple syrup and cigarette smoke.

Once every inch of her was out of view, she lay on her stomach, chin to the floor, angled toward the foot of the bed, with her fingers slick and clammy around the hilt of the knife.

No amount of knocking would convince her to come out and open that door. If local law enforcement wanted to talk to her, they could send a guy who looked like a small-town detective during daylight hours.

The wait was petrifying, the silence deafening. Perspiration beaded on her brow as her panic-stricken heart tore through her chest, searching for a way out.

She didn't detect approaching footsteps. Didn't hear a fist against the door. When the hush broke, it detonated in a spray of splintered wood.

The door swung open, pieces of it scattering the floor inches from her face. A bullet had done that. Without the report of gunfire.

His weapon had a suppressor, like something out of a fucking mafia movie.

He was going to kill her.

She slapped a hand over her mouth, smothering the burst of her breaths as she slid the knife across the carpet in front of her.

The intruder strode in, making a beeline for the bathroom. Shiny dress shoes blurred by. Soundless footsteps. Determined. Deadly.

If she slipped out of hiding now, he would shoot her. Not that she could move. Ice encased her joints. Tears leaked from her eyes, her dread so cold and heavy it pressed her into the floor.

He stopped at the bathroom door and quietly opened it. Then he stepped back and fired into the cloud of steam.

Phut. Phut. Phut. Phut. Phut.

She flinched with each muffled shot, shaking violently as bullet casings dropped to the floor.

He paused. She stopped breathing.

Right about now, he was coming to the realization that a body hadn't fallen in the shower. He would have to go in there and investigate, and that would be her only opportunity to escape.

Her muscles clenched, her entire being fraught with fear and braced to run. How many bullets did he have left? Was he carrying extra magazines?

His shoes pivoted, angling toward the bed.

No, no, no. Oh, God. Please, don't walk this way.

He stalked straight toward her, sending her into a hyperventilating fit of terror.

EIGHTEEN

A tear trickled down Rylee's cheek and dangled from her chin with maddening endurance. More fell as the gunman closed in, his shoes following an invisible line to her hiding spot.

Lying on her stomach in a puddle of breathless terror, she readjusted her grip on the knife and poised it just out of view.

He paused at the foot of the bed, and her pulse went berserk. He lowered into a squat, and her adrenaline kicked in, muffling all sound. Then she lunged, slashing the knife, fast and deep, across his ankles.

With a guttural cry, she hacked again, less effective this time as his legs whirled, soaking her hand in hot blood.

The gun fired with a suppressed pop. She didn't slow her attack. Swiping the blade across his shins, she scrambled out from under the bed. The metal frame ripped along her back, but she didn't feel the pain. Right now, all she felt was the driving urgency to eliminate the threat.

She kept the knife in constant motion, lacerating his legs again and again. Raging fear and frustration constricted her chest. How was he still standing?

A dry click sounded from the pistol. Out of bullets.

His body crashed onto hers, heavy and uncoordinated. She'd maimed him, but he wasn't giving up.

"Who are you?" She twisted beneath him and buried the blade in his thigh. "How the fuck do you know me?"

He roared in agony and grabbed for the knife. She yanked it away and stabbed him in the stomach.

His hand collided with her face, smashing her jaw with a force that sent her flying backward. She didn't have time to control her landing. The impact with the floor snatched the breath from her lungs, and her head bounced off the corner of the wall, shooting stars across her vision.

She blinked rapidly, panting and disoriented. When her eyes came into focus, he was on his knees, crawling toward her with a hand wrapped around the knife in his gut.

"Why won't you fucking die?" she screamed and threw herself at him, pounding her fists in his face. "What do you want? Why are you here?"

He fell onto his back, choking and smiling through a gurgle of blood. "The bridge."

Her heart stopped and restarted. "How do you know about that? What does it have to do with you?"

With a strangled laugh, he grabbed her throat and wrenched her ear against his mouth.

"Thur…nnnn…eee."

She tried to jerk away, but he had a death grip on her neck. He'd lost too much blood to be this strong.

Her hands moved without thought, grabbing the knife, sliding it from his belly, and thrusting it back in. Again. Again. The fist on her throat dropped away as she continued to stab him.

Over and over, she aimed for vital organs — stomach, heart, neck, lungs. She was hitting ribs, struggling to spear the blade past bones. But he wasn't moving. Didn't appear to be breathing.

With a jolt, she broke out of her fugue and scooted away, taking the knife and his gun with her.

Numbness spread over her as she sat in the dark, gulping, unmoving in a crippled state of shock and horror.

She needed to do something. Close the door. Wash her hands. Turn off the shower. Check his pulse.

No. Fuck, no. She didn't want to touch him.

Blood soaked his clothes, the floor, her fingers, the knife. So much of it. Everywhere. He couldn't be alive. No way.

Still, she didn't twitch a muscle, too terrified a sound might resurrect him.

He'd come here to kill her. If she hadn't checked the window, he would've succeeded.

Who in the hell would go through the trouble of killing her? Why? He'd mentioned the bridge, but it didn't make sense. Was someone offended that she contemplated suicide ten years ago?

Mason didn't know about that. No one knew about it.

Except Tommy.

No. It wasn't possible. Tommy wouldn't have sent this man. If he wanted her dead, he would've done it himself.

Minutes passed, and the flow of her adrenaline slowed, bringing awareness to her body, to the pain in her face and back and the uncontrollable shaking in her limbs.

She wiped the knife on her pants, cleaning off the blood. More covered her hands. She needed to get moving.

The sound of an approaching car pierced through her daze. Headlights illuminated the open doorway. Doors slammed. Footsteps advanced.

Her stomach tightened, and she whimpered.

More hitmen? A backup team for the man she'd just killed? Goddammit, she couldn't fight off another attack.

Scooting backward in the dark, she slid between the mattress and wall, set the knife under the bed, and aimed the gun with both hands. It was out of bullets, but they wouldn't know that.

Hidden by the bed, she ducked down low, tucking into a ball, and tried to control the torrent of her breaths.

The tread of heavy boots crossed the threshold. Multiple intruders.

Oh, God, I'm dead. I'm dead. So fucking dead.

The overhead lights illuminated, blinding her eyes. Curled up on the floor, she aimed the gun upward, and another gun pointed back.

"Rylee." Tommy stood over her, his face set in stone, eyes bloodshot, and posture vibrating with unleashed fury. "Lower the gun."

Relief, distrust, fear, anger—so many emotions

battled inside her. She didn't move.

"He's dead," a deep, masculine voice said. Chillingly deep. "No wallet or ID."

"Rylee, lower the gun," Tommy said in his domineering tone.

"Fuck you."

The owner of the unfamiliar voice stepped into view and snatched her next breath. "You're one woman against a gang of bloodthirsty savages."

Savage was one way to describe him. Short brown hair. Razor-sharp eyes. Powerfully built. The faded scar that divided his cheek didn't detract from his chiseled beauty. His smirk did. A lethal smirk, that curled arrogantly around a toothpick.

Van.

The monster who had captured and raped Tommy nine years ago.

"Don't underestimate her." Tommy gave her the full force of his eyes while addressing Van. "I'd rather take on you and your attic than this hellcat."

What the fuck? He must be joking.

"I can arrange that." Van clapped him on the back and ambled toward the bathroom.

The shower turned off, and he prowled back through the room, joining the din of footsteps and hushed voices that gathered outside the door.

Tommy unchambered the live round in his gun and wedged the weapon into the back of his jeans.

She tightened her grip on the pistol in her hands. "How did you find me?"

"We had a tail on the hitman." He tipped his chin in the direction of the corpse, his expression unreadable. "You butchered him."

"He deserved it."

He went still, no part of him moving except his gaze, which darted over her, probing, flaring darkly. Deadly eyes. Hypnotic. God, the man was beautiful when he was contemplating murder. "Did he hurt you?"

"I've been hurt worse. Most recently, on your watch."

"Yeah, I hurt you. Unjustly. Unforgivably. So shoot me." He lowered to a crouch, leaning into the crack where she huddled, sucking all the oxygen. "Pull the fucking trigger."

The gun rattled. Her breaths shook.

She couldn't do it. Even knowing the gun was empty, she couldn't take the risk. "I hate you."

"I know, and I'm going to fix that."

She blinked, unsure she heard him correctly. "Fix what?"

"I was wrong about some things." He drifted closer, pressing his chest against the barrel of the gun. "You and I, we're going to start over, but right now, I need to get you out of here."

"No. Fuck that. I'm not going anywhere with you."

"You're in danger."

She met his treacherous stare. "You think?"

In a blink, he snatched the gun from her hand, aimed it at the ceiling, and fired a dry click, without a twitch of surprise.

He'd known the whole time it wasn't loaded.

"Let's go." He held out a hand in the narrow space between them.

More footsteps entered the room. More ruthless friends to aid in her mistreatment.

Reaching under the bed, she grabbed the knife and

angled it at his throat. "Back up."

His eyes glinted, and he pressed forward, cutting his neck on the blade. "You can do better, Rylee." He dropped his voice to a heated whisper. "Hate me with your body. It's far more satisfying."

She was struck by how much sharper his words were than the weapon in her hand. He bled from a small cut in his throat while she hemorrhaged in endless, agonizing bitterness.

For reasons she didn't understand, someone wanted her dead. Maybe that someone wasn't Tommy, but... "You starved me."

"A decision I regret. Tonight, I have a new priority, and that is protecting you."

"You can't protect me from yourself."

"No." His gaze, warm and richly gold, never wavered from hers. "You'll have to weigh that risk."

His throat didn't bob against the knife. His hand didn't swing to overpower her. He just waited her out while his friends searched the dead body.

She leaned in and tipped up the blade, lifting his chin. "No shackles."

"Not unless you beg."

"Never. What about the last rule in the rules of three?"

Three months without hope.

"We were ten minutes behind the hitman. I knew I would arrive too late." His face took on an expression she'd never seen there before. *Torment.* "The whole way here, I knew I would hold your dead body, look into your lifeless eyes, and never experience hope again." He touched the pads of his fingers to her throbbing jaw, featherlight. "I don't know what you've done to me, but for the first time in ten years, I have hope in my grasp, and I'm going to fight like hell to keep it."

Just words. Nice words. Profound words, if she were honest. But they wouldn't keep her safe. "I will never forgive you."

"I look forward to all the ways you're going to never forgive me. Lower the knife, Rylee."

He could take it himself. He was stronger, faster, expertly trained in disarming opponents. But for some insane reason, he wanted her to make this step.

It didn't mean anything. She was in danger, and he was the only person who could help her.

She tossed the knife.

With a nod, he rose and held out his hand.

"You should clean that cut." She rejected his waiting hand and pushed to her feet. "Someone else's blood was all over that blade."

He stepped back, giving her space to move out of her hiding spot. The room was empty, the corpse covered with a blanket. Everyone waited outside.

"You have two minutes to clean up." He nodded at the bathroom.

She didn't have to look down at her body. Her skin shivered beneath a sheen of cold, wet blood.

"Who's here with you?" She strode into the bathroom, grateful to find the clothes she'd left in here earlier.

"Half the team." He followed her in and gripped the hem of her bloody shirt. "Arms up."

Sensing the tension in his posture, she let him undress her. "You're expecting more hitmen?"

"Yes." He traced a finger along the torn, burning skin that ran the length of her spine. "How did this happen?"

"The bed frame. I saw the gunman talking to the motel clerk. It gave me time to hide." She washed her upper body in the sink, thinking through the ramifications. "The clerk might've called the cops."

"The clerk was dead when we arrived."

She froze in horror.

"Keep washing, Rylee." He crouched behind her and carefully lowered her filthy pants. "You have one minute."

Another dead body. Three in one week. Because of her. Who would be next?

Shoving down a thousand questions, she focused on scrubbing away the blood.

As Tommy helped her step out of her pants, she was viscerally aware of how close his mouth hovered to her bare backside. His breath caressed her flesh, prickling goosebumps, and his hands ghosted down the backs of her thighs, too tender to belong to the man who'd viciously fucked her in the desert.

"What are you doing?" She jerked her hips, trying to dislodge his touch.

With a firm grip on her butt, he gave her a warning squeeze. Then he released her and grabbed a clean towel.

Seconds later, she was wiped down and dressed in clean lounge pants and a t-shirt.

As he soaped up his neck and scrubbed the cut she'd inflicted, his gaze locked on hers in the mirror. There was something different about him. Something softer in the way he looked at her. It put her on edge.

When he clasped her hand to lead her out, she yanked free from his grip.

"Rylee." He reached for her again, eyes hard.

"I'm not going to run."

She walked out ahead of him and slammed into potent, eye-burning fumes of gasoline. The room had been doused in it.

"Where's my ID? Clothes?" She spun in a circle.

"They grabbed it." He caught her shoulders and pointed her toward the door.

With a hard swallow, she stepped around the covered corpse and into the dark parking lot.

Someone had killed the outside lights, but the moon was bloated and bright, illuminating a motorcycle, two SUVs, and two…four…*seven* human-shaped silhouettes.

The desert heat clung to the night air, but the atmosphere exuded a chill that seeped into her bones. All eyes turned to her, and she stumbled back as if she'd been shoved, crashing into Tommy's broad chest.

"You're safe." He curled a hand around her hip and put his mouth at her ear. "You know them."

Cole was easy to spot with his beard, leather jacket, and formidable lean against the motorcycle.

Next in line was a man with sloping shoulders, a stern expression, and red hair. That could only be Luke. Van stood beside him, gnawing on a toothpick.

Her heart thudded as she took in the others.

A Latina woman sat on the curb, cuddled in the arms of a man with dark blond hair and crystal blue eyes. Lucia and Tate? If they hadn't been joined at the hip, she might not have guessed who they were. But Tommy's emails often talked about how the two were never apart. He'd joked that they probably took their daily shits together.

Which brought her gaze to the imposing figure

who stood away from the rest. Stubble shadowed a
squared jaw and outlined sculpted lips. Dark hair, dark
eyes, Hispanic features — all carved into the image of a
shockingly attractive man. But his presence bespoke of
something other. Something egregious, inhuman, and
evil down to the morrow of his soul.

A shiver snaked through her, for she knew,
without looking at the self-inflicted scars on his arms,
that she was standing in the withering stare of one of the
most ruthless crime lords in Venezuela.

In the name of all that's holy, why is he here?

"I thought you…" Damn, her trembling voice. She
cleared her throat. "You live on the other side of the
world."

"While I'm honored to make the cut into Tomas'
diary of angsty feelings, where I live is none of your
goddamn concern, little girl." He grinned, and it wasn't a
grin at all.

Her mouth went dry, and her pulse careened into
hysteria.

"That's enough, Tiago." Tommy shifted her behind
him and gripped her hand.

This time, she allowed it, squeezing tight to his
fingers as he removed a set of keys from his pocket.

"If you let him intimidate you, he'll never stop," a
woman spoke from the shadows of the SUVs. "He gets
off on it."

The striking image of the last silhouette emerged
from the darkness, striding forward.

Dressed head to toe in black, she wore badass
buckled boots, guns on her hips, and straight black hair
to her waist. Slender limbs, all long and graceful, gave
her the appearance of delicate femininity. But her bearing

commanded attention. Her aura controlled the very air. Authority beamed from her glacial eyes.

Liv.

The queen of depravity and dominance.

She'd molded Tommy into the sexual deviant he was today, and Rylee felt an irrational stab of jealousy over that. But she was also wonderstruck, tongue-tied, and instantly enamored.

The scar that hooked across Liv's cheek replicated Van's in its appearance and story. And like Van's, it only added to her allure. The woman looked like Kate Beckinsale of the underworld—all sexy power, intimidation, and seduction.

"We'll talk in the car," Liv said in greeting and plucked the keys from Tommy's hand. "I'm driving."

This was happening.

Surrounded by criminals, Rylee felt the shadows closing in, tingling her nape and smothering her chances of survival. What had she gotten herself into?

Too late to run. She was outnumbered eight to one.

Eight darkly corrupted felons had traveled all the way here because of her. Because she'd invaded their privacy and gotten herself mixed up in something terrible.

She would have to go with them, wherever that might be, and hope to God they weren't plotting her death.

Tommy held onto her numb hand and led her to the SUV.

Behind her, someone struck a match, and the motel erupted in flames.

NINETEEN

In the darkness of the SUV, images of Rylee's injuries worked through Tomas' conscience. Something had struck her jaw with enough force to leave it swollen and red, and a nasty gash marred the length of her spine. Numerous marks cut and bruised her gorgeous flesh. But the other guy looked much worse.

She'd fought for her life and defeated a professional hitman. Admiration didn't begin to express how he felt about her. A heady, complex cocktail of emotions hammered at him, mixing with adrenaline and twisting in his stomach.

He'd lost her four days ago. Almost lost her for good today.

Just like that, he forgave her for invading his privacy. Her life was in danger, and he felt responsible for that. He shouldn't have let her leave with the detective. He should've fucking protected her.

She wasn't the enemy.

Fate was giving him a second chance. A chance to

right his wrongs with her and maybe, just maybe, find happiness again. He wouldn't fuck it up. He'd meant what he told her. Tonight, he would begin anew.

A fresh start.

With her.

His mind had gone there so quickly. The instant he thought she was dead was the exact moment he realized she was more than the best sex of his life. More than a throat he wanted to throttle. More than any word he'd ever written in an email.

He survived Caroline's death. But he knew, deep in his fractured soul, he wouldn't survive Rylee's.

The simmering sensations at the base of his throat, behind his breastbone, and in the pit of his stomach were an accumulation of violence and desire, chemistry and possessiveness, fire and rage. The extreme passion she produced in him was the antithesis of the tender, doting innocence he'd felt with Caroline.

It was difficult to think about, but he couldn't help but wonder if he and Caroline would've been as compatible as adults as they'd been as children. Caroline had been a gentle soul, sweetly passive, always smiling. If she hadn't died, he probably would've still gone to Austin, grieving the loss of his mother, and ended up in Van's attic.

That experience had fundamentally changed him. Ten years later, he didn't want Caroline's kindhearted brand of love. He wanted explosive, no-holds-barred, raging, brutal passion.

He wanted Rylee.

But she wasn't ready to hear any of this.

"Where are we going?" She sat beside him in the backseat of the SUV with her hands balled on her lap.

Liv drove in silence with Luke in the front seat next to her.

"A safe house." Tomas would eventually have to tell her it was thirteen hours away.

"How did you find me?"

"When you left with the detective," he said, "I called in my team. We traced your credit card and identified the cash machine you used. It took us several days to track down the motel employee who helped you."

"She told you where I was?" She heaved a frustrated sound. "I paid her an extra two-hundred to keep her mouth shut." Her shoulders tensed, and her gaze flashed to him in the dark. "Tell me you didn't hurt her."

Rule number one in this business: *Never leave loose ends.*

But Rylee didn't live in his world. She didn't know.

"The motel clerk took her bounty of cash and drove to San Antonio," he said. "A spontaneous vacation to visit a friend. If she hadn't left town so quickly, we would've located you within twenty-four hours."

"What did you do, Tommy?" She shifted to face him, her voice rising. "Answer me."

He had a lot of bad news to give her. Christ, she'd already been through so much. He wanted to spare her this. For just a little while longer.

"She just butchered a man, Tomas." Liv met his eyes in the rearview, her voice melodic yet icy in its command. "Don't coddle the woman. She can handle it."

He knew that. Fuck, he still wore the vicious marks of Rylee's claws and teeth. He knew exactly how she handled things.

With a steeling breath, he turned toward her.

"The hitman located the girl before we did." He reached for her face, her expression falling, collapsing in agony before his eyes.

"No." She jerked away, shaking her head. "No, no, no!"

"She's dead."

Killed slowly. Body parts removed. All left for his team to find.

Her eyes glistened with tears, but she didn't let them fall. "So the hitman learned my location and killed that poor girl." She inhaled deeply. "How did you follow him?"

"Cole and I stayed behind, working it from a different angle." Tomas hadn't been much help, his technical skills no match for Cole's. "It took days, but Cole managed to trace Paul Kissinger's phone to multiple other devices. I still don't know how he did it, but one of the devices he locked onto was traveling from San Antonio back to this area. We knew that was our guy and scrambled to catch up. When the phone stopped moving at your motel, we were still ten minutes out." A hot clamp squeezed his airway. "Ten minutes too late. I'm so sorry, Rylee."

"I got myself into this." She leaned back and looked out the window. "I won't forgive the way you treated me, but I know you didn't send that hitman after me. That is a result of something I've done, evidently. Not your fault."

"What do you mean?" Suspicion thickened his voice. "What are you hiding?"

"Nothing!" Her gaze shot to his, wide and urgent. "I don't know what's going on, but when I was stabbing that man, he mentioned the bridge." She nervously glanced at Liv and Luke in the front seat and whispered, "He was smiling like he knew a dirty secret. But you're the only person I've ever told about that night."

"Start from the beginning. Tell me step by step what happened from the moment you saw the hitman talking to the motel clerk."

She explained how she left the shower running and hid beneath the bed, hoping to distract him long enough to escape. She had the knife and her wits—two things that saved her life. While it was hard to hear the details of her struggle, he was so fucking proud of her.

"I asked him about the bridge. How did he know about it, and what did it have to do with him?" Her brows pulled together, and she chewed her lip. "He was pretty much dead at that point, but he mumbled something about Thur… Need? Like Thursday? Or thirsty? He never finished."

Baffled and agitated, he drummed his fingers on his knee. He'd briefed his team on everything he knew about Rylee Sutton, including her ex-husband, the suicide bridge, and her sexual history, as well as her hate-fuckfest with him.

That had been a strange conversation. He never shared shit like that with anyone. But his secrecy in writing emails for ten years had started this mess. They deserved to know all the facts, no matter how personal.

The consensus among everyone was that this had nothing to do with Rylee. They were dealing with a team of sophisticated spies and assassins who were likely using her to get to the Freedom Fighters. Probably a loose end from a sex trafficking ring they'd taken out in recent years.

So how would her near-suicide on a bridge a decade ago have anything to do with this?

The emails.

That was the night he'd started writing.

"I called Mason yesterday," she said into the silence.

Luke's gaze snapped toward Liv, and every tendon in Tomas' body went rigid.

He wanted to bend Rylee over his knee and show her luscious ass just how foolish it was to contact anyone right now. But the damage was already done.

Now he needed to understand the repercussions. "Tell me what was said. Every word."

"I used a disposable phone."

"Purchased from a corner store? It can be traced."

Despite the darkness, her face paled. Then she breathed in and walked through the conversation — Mason's confession that he loved her, kept tabs on her, and wanted her back.

"He reported me missing because Evan called him with claims that I was acting scared and disappeared." She rubbed her temples. "That just isn't true. Even weirder, Evan admitted to Mason that we were sleeping together. Why would he do that? To enrage Mason? To bait him?" She dropped her hands, her voice monotone. "I think Evan is behind all this. It doesn't fit his personality, but there are too many things that don't add up."

He exchanged a look with Liv in the rearview. Her gaze crystallized, issuing an order that shriveled his balls.

Yeah, he knew what he had to do and didn't need her controlling the situation from the front seat.

Fuck, this was going to hurt.

214

"Rylee, listen." He clasped her hand, clenching tight as she tried to pull away. "Evan died at work today. He fell off a six-story building at his construction site."

"What?" She yanked frantically on her hand, her breaths gusting hard and angry. "No. It wasn't on the news. They would've reported it. He wouldn't fall off a fucking building. He's smarter than that."

"His death is being investigated. They'll rule it accidental, but you and I both know it was foul play."

"He's not dead." Her voice shook, her gaze brimmed with anguish and denial. "He's not dead, Tommy. He's not."

He would give anything to order the caravan off the road and chase everyone out of the car so she could wrap her emotions around this in private.

Nothing like breaking down in front of strangers. He hadn't been able to do it when he lost his mom and Caroline. He didn't leak a tear at their funerals. Couldn't open his soul to a therapist, either. He still didn't know if he had it in him to show weakness in front of his closest friends.

He felt her fighting it, battling the sobs in her chest, and pushing it all down. She trembled with the effort.

She needed to let it out. He knew that from experience.

All those years of writing emails, pouring his fears, sadness, and loneliness into the ether, and to think, someone had been listening to him after all. While he'd mourned his dead girlfriend, Rylee had been there for him through every word.

Now the tables had turned. While she grieved her friend, her *lover*, he wasn't jealous. He only felt an overwhelming, protective need to take away her pain.

Gathering her in his arms, he fought her snarls and weak attempts to break free. Once she settled down, he held her on his lap, cradling her, wrapping her up with his body, and kissing the tears on her cheeks.

"I hear you, Rylee." He pressed his lips to her ear, breathing her in. "All of you. We're still here. Our lives matter. Don't shut down on me."

She stared up at him, her eyes swimming in rippling silver waters. A choking sound strangled in her throat. Another smothered sob. Then she circled her arms around his shoulders, buried her face in his neck, and wept silently, softly. Each painful hitch in her breath ripped him open and pulled her in.

From the moment he met her, she'd sworn her intentions were innocent, claiming that all those years ago, she'd hurt with him, cried for him, and changed her major to psychology. For him. She'd taken a sabbatical and driven to his house because she wanted to help him.

And he'd treated her like an enemy. Now that he knew the truth, he had to live with his crimes. But he wouldn't live without her.

Once they escaped the present danger, and they *would* escape it, he was going to smash through her intimacy issues and convince her she needed him as much as he needed her.

"Evan Phillips didn't make that call to her ex-husband." Luke twisted in the front seat and met his eyes.

"No, he didn't." Tomas didn't have proof, but he knew at gut level her neighbor was an innocent casualty.

Either Mason was lying about Evan's phone call, or someone had called Mason, pretending to be Evan.

The reason for Evan's murder wasn't apparent. It

could've been retaliation of the jealous ex-husband, or a message sent to Tomas' team, or just a loose end that needed to go away.

For the next hour, he spoke quietly with Liv and Luke, speculating about possible enemies. Rylee didn't try to push off his lap, her soft whimpers sinking into stunned acceptance. He sat with her in her sadness, his arms tight around her, exactly where he belonged.

If he didn't fuck this up, he could have more moments like this. Moments when he held her while she was happy, scared, excited, or just wanted to sleep.

He hoped she would sleep now, but he sensed too much alertness in her muscles. She was listening, always eavesdropping, as he and his friends reminisced about missions gone by and gossiped about family drama.

Liv had deliberately confined Van, Tiago, Tate, and Lucia in the same vehicle for thirteen hours.

"Forced proximity," she said. "They need to work out their shit."

While that was true, he didn't believe Tiago's crimes would be forgiven anytime soon. The crime lord had poisoned Lucia to keep her sick, forced Van and Tate to have sex, and scarred up Tate's back beyond physical and emotional repair.

Some crimes just weren't redeemable.

While Rylee sat lethargically on his lap, he used the opportunity to dig out the first-aid kit and treat the laceration on her back. For once, she didn't fight him. A testament to the despondent state of her mind.

Three hours into the drive, she lifted her head from his shoulder and squinted at the blackness beyond the window. "Where is this safe house?"

"Missouri." He braced for the backlash.

"What?" Her voice pitched with outrage, and she shoved out of his embrace. "I can't leave Texas."

"Too late."

She scrambled toward the far door. To do what? Jump from the moving vehicle?

He caught her throat, wrenched her forcibly back to him by the neck, and took her mouth. She fought him. Hot damn, she always fought. He groaned against her teeth and kissed her deeper, harder, wordlessly ordering her to return the kiss.

With a hand cradling her ass, he pulled her roughly against him and held her nape in a firm lock.

"Let me go." Straddling his lap, she seethed against his mouth and shoved at his chest. "You're kidnapping me!"

"Shut the fuck up and kiss me." His stomach heated, his mind spinning to untangle the knots of her venom.

Battling her rage with more rage wouldn't yield a lasting relationship with this complicated woman. While his cock loved her ferocity, they were more than sex. More than her hatred.

She told herself she was done with commitment and love and all matters of the heart. But that wasn't true.

"You fear intimacy." He restrained her hands against her back and held her close, chest to chest, mouth to mouth. "But you've been in a relationship with me for ten years."

"You didn't even know I existed."

"That changed the moment you walked into my house and upended my world."

He covered her mouth with his, his tongue insistent, pushing past the stubborn line of her lips. He refrained from using aggressive, overpowering strokes and instead delivered a languorous caress, tipping her expectations into bewilderment.

Her mouth opened on a gasp, and she gave way to his adoring licks. He suckled and worshiped, pressing in and releasing her hands to cup her head and palm her tight, round ass.

For a moment, she melted into him, welcoming his tongue moving in her mouth, against hers. She gripped his shirt and angled her head, delving deeper and whimpering. Not sounds of hunger, but distress.

Intimacy was her limit, and a tender kiss came way too close to that. So when her hands balled into fists on his shirt, he was ready for the blowback.

She punched his chest and sank her teeth into his lip. More strikes. Rabid bites. He absorbed it for a few seconds, knowing she needed an outlet for the pain inside her. He also knew she'd have him covered in blood if he didn't defuse her soon.

"Behave." With his hands framing her face, he slowed down the kiss and earned himself a vicious bite on the tongue.

"Fuck you." She went at his mouth, attacking him in a firestorm of feral heat and scorn.

He nibbled when she bit, caressed when she scratched, and hummed when she growled. He dominated her mouth with devotion, overpowering her hostility with sensuality and sliding her temper into a languid embrace of exploration and affection.

Until she shoved him back against the seat. He allowed it, soaking in her fury and grief, her fists pounding upon his chest, her fingernails scoring his flesh. He caressed her everywhere, softly, compassionately, his touch in extreme opposition of hers.

She tore her mouth away, panting. Angry and confused. Then she fused their lips again.

Her kiss was war and retribution. Punishment for everything he'd done to her. But it was also redemption, heaven, and desire. He loved the fiery taste of her, the all-consuming fervor in her breaths, and the curling of her claws in his hair, ripping, pulling, and holding him close.

He loved that she didn't do anything half-ass, especially when it came to him.

"If you put this much energy into hating me," he breathed against her mouth, "I can only imagine the amount of intensity and passion you'll put into loving me."

"Never." Her eyes glinted like steel blades. "I'll never love you."

"Oh, boy," Liv said from the front seat. "I've heard those words before."

"Me, too." Luke sighed and shifted to glance at them over his shoulder. "Rylee Sutton, you just sealed your fate."

TWENTY

An indignant cloud darkened Rylee's expression, and Tomas wanted to kiss it right off her face. She didn't like hearing that her fate was sealed. She'd fought too hard for her independence and was too protective of her heart to believe her efforts had been for naught.

Tomas, on the other hand, held tight to his newfound hope.

She was stuck with the Freedom Fighters, whether she forgave him or not. She knew their identities, their secrets, and once they arrived in Missouri, she would know the location of Cole's safe house.

Even if Tomas let her go, his friends would not. *Loose ends.*

None of that mattered. She was his now. If she tried to leave, he would go with her. She just didn't know it yet.

Cole led the caravan on his motorcycle, shooting down the dark highway in the dead of night. Around one in the morning, four hours into the thirteen-hour drive, he pulled off at a vacant rest stop.

"Bathroom break." Tomas nudged Rylee beside him, reluctant to wake her after it had taken her so long to fall asleep.

She rubbed her eyes and followed him out of the car.

Parked behind them, the second SUV rocked wildly on its frame.

What the hell?

The doors flew open, exploding in a whirlwind of swinging arms and heated voices. Lucia's roar was the loudest, her rapid-fire Spanish shuddering the air.

With a snarl, she raced around the vehicle and attacked the smirking driver.

Tiago.

"Oh, shit." Tomas gripped Rylee's hand, prepared to toss her into the SUV if guns were drawn.

Tiago stood like an impenetrable mountain, chin up, feet braced apart, as he absorbed the force of Lucia's punches.

"They need to knock that shit off." Cole charged toward the commotion.

Liv's hand shot out, stopping him. "There's no one around for miles. Let it play out."

Tate and Van yelled, too, quieter, calmer than the woman who unleashed unholy hell on her nemesis.

"Deep down," Luke said to no one in particular, "Tiago feels regret for what he did to them."

"No, he doesn't." Cole scoffed and walked off.

"Yeah, you're right." Luke started toward the small building of restrooms. "Satan has no feelings."

Rylee tilted her head, eyes locked on the fight. "If everyone hates Tiago, why is he here?"

"He's here for Kate." Liv lit a cigarette, inhaling deeply. "The longer he avoids us, the more he isolates her from her family. Isolation breeds resentment. He might be the devil, but the devil is intelligent."

"Happy wife, happy life," Tomas said.

Rylee cast him a strange look. "So he wants to be part of this family?"

"I don't know if *want* is the right word." He tensed as the fight grew more unruly.

Tiago's patience was dwindling. He caught Lucia's next punch, knocked it away, and cuffed her throat, choking her. Tate went ballistic, jumping into the fray and tackling Tiago to the ground.

"As an outsider," Rylee said, hugging her waist, "it looks like you're your own enemies."

"You're wrong." Tomas turned toward her, putting his face in hers. "Forget everything you learned in school. We're not your case studies. We don't need your therapy." He stabbed a finger at the brawl. "*This* is how we deal with things."

"With your fists?" She stood taller, meeting his glare head-on. "That's going well, I see."

"We work out our issues with communication. Yes, we communicate with fists. And words. And *sex*."

She pressed her lips together, but her eyes argued loudly.

"We don't want to be fixed, Rylee." He straightened, glanced at Liv, and returned to her. "We can't do what we do and be normal or safe or sane. Think about it. We hunt monsters. We break laws. We torture and kill. Hell, we even fall in love with our prisoners. Or *abductors*, depending on the perspective."

Her eyes widened as they darted around, taking in

his team. He could see her mind working, recalling the stories of how each of his friends found love. Liv and Josh, Van and Amber, Camila and Matias, Tiago and Kate, Luke and Vera—they all began as captor and captive, evolving from vicious enemies to lifelong mates. Every single one of them.

The Freedom Fighters needed to be coldblooded and crazy to do their jobs. They also needed some of that madness to fall in love, evidently.

"Our story isn't any different." He caught and held her gaze.

"We're not in love, Tommy."

"I'm not opposed to the idea."

She set her jaw. "You're an idiot."

"Call me that again, and I'll kiss the shit out of you."

Her breath stuttered, and she cleared her throat. "I need to pee."

He glanced in the direction of the restrooms just as Luke strolled out. With a chin lift, he signaled Luke to wait. Having already swept the small building, his friend would stand by while Rylee was inside.

"Go ahead," he said to her.

"I wasn't asking." She strode off, stubborn to a fault.

Behind him, the drama with Tiago fizzled from smacking fists to emotional words.

A quick sweep of the perimeter gave him a view of shadows, dark tree lines, and in the distance, an empty highway. Everyone present carried weapons, and no matter what they were doing, they were all on high-alert.

"We'll get through this." Liv touched his forehead, brushing the hair from his eyes. "No matter who we're fighting. There will always be another fight, and we'll always stand together, righting our wrongs."

"And the wrongs of others." He glanced over his shoulder, finding Van, of all people, standing between Tiago and Tate, speaking to them in calming tones. The argument was over. "Van's come a long way."

"So have you."

"What's that supposed to mean?"

"You've always been more closed-off and secretive than the others. I used to worry about your happiness." She smashed her cigarette beneath a boot and offered him a rare smile. "I'm not worried anymore."

Her sharp brown eyes used to give him nightmares. Now they regarded him with an affectionate sort of intensity that told him their decade-long friendship was invaluable to her.

"I've always been your favorite." He grinned.

"Josh might have something to say about that."

"I can't believe the boy scout let you out of the fortress without him."

"He wasn't pleased. But Matias' plane won't hold all of us, and I'm sick of being the one who stays behind."

She'd spent the better part of the past decade raising her daughter. Livana was an adult now. A badass little vigilante in training. Considering who her parents were, he wasn't surprised.

"Everyone wanted to come on this mission." Liv stared at the dark horizon, the scar on her cheek glinting in the moonlight. "To be back in Texas, where it all began? It's nostalgic."

"Most of us grew up here, but honestly, I never had a desire to return."

"Well, we're headed to Missouri now. I didn't even

know Cole had a safe house there."

None of them knew. Cole was a goddamn mystery.

He was also a lifesaver. They needed a safe place to regroup, analyze the evidence they'd collected, and determine how to proceed. That could take weeks, and Tomas' shabby little safe house in the desert was too small and no longer safe. When he'd suggested that they camp out in the desert, Cole shot down that idea and offered his house in southern Missouri.

Tomas' attention flitted to Luke, who paced in front of the restrooms. "I'm surprised Luke left Vera in Colombia, given how new their relationship is."

"She was pissed. But he wanted to be here for you."

"Vera stayed behind because she has a gunshot wound?"

"He refused to let her travel. He'll have a lot of groveling to do when he gets home."

Home. In Colombia, Texas, or Timbuctoo, it didn't matter. Home was wherever his fucked-up, overprotective family was. And Rylee.

"She's one of us now." He nodded at the restrooms.

"You think she's a good fit?"

"For the team? Or for me?"

"Both."

"She's mean enough." He chuckled. "Yeah, she fits. She's carrying her weight in issues."

"Oh, good. I was starting to think she might be too normal for this crowd."

"Nah, she's batshit crazy." A warm whoosh filled his chest, lifting it. "She wouldn't be a psychologist if she wasn't."

"Look at you." Her enigmatic brown eyes roamed over his face. She stepped closer and trailed her fingers along his jaw. "You're falling, and my God, it's stunning." She smiled wickedly. "You're so fucked, Tomas."

He cupped her hand to his cheek, cherishing the connection.

Footsteps approached, and they turned.

Rylee breezed past them, followed by Luke. She shot Tomas a withering glare and stormed to the SUV, slamming the door behind her.

"Jealousy. I don't miss that stage of a new relationship." Liv patted his cheek. "Good luck."

She strolled toward Van and the others, where they'd calmly gathered near the other SUV. Tomas headed to the bathroom to take a piss. Then he joined Rylee in the backseat.

"You want me," he said in greeting.

"I want you to fuck off and leave me alone."

"I'm not him."

"Excuse me?"

"You heard me."

"Yeah." She huffed. "You think I'm hypersensitive and over-reactive because the man I loved cheated on me. Here's a news flash. You can fuck whoever you want because I. Do. Not. Love. You."

"Love me or hate me. Either way, I'm yours." He grabbed her jaw and forced her eyes to his. "I will *never* fucking cheat on you."

Her swallow jumped against his hand, her eyes round and heartbreaking.

He was pushing too hard, too fast.

"Get some sleep." He released her, giving her

space. "We have a long way to go."

TWENTY-ONE

Cole's safe house was a lakefront estate in rustic Missouri. Any doubts Tomas had about finding a place to comfortably and safely accommodate their party of nine were immediately quashed when he stepped inside the sprawling mansion.

It sat on a dead-end road, where the asphalt met acres upon acres of woodland. No other houses. No sounds of traffic or life for miles around. Total isolation.

"Bedrooms are down that hall." Cole paced through the main living area, flicking on lights and tapping codes into a screen on the wall. "Eat. Get some rest, and we'll reconvene tonight."

No one moved. Tomas didn't know what the others were thinking, but Jesus, it was surreal, this glimpse into Cole's private life. Even Rylee, who had only met Cole a week ago, looked shell-shocked by the grandeur of the place.

Fireplaces dominated both ends of the living room. The cathedral ceiling and natural color schemes directed all attention to the wall of picturesque windows between the hearths.

The view of a private cove, illuminated by the late morning sun, was nothing short of mesmerizing.

"You own this? The estate? The land?" Tomas watched Cole move through the open kitchen. "By yourself?"

"Yes."

"Clearly, we paid you too much for your services." Van prowled along the windows, gnawing on a toothpick and taking in the view.

"Seeing how I've been saving your asses for free for the past year, I'd argue you're not paying me enough."

"You're either with us, or you're not." Liv lowered into an overstuffed chair. "It's not a monetary decision."

"Am I with you?" Cole stalked toward her and bent into her space, nose to nose. "Spell it out. What do you want?"

"Secrets don't keep well for long in this family." She was a fraction of Cole's size and managed to look more threatening as she leaned in, forcing him back. "We hide nothing from one another."

"Except Tomas' emails," Cole said.

"Which are no longer a secret." Tomas clenched his jaw.

"Like I said." Liv raised her chin. "Secrets don't keep in our family."

"If you let me in, I'll do the same." Cole straightened and shrugged off his leather jacket. "This property is the entirety of my wealth. An accumulation of the side jobs, the *risks* I've taken over the past twenty years. But it's more than that. This is my retirement. My sanctuary. And now, I'm offering it to you. To the cause."

Tomas glanced at Rylee beside him, the surprised look on her face mirroring his thoughts. For whatever reason, Cole had just made an exorbitant bid to be part of their exclusive team.

He'd been working alongside them for a year, but always as an outsider. He wasn't forced into this by way of Van's attic. Nor was he marrying into the family. Before now, those had been the only avenues into becoming one of their kindred.

But apparently, he wanted this badly enough to invest his entire future in them.

"How is the kitchen already stocked?" Tiago rummaged through the built-in commercial fridge, his nefarious presence as out of place as his question.

"You're worried about my secrets," Cole said to Liv, "when you should be worried about the Venezuelan kingpin who carries razors in his pocket." He turned toward a scowling Tiago. "I have a caretaker, vetted and trusted, who's been looking after this property for fifteen years. He prepared the bedrooms and stocked the kitchen this morning."

Tiago nodded, his expression brooding. Pensive. "You're already in the fold, Hartman. They need you. Most of them care about you. Trust will take time." He grabbed his bag and strode into the hallway, vanishing around the corner.

Silence descended in his wake. Looks were exchanged. Someone blew out a breath.

"That was awkward." Tomas rubbed his nape.

"Fuck him." Lucia crossed her arms. "He's just sore because he has no friends."

"Fix it." Van pointed a toothpick at her.

She made a growly sound. "Why me?"

"Because Tate and I made our peace with him. You're still hanging onto the past."

"Fine." She slung her backpack over her shoulder and turned to follow Tiago. "I'll do it for Kate."

"You'll do it for *you*." Tate swatted her butt. "And not until you're ready. Let's grab a room."

The massive living space slowly emptied as everyone wandered off. Between Colombia, Texas, and Missouri, the team had been traveling nonstop for four days. Two weeks before that, they'd been in California, taking down La Rocha Cartel.

Now that they were safe, the first order of business was food and sleep.

Within minutes, only Tomas and Rylee remained.

"I'm hungry, not tired." She stepped into the kitchen and snatched an apple off the counter.

She'd slept most of the way here and missed the meal they'd grabbed through a roadside drive-through.

"Eat." He collected their bags and ambled toward the hallway. "I'll claim a room."

"Two rooms."

He didn't bother acknowledging that ridiculous request.

A gradual slope of stairs ascended into a long corridor, the flooring tiled in an artistic mosaic of slate stones. He lost count of how many doors he passed, all with keypad entry. Christ, there must've been eight or nine bedrooms in total. Unless something else was hiding behind these locks.

He stopped at the first open door and gaped.

Inside, racks of guns covered one wall. Dozens of firearms of every size, shape, and caliber. File cabinets, desks, and worktables filled the rest of the dimly lit room, the surfaces covered in laptops, camera equipment, and high-tech clothing and gear.

Cole stood at a table, sifting through stacks of burner phones, all plugged into a power strip that ran along the wall.

"Last room on the right is mine." He didn't look away from his task. "The one on the left is still open."

"Thanks." As Tomas turned to leave, his gaze caught on a transparent garment bag that hung from a hook behind the door.

White satin and lace.

A wedding gown.

Damn, it looked eerily spectral and downright sad amid the plethora of guns and spy tech.

"I should burn it," Cole said behind him.

"I don't know, man." He pivoted, meeting the starkness in Cole's brown eyes. "I burned everything, but the ghosts clung."

"Are they still clinging?"

"Yeah." He scratched his jaw, rethinking his answer. "Actually, I've been too distracted to notice."

"Your dick's been distracted."

"More than usual, and more than just my dick. That woman has her claws in every part of me. Now that I think about it, I'm pretty sure she scared the ghosts away." He chuckled and quickly sobered. "Do you think her ex-husband hired hits on her and Evan Phillips?"

"I don't know yet." Cole turned back to the table of burner phones. "Get some rest. Recharge. We have a lot of work to do and need to be clearheaded."

With a nod, Tomas made his way to the last room on the left. An airy, tidy space with a large bed and private bathroom—all decorated in simple, natural hues. Beyond the windows, trees rippled on hillsides that stretched to the horizon.

He could see why Cole chose this place to retire. It was lush and green. Peaceful. Calming. Completely void of sand, desert heat, and hatred.

With Rylee, he would take her hatred over indifference. Her fire was irresistible, addictive, and he wouldn't dare try to control it if it made her happy.

But it didn't. Her anger made her miserable. He accepted the blame for some of that, not all of it. Nine days ago, she walked into his house with a block of ice around her heart and a grudge against men that was ten years in the making.

Enough was enough.

He dropped their bags near the door, brushed his teeth, and found his angry little hellcat sitting alone at the kitchen island. She'd fixed herself a salad with pre-grilled chicken.

Lowering onto the stool beside her, he reached toward her bowl to steal a meaty morsel.

"No!" She jerked it away, hugging the dish protectively to her chest. "Please, don't."

He yanked his hand back, scalded by her reaction. "Jesus, Rylee. I'm not going to take your food away."

She didn't move, her glare distrustful and defensive.

He'd done that. Adding to her fears of intimacy and commitment, he'd instilled a new one.

Starvation.

What kind of monster was he?

"Fuck." He shoved away from the island and paced through the kitchen. "I fucked up. Cole warned me. He told me if I harmed you and learned you were innocent, that I would wear the scars." His chest hurt, and his stomach coiled in a turmoil of guilt. But he wouldn't give up. Pausing a few feet away, he looked her square in the eyes. "You have every right to hate me. I know you're pissed. So yell at me. Let me hear it. Act like a fucking adult and confront me."

Her lips parted. "The day I walked into your house, those were my words."

"I've been listening." He lowered his head and ran a hand through his hair. "I'm not going to apologize. I won't beg for your forgiveness. Instead, I'm going to make you a promise." He lifted only his eyes, pinning her with a stare she couldn't ignore. "I will *not* repeat my mistakes. Let me be clear. My only priorities are to protect you and keep you healthy. I will not cheat on you. I will not starve you. But I will *hurt* you."

"Why?"

"Because when we're in love, we will hurt each other as much as we save each other."

She sat still for so long he thought he'd lost her inside her head.

At last, she released her death grip on the bowl, set it on the counter, and tucked back into her meal.

He returned to the stool beside her, bracketing her rigid body in the *V* of his thighs. "Tell me what you're thinking."

"I should be in Texas, helping Evan's parents bury their son."

"And get yourself killed in the process? I won't allow it."

"Of course, you won't. You're a domineering prick." She chewed slowly, eyes on her salad and voice soft. "I don't belong here. I'm not a vigilante. I have nothing to offer."

"You just took out an assassin. The man who killed an innocent motel clerk. You succeeded where we failed. I'd say you've more than proved your value in this fight."

"I don't want to be here."

"Tell me why."

She finished the last bite of salad and stood, carrying her bowl to the sink. "I didn't choose this."

"None of us *chose* it. You know our histories. This life chose us."

"I work in law enforcement."

"Van's father was the Austin Police Chief."

"I don't carry weapons."

"Amber, Kate, and Josh don't carry weapons." He rose from the stool and prowled around the island to stand behind her. "You carry a shotgun in your truck, and let's not forget the butcher knife you stole from my house."

She stiffened at his nearness. "I was in danger."

"You're still in danger." Lowering his nose to her hair, he breathed in her mouth-watering femininity. "That's why you don't want to be here."

"Because I'm in danger of getting killed by one of your homicidal friends?"

"No, Rylee." He trailed the backs of his fingers down her arms, making her shiver. "Because you're in danger of falling in love."

"Oh, my God." She shot out from beneath the press of his body and scurried around the island. "What is this obsession you suddenly have with *love*? The man who wrote those emails plowed through hundreds of women and couldn't emotionally connect with any of them."

"None of them were you." He stalked after her. "You blindsided me. Knocked me on my ass."

"I can't stand you." She backed away, rubbing her arms, looking for all the world like she wanted to run.

"You can't stand the thought of me getting too close." He closed the distance, backing her into the corner of the kitchen. "Because I *am* getting too close, and when I ram through that armor around your heart, you think you're going to get hurt again."

"You don't know me." Her back bumped into the pantry door, her eyes darting, searching for a way out. "You don't love me."

"You'll deny it. You'll fight it with every breath in your body." He braced a hand on the door above her head and leaned in. "But having already experienced it once, you know it's a fight you can't win."

"Stop throwing my words back at me!" She shoved at his chest, ducked under his arm, and darted toward the hallway.

"Stop running from them like a hypocrite."

"I'm not running." She held up her middle finger without slowing.

She wasn't *literally* running. But that speed-walk of hers wiggled her ass in a spellbinding way. He followed it like a tractor beam, locked onto the diabolical, heart-shaped curves. Fucking hell, she was built. All toned muscle, flawless skin, fiery temper, and *his.*

The tightening heat in his stomach was a primal demand, his body thrumming for a fight and his eyes fixed on his meal.

"Last door on the left." He trailed after her, chasing, hunting his chosen with a determination that couldn't be extinguished.

She reached the bedroom two paces ahead of him. As the door swung closed, he stopped it with the toe of his boot. Then he kicked it open.

"Get out." She tried to re-shut it, pushing him back, her resistance at odds with the raw lust in her eyes.

He wasn't imagining it. Her breathing unfurled at a ravenous speed, noisily heaving from her chest. Her nipples pebbled beneath the tight shirt, her pupils dilated. She licked her lips, stared at his mouth, and shoved him again.

With a hand holding the door open and his boots planted on the threshold, he didn't budge.

Wild brown hair fell in disarray around her shoulders, the upthrust of her tits so round and tempting. Lashes, sprinkled in dark hues of animosity, hooded the molten silver of her eyes.

He leaned in, shaking with excitement and hard as a rock.

She leaned in, too, angry and gorgeous and not above ruthlessness when it came to getting what she wanted.

Right now, she wanted *him.* The dip of her gaze to his straining fly confirmed it.

"When I shove down your pants," he said, "and sink my fingers in your pussy, you're going to drip all over my hand."

"Doesn't mean anything. I love your monstrous cock."

He throbbed behind his zipper, engorged past the point of pain.

Tension mounted. He didn't force his way in. She didn't push him out. They just stared at each other for an endless, unblinking moment.

Then they moved. He grabbed her as she climbed his body. Lips colliding and hands grappling, they locked in a battle they would both win.

The door hadn't even closed before he had her pinned against the wall. She tore his fly. He wrenched down her pants. In a frenzy of shredded fabric, they managed to rip enough clothing out of the way, and he was in her.

Christ almighty, he was all the way in, plunging to the root and submerged into soaking wet heat. Her hips rose to meet his, questing, demanding, and he gave it to her. Nailing her against the wall, he fucked her with the unbridled force of his strength.

It was so incredibly hot, this unhinged frenzy between them, this mutual, maddening urgency to climb closer and closer until they dug out their souls. They couldn't keep their hands and mouths off each other. Ripping at clothes, kicking away shoes, they were naked and tumbling across the floor in a matter of seconds.

She thrashed beneath him, her eyes the color of rainclouds. Perky, flushed tits. A complexion so pristine and fair. Sinful pink lips — one set bruising his mouth while the other swallowed the full length of his hunger.

His hips moved like a piston, chasing his release. The sensations blew his mind, the pleasure out of this world. He was going to come. Really fucking hard and soon.

He broke the kiss and held her gaze, his balls tightening, the pressure nearing detonation. "Tell me you don't need me."

"I don't need you."

He pulled out, rose up, and finished all over her

chest and face, grunting and shaking in a surge of liquid ecstasy. With a firm grip, he continued to stroke from base to tip, milking every drop and spraying jets of come across her shivering flesh.

When his nuts went empty, he climbed to his feet, his insides jumping with wild anticipation of her reaction.

She sniffed haughtily, sat up, and reached blindly behind her. Her hand landed in his bag near the door. Without a word, she pulled out his favorite fur-felt cowboy hat and wiped it across her chest, collecting his come on the expensive fabric. She used the underside on her face, cleaning every drop of him from her skin. Then tossed the hat back in his bag.

He stood there in absolute disbelief, staring at her. His hat would forever be traumatized.

Opening her legs, she ran two fingers along her slit and slipped them inside, her wicked eyes fixed on his. "I don't need you."

The fuck she didn't. She needed his cock, his protection, and above all, she needed his love. But rather than forcing any of it on her, he turned on his heel and strode toward the bathroom.

One round with this woman would never be enough. Already, his dick was swelling with blood, pulsing to get back inside her.

Halfway to the bathroom, her footsteps hit the floor, sprinting after him. He didn't have time to turn before she was climbing up his back and biting down on his shoulder hard enough to draw blood. Then she slapped him across the head.

His temper flared, and he spun. She spun with him, sliding to her feet while landing a torrent of punches on his spine and ribs. His seething frustration culminated in World War III when her open palm collided with his ass.

She fucking spanked him.

He froze and felt her go deadly still behind him.

"Rylee."

"Tommy." Her voice shook.

"You better run."

TWENTY-TWO

The mad ravings of Rylee's thoughts withered beneath the impact of Tommy's searing glare.

Oh, shit. She'd done it now. He was going to kill her.

Her heart rate spiked, hammering at her to flee. But with Tommy, she never did the smart thing.

In a bristling surge of fear, she slapped his face, making his cheeks bloom redder, hotter, madder than ever.

His hands balled at his sides, his cock outrageously long and swollen between his powerful legs.

Beautiful.

Dominant.

Terrifying man.

"Go ahead." She stood taller, despite her knocking knees. "Hurt me just like you promised."

His nostrils flared, and he closed his eyes. When they opened again, his anger was leashed, focused.

"Love hurts," he said. "It lashes out when tempers

erupt. I might say shit I don't mean, but I will not strike you when I lose control."

Like she just did.

Her face tingled, chilling at the implication.

"You want me to hit you out of anger, so you can push me away." He touched her chin, lifting it. "You want me to cheat on you, so you can blame me when you run." He lowered his hand. "I won't do it, Rylee. I'll grab your throat in the heat of passion because it burns you up. I'll beat your ass because it makes you wetter than sin. But I will never cheat on you, nor will I ever hurt you out of anger."

"You hurt me when you fucked me in the desert."

"Weak argument. We were both raging. *With hunger.*"

Buzzing ignited in her ears. She shook her head, unable to escape the thrashing of her pulse. "I don't trust you."

"You're too scared to try."

"I'm old enough to be your mother. A hard pass."

"*That* was a lie. A bullshit attempt to chip away your confidence. There's no excuse for it. I was in the wrong. You know all my secrets, and I felt cornered, embarrassed by my mistakes. You had the advantage. You still do. You have the power to destroy me."

"I do not!" She drove her fist against his stone-hard chest. "See? You don't even move!" Another punch. "You chained me in the desert." *Punch, slap, punch.* "You strangled me until I passed out, left me with no water, and starved me for days." She pounded her knuckles in a fit of fury, her eyes hot with tears. "I can't forgive you. I won't. What kind of woman falls in love with a sadistic bastard?"

He stopped the barrage of her fists with a bear-hug, lifted her off her feet, and brought her down on her back on the bed.

"A sadistic woman, that's who." He lay atop her, trapping her hands and hovering his face an inch from hers. "And this bastard loves you."

She felt a cracking, rupturing sensation around her heart, and all at once, something burst, letting in air and warmth and terrible possibilities.

"No." She was breaking open, falling apart. "Stop playing with me, Tommy. If you're going to hurt me, just do it. Get it over with!"

He kissed her. Open mouth. Sweep of tongue. Gentle strokes, slipping along the inside of her lower lip. It hurt. Not like a fist. It hurt like hunger pangs. It was a helpless, gnawing, painful need way down deep inside.

Delving deeper, he roamed the caverns of her mouth with a skill that electrified. Her knees turned to water. Her arms went slack between them, and currents of insidious heat flooded her breasts, prickling the peaks.

He kissed her with tenderness, his hands flowing over her body with devotion, drawing pleasure beneath her skin, making her hungry, needy for more. He tasted of warmth and something rich and masculine and *loyal*. He tasted like her fantasies.

Never, *never*, had she been touched or kissed with such sublime adoration. His tongue moved in her mouth with agonizing respect as his fingers traced her breasts with reverence. His cock lay hard and thick against her belly, leaking from the tip but not stabbing. Not taking.

She could battle his cruelty with fists. She could fight his ruthlessness with hateful words. She could sink her teeth into his stone-cold rage.

But she couldn't attack his affection with violence. She couldn't hit him when he kissed like this. When he kissed her like he well and truly loved her. She wasn't that hard-hearted.

But she wasn't naive, either.

He would grow bored. Whatever this infatuation was, it wouldn't last. He would miss the excitement of the chase.

His mouth trailed down her neck and suckled her breasts. The pressure of his lips, the swirl of his tongue, it was too perfect, too familiar, as though she'd spent her entire life in his arms.

His hand, strong and long-fingered, slid between her legs, tracing the shape of lower lips and rousing sensitive nerve endings. She throbbed, and his mouth nuzzled her quivering belly. Liquid heat flooded her pussy, and he continued to explore, tease, and slowly dismantle her kiss by kiss.

She wasn't stopping this. She couldn't. He was too talented, and she wanted it too much.

"This is just sex." She twisted her fingers in his thick hair.

"This is our bodies following the demands of our hearts."

"I bet that line gets you laid every time."

"My heart" — he sank a finger inside her — "never felt a damn thing during sex. Until you."

"That's a lie. Everyone's heart pounds when they fuck."

"My heart pounds when you walk into the room."

"You're deranged."

"No, merely in love. With you." He nipped her inner thigh. "Hurry up and love me back so we can do this without fighting."

"You can't love me, Tommy. I'm too broken."

"If you're broken, I'm broken. Christ, you look good enough to eat."

With his shoulders wedged between her legs, he stared at her cunt. Then he caressed her, stroking wickedly and stealing back, gentle around her opening and firm thrusts straight through the center.

Her eyes rolled back in her head, her entire body shaking with the need to come.

"You're not thinking through this." She gasped, clenching around his curling fingers. "You love women."

"I love you."

"You love pussy."

"Yours, no question."

"Do you love my pussy enough for it to be the only one you touch for the rest of your life?"

"Yes." He met her eyes. "I'm one-hundred-percent devoted to the stunning artwork between your legs and the beautiful stubbornness between your ears. So much so that I will answer these infuriating questions honestly every time they arise for the rest of our lives."

He buried his face in her cunt, scattering her thoughts on the tide of her gasps. The heat of his breaths was heaven, his lips firm, the voracious strokes of his tongue exceeding her desires and filling her with more.

Blazing light spread beneath her skin, stirring and shimmering and lifting her higher, higher, higher. Just as she reached the brink of climax, he pulled back. His heat, his kiss, all touch was gone.

"Tell me you need me." He stared at her, his mouth glistening, waiting.

Stunned, she stared back. Confusion crashed into

realization and simmered into outrage.

He was trying to control her through orgasm denial? Kissing her with an agenda? Toying with her to get what he wanted?

Fuck him. She refused to surrender like a doormat. She also knew she would never win this fight. He had the stamina and willpower of a superhuman machine.

No more games. She was done.

Done with the manipulation and the cheating and the emotional pain.

"I don't need you." She reached between her legs to get herself off.

He watched her hand but didn't smack it away. His body tensed, but he didn't overpower her with his strength. Didn't try to dominate her in his Draconian way. Something flashed across his expression. Disappointment? Frustration? But he didn't leave.

Instead, he lowered his head and placed his mouth against her hand. His tongue joined her fingers. His fists gripped her thighs, holding her open, and before she could process the unexpected turn of events, he pushed her, hard and fast, through an unstoppable climax.

Rippling waves of pleasure poured through her, trembling her limbs, her moan of completion one of barely contained victory.

But she didn't feel victorious.

She felt like shit. Made worse when he pressed a loving kiss between her legs.

His eyes lifted to hers, blinking, raw, stark with vulnerability. "You're not the only one who's afraid of getting hurt again." He pushed off the bed and stood before her naked, open, his hands hanging at his sides. "It scares me how much I need you."

I need you.

Three words, so simple and ambiguous, reached into her chest and shook her. They sneaked under her guard and gathered up the most broken parts of her.

I need you.

"Ten years ago," she said, voice cracking, "you wrote those words to your girl."

"And my girl heard them. She listened to me. She was there for me. I need my girl to keep doing that. I need you, Rylee."

"I'm not..." She pressed her fingers to her brow and released an anguished breath. "You were livid because I invaded your privacy."

"I'm an idiot."

For a man who'd spent most of last week glaring instead of talking, she couldn't fathom what the fuck had changed.

Except she knew.

He was telling her, showing her, and she just couldn't accept it.

"Someone else could've bought Caroline's jacket and logged into her account," she said. "I could've been anyone. You can't hinge this on the emails. Why do you need *me*?"

"You challenge me at every goddamn turn. You keep me in check, never backing down. You don't cower in the face of fear, not even when you're trapped under a bed and hunted by a hitman. You're crazy as hell, but you have a levelheaded grip on your moral compass. You think your heart is subtle? That you don't show it or share it with anyone? That's not true, Rylee. I watched you cry for your neighbor. You cried for that motel clerk. And you cried for me when I burnt Caroline's house." He dragged a hand down his brow, his nose, his mouth. "As if all that wasn't enough to send me off the rails..." He looked up, his gaze touching, stroking, heating her body. "You're so wildly, immeasurably, astonishingly beautiful it physically hurts."

Heart thundering, she lowered her eyes to the engorged erection hanging between his legs.

A swallow stuck in her throat.

There was no gain without pain. No reward without risk. She would never know how good it could be unless she got out of her own way.

The truth was she *did* need him. She needed his intensity, his honesty, his possessiveness, his passion.

She desperately needed him to need her.

But she was scared. Yes, she was thinking about Mason and the ten years of pain he'd caused her. How could she open herself up and expose her heart to another decade of agony?

And there would be agony. Over the last nine days, Tommy had proved just how vicious he could be.

He steadily watched her, his demeanor cooling by the second, along with his arousal. She held his gaze, locked in a standstill that made no progress.

With a deep breath, he shot her a shivering look and turned toward the bathroom.

She summoned her pride and remained silent as he walked away, leaving her on the bed with her disparaging thoughts. The door shut behind him, and a moment later, the shower turned on.

Tears threatened as her stomach twisted, but through the churning and lurching, she felt something stronger, more profound. *Longing.*

There was no one more capable of love than Tomas

Dine. He'd been devoted to Caroline Milton at a level that had made Rylee envious. At the peak of his sexual prime, years after Caroline's death, he'd remained faithful to her. His emails spoke of nothing but love for the girl.

He'd never blamed her for his pain. Never let her loss define him. He grieved without allowing it to control his life.

If he'd married Caroline, he would've never cheated on her because betraying someone he loved wasn't part of his chemical makeup.

Nine days ago, Rylee drove to Tommy's house with a plan. She wanted to help him move on from his ghosts. But he wasn't the one who needed help.

Her chest constricted, and she rubbed her breastbone.

The truth was there, waiting.

I need help.

I need him.

Deep down, she still dreamed of finding a life partner, someone who loved her enough to be loyal. Faithful.

I found him.

Her winding, battling thoughts went on through his absence and carried through her own shower. He let her have the space, and like a coward, she lingered in the bathroom long after she finished. If she avoided him long enough, he would realize she wasn't worth the effort and seek out someone younger and easier to manage.

A voice in the back of her mind hissed, *You stupid cow. He loves you.*

She hid in the bathroom until her hair was air-dried. Until she was confident he was asleep. He'd been running for days without slowing down. He needed the rest.

Nothing would be decided now.

Wrapped in a towel, she opened the door and froze.

He sat on the floor just outside, his back to the wall and head hanging between his bent knees. Waiting for her.

Her lungs caved in as his golden eyes lifted, searching hers for a specific answer to a specific question.

She clutched her throat. "I hold onto grudges forever."

He rose to his full height, wearing briefs and nothing else.

"Then I'll wait." He held out a hand.

"Forever?"

"For as long as it takes."

Her heart keeled and bucked and pounded, the painful beats speaking to her, telling her something important was within reach, and she should grab it before someone stole it away.

Her damn heart bayed for his.

Fingers trembling, she grasped his hand. He led her to the bed, undressed, and wordlessly slid beneath the covers. She dropped the towel and followed him in.

Their bodies came together on instinct, chest to chest, hips to hips, legs entwined. He held her with arms of corded brawn, his muscular torso and soft, thick cock pressed tight to her body.

She had a full belly, a warm bed, and a beautiful man with his hands wrapped around a part of her she'd never imagined a man would touch again.

Her heart.

"Tommy." She touched his strong, whiskered jaw and sank into the golden rays of his eyes. "I'm your girl."

"From the moment you read my first email." He cupped her face and rested his forehead against hers.

"I need you."

She felt his brows pull together, his muscles tightening around her. Then his hand lowered, drifting down her body to slide between her legs.

"No." She gripped his arm and flattened his hand against her chest. "I need all of you, Tommy. I need *us*. I don't know what that looks like tomorrow or ten years from now, or how our worlds fit together, but knowing you, you already have all that worked out."

"You're mine." His strange expression suggested he was trying out the words, tasting them. "*Mine*."

"And you're mine."

He smiled, a brilliant, lustrous, heart-stopping smile, and caressed his palms along her shoulders. His fingers laced through her hair, and his mouth captured hers, kissing her senseless.

His happiness felt elemental against her lips, stirring a fluttery, whirling, delicious warmth in her chest. They made out without hurry or expectation, touching, kissing, grinning, *living*.

She was reborn in his arms, alive and unrestrained, her emotions unfurling in staggering abandon. So many feelings, sensations, the good and bad, the pain and pleasure, the past and present—all of it mounted and spilled out in a shocking flood. She gave a harsh cry, her body convulsing and belly clenching, untying knots as sobs tumbled from her throat, along with wave after wave of relief.

He held her through it, kissing away her tears.

Then he lowered himself onto her, his mouth hungry against hers as he worshiped her, caressed her everywhere, and prepared her to take him.

When he finally pushed inside, it was with slow, rocking thrusts, fitting his hard length deeper, deeper. At last, he hilted himself, bottoming out, filling her with unholy pressure and pure satisfaction. She gasped, then groaned, matching the growls rumbling from his throat.

He paused, their breaths rushing, colliding, eyes locked in wonder.

God, he was so gorgeous—chiseled features, squared jaw, a shadow of sexy stubble, and tousled brown hair dangling over his stern brow.

"You should know," she said, "I might act like all is well, but beneath the surface, I'm dreaming about running my own cartel and pistol-whipping every woman who looks in your direction."

His eyes danced, his smile beaming. "I'll provide all the pistols you need."

By now, she should've been immune to the deep timbre of his voice. But the low, throaty vibrations were as intoxicating as the stretch of his cock.

He circled his hips, forcing her to feel every inch, driving shivers of pleasure through her limbs. Her head fell back. She dragged in air, and his mouth fell upon her throat, licking and kissing and showering her in sparks of love.

Desire stirred along her spine, spreading outward like a slow, burning flame. His strokes caught a timeless rhythm, sinking deep, masterfully controlled and wickedly orchestrated.

He fucked her slowly, loved her thoroughly, his stamina and youth carrying her through hours of unadulterated pleasure. He was a mean son of a bitch, a carnal beast, but without a fog of anger driving their hunger, they took their time and savored the explorations of each other's bodies.

She didn't know how long they played or how many orgasms she'd chased into the rafters. But she knew he was spent when a hoarse groan brought him to a languid, sweat-slick halt.

Rolling to his back, he took her with him. With their bodies still joined, she gently rocked, reluctant to relinquish the motions that brought them so much pleasure.

Eyes closed, with an arm thrown over his brow, he lay limply beneath her, chuckling softly.

"You're insatiable," he murmured and trailed a knuckle along her thigh.

"Get used to it. I hear women only get hungrier with age."

"Can you have a baby?"

"I don't know." Startled, she slid off of him, staring at his closed eyes. "I've never tried. Can you?"

"Never tried."

"Do you want a baby?"

"I want you." He cracked open an eye, lazily watching her. "Children. No children. Whatever happens, happens. We're going to have an amazing life together."

She nodded, wanting that with a healthy amount of fear and excitement.

Tenderly, she ran her palm down the corrugated ridges of his abs, the skin taut and slick over steel. When she reached the trail of soft, wiry hair, he sighed, relaxed.

As relaxed as his cock. It lay along his thigh, wet

with their mingled come, and long. Even flaccid, he was at least seven inches. But she could fit that much into her mouth.

Her fingers moved on their own, encircling him, her mind full of wonderment. She'd spent hours exploring every inch of his body, but this part of him still intimidated her. She hadn't dared to take him into her throat.

She moved between his legs, roving her thumb over the velvety knob. The muscle jerked, but didn't harden.

He lowered his arm, staring at her from beneath hooded lids. "Are you going to suck the life out of me?"

"I'm going to try."

He started to swell in her hand, so she hurried, lowering her head and drawing him into her mouth. The tang of their arousal hit her taste buds, the sound of his grunts spurring her faster.

She lapped and sucked, rushing against the clock as he grew harder and longer against her tongue. This wasn't an act she'd ever been particularly fond of. But the tremors in his thighs, the clench of his hands in the bedding, and his groans… Oh, Jesus, his groans were everything.

Eyes shut tight, he rode out the contractions that rippled along his flat abdomen. *Extraordinary.*

He was too gorgeous, too sexy, too fucking huge in her mouth. But too much of this man was the perfect amount. The perfect amount of gagging, choking, thrusting…

With a growl, he flipped her onto her back and fucked her until neither of them could move.

Then they slept. Hearts beating in sync, bodies

entangled, blissfully content, they slept until nightfall.

She woke in the dimly lit room, dying of thirst. Tommy didn't stir beside her.

Careful not to disturb him, she slipped from the bed, dressed in the bathroom, and crept into the hall in search of something to drink.

Voices drifted from the living room at the far end. Soft whispers. The team was awake.

She wasn't keen on facing a gang of armed criminals alone. But if she wanted a life with Tommy, they would have to accept her. She would have to trust them.

Steeling her spine, she adjusted her t-shirt and jeans and strode down the hall.

Halfway there, a partially opened door gave her pause. Light glowed from within, the flooring different from the rest of the house. Polished hardwoods.

No furniture was visible through the crack. Was that…a mirrored wall?

She shifted, stealing another angle, and spotted Cole sitting on the floor near the back wall, surrounded by beer bottles.

Curiosity and concern pulled her closer. She opened the door.

A dance room. Holy shit, it was beautiful. Massive. Twelve-foot-tall seamless windows soared to the rafters. Mirrors covered the other walls, and ballet bars wrapped the entire room. There was a lounge area with a leather couch, a built-in stereo system, and a dancing pole in the back corner.

All built for the dancer who was tattooed on his arm.

Her heart sank to her stomach.

Cole glanced at his watch and dropped his head back against the wall, eyes shut. "Forty-five seconds."

"What?"

"There's a rumor going around that Tomas is packing a ten-inch dick."

The random comments gave her whiplash. "It's not a rumor."

He nodded, finished off his beer, and grabbed two more. "Want one?"

"Sure?" Uncertain, she left the door cracked behind her and joined him on the floor.

They drank in silence.

Out of the corner of her eye, she watched him look around the room, his eyes flickering as if he were tracking an invisible dancer as she swayed through her routine, her feet scuffing and bouncing across the shiny flooring.

Shadows crept over his expression, and he blinked, looking away.

"Do you want to talk about her?"

"Nope." He popped the *P*.

"How long has it been, Cole?"

How long have you been hurting?

"She married my best friend seven years ago." He tipped his beer toward the door, his voice gruff. "Your forty-five seconds has arrived."

She followed his gaze and found Tommy standing on the threshold.

TWENTY-THREE

Tomas couldn't ignore the territorial feeling in his gut as he took in the unexpected room filled with ballet bars, mirrored walls, empty beer bottles, and his girl.

His gorgeous girl. Swigging beer. With the only single man in the house.

Yeah. He was feeling territorial. They'd just made a monumental step in a fragile, new relationship, and she'd sneaked out of their bed to chug beers with this guy.

Drawing in a deep breath, he slowed his roll and leaned a shoulder against the door frame.

Rylee sat on the floor with her legs crossed, her gaze ticking between him and Cole before settling on Cole. "Forty-five seconds…?"

"The time it took Tomas to throw on his clothes and chase after you." Cole rested an arm on his bent knee, a beer bottle dangling from his hand. "I know the drill. I used to be just like him."

"You used to be overbearing, unpleasantly arrogant, heavy-handed, and moody?" A twinkle lit her eyes.

"All of that and worse," Cole said, expressionless.

"He still is." Tomas slipped his fingers into the pockets of his jeans, fighting the urge to drag her back to bed.

They had a lot of work to do—phone tracking, computer hacking, and high-tech spying—that heavily relied on Cole's expertise. The man shouldn't be drinking, but Tomas wasn't here to nag him. The guy was dependable.

"Do you want me to leave?" she asked Cole.

"I don't care what you do." He leaned back against the wall, settling in with a long draw from his beer.

Turning toward Tomas, she shot him a look that said she wasn't budging from this room. And she wasn't asking him to stay.

The instinct to haul her out and spank her ass warred with all logic and reason. He needed to eat. His friends were already gathering in the living room, and he trusted her.

Proving it, he gave her a smile that caught on her face. She smiled back, and he shifted away, heading toward the kitchen.

As he stepped out of the hallway and around the corner, he paused, tensing.

Across the room, Lucia stood near the windows, crying in Tiago's arms.

What the fuck?

He searched the living room and found Tate sitting off to the side, perched on the edge off a chair. Leaning over his lap, he braced his elbows on his knees, head down, and eyes up, watching the bizarre embrace like a hawk.

Tiago didn't look up, didn't say a word. His attention was engrossed in the weeping woman he held. Lucia wasn't a crier, so to see her sniveling softly against the madman's chest, to witness him gently shushing her, stroking a hand over her hair, and hugging her tight, it was fucking weird.

And heartening.

It was a good sign if Tate wasn't interfering. He didn't look pleased, but he wasn't tearing off Tiago's arms, either.

Everyone knew Tiago harbored a deep affection for Lucia. Nothing like what he felt with Kate. But he and Lucia shared a history. An ugly, brutal history of lies and deception. He'd poisoned her for years. She'd smashed his head in with a lead weight, and through it all, he'd kept her alive, protecting her from enemies and allies in his dark underworld.

Lucia leaned back and wiped her cheeks. Tiago released her, clasped his hands behind him, and stared down at her, speaking softly.

Their relationship was a twisty, complicated knot to unravel, but they appeared to be making progress.

Tomas veered toward the kitchen, grabbed a sandwich from the fridge, and spotted the others outside. Leaving Tate to supervise Tiago and Lucia, Tomas stepped out onto the terrace.

The evening autumn air chilled his skin. Not cold, but so very different than the desert.

Liv, Van, and Luke sat around a table, deep in conversation about the mission that Matias and Camila just finished in Mexico. Another sex trafficking ring annihilated.

The thought brought a smile to his face. Fuck, he

loved his job.

Lowering into the chair beside Van, he wolfed down the turkey sandwich and admired the exterior view of the massive one-story manor. Veneered in stone, it wrapped around several outdoor living spaces with walkways that led into the woods.

From the largest terrace, a bridge arched over a ravine, providing access to the covered dock on the lake below. A vista of forest and high bluffs surrounded the calm inlet of water. It was majestic and comforting and felt almost as secure as Matias' fortress in the Amazon rainforest.

"Where's Rylee?" Luke asked.

"Talking to Cole. Did you know he has a full-blown dance room down the hall?"

"Not surprised." Liv leaned back in the chair. "The tattoo is telling."

"Are you surprised by his pushy bid to join our team?"

"He's already with us." Liv shrugged.

"He just wants us to recognize that." Van tapped a toothpick on the table.

"Why? What does he get out of it?"

"Purpose. Belonging." Luke stretched out an arm, indicating the sprawling mansion. "This was built as a safe house. He told me that he used to let people in his profession stay here to recharge and regroup. He gave up that job for a girl, lost the girl, and now all he has is the house. A nine-bedroom estate with gear and tech, designed for people like us. He supports our cause, trusts us enough to bring us here. We give him purpose. A place to belong."

"Makes sense." Tomas looked at Van. "You

recruited him how long ago?"

"Six years." Van met Liv's eyes. "When I hunted down Traquero."

Traquero, the slave buyer who brutally raped Liv in front of Josh.

When Van had learned about the assault, he lost his fucking mind and dismantled his sex slave operation. Then he hired Cole to find Traquero so Van could kill the monster, which he did. *Gruesomely.*

Cole didn't show up again until a year ago, when Tate hired him to locate Lucia and retrieve her from Tiago's clutches.

"What do you think we're dealing with, Tommy?" Luke scraped a hand through his messy red hair, his gaze focused. "This can't just be about a jealous ex-husband."

"Occam's razor. The simplest explanation is usually the right one, and the simplest explanation is Mason Sutton." The tension at the base of his skull disagreed. "I feel like we're overlooking something. Can't put my finger on it."

"If Rylee hasn't told anyone about the bridge except you," Luke said, "how did the hitman know about it? What does it have to do with anything?"

"We won't know those answers until we have a motivation. We need the hitman's identity and that of who hired him."

"That's Cole's expertise." Van reclined back, propping a socked foot on his knee. "Depending on who's behind this, it could take weeks to uncover."

"I talked to Matias an hour ago." Luke traced a finger along the edge of the table. "If this gets drawn out, he and Camila will fly in with the rest of the team."

His friends were restless, itching for action and the

thrill of a fight. And missing their other halves.

"We need to put our heads together." Tomas scratched his jaw, gathering his thoughts. "Paul Kissinger started watching Rylee six months ago. Three months before that, she filed a protective order again Mason. Paul found me through a tracking device on her truck. A standard device that is widely available. Far different than the tech that was planted in her house."

"Do we know when that tech was planted?" Liv asked.

"Recently. The components are so new that Cole has never seen its kind before."

Her eyes hardened. "Do you think we're dealing with two unrelated threats?"

"The hitman made contact with Paul's phone. We're still waiting on the analysis from the call logs, but we know there's a connection."

"It could be a criminal Rylee testified against," Luke said. "Or a family member of one of those criminals. Someone with a vendetta against her."

"Or it could be any of the hundreds of traffickers we've taken out. We never leave loose ends, but mistakes happen."

"Whoever this is, they're not after your emails. Rylee's house hasn't been ransacked. No one seems to be searching for the copies she made."

"Unless they already have them." His insides tightened.

Her house was compromised. At some point, very soon, he needed to get those email copies and talk to her about selling the property and moving to Colombia.

He went back and forth with his friends for the next hour. The conversation circled, discarding theories and forming new ones. Eventually, Tate rapped on the window, announcing dinner, and they moved the discussion inside.

Tate and Lucia had prepared a spread of Mexican food — enchiladas, tacos, and other fixings Tomas could name.

Cole breezed around the large dining table, setting up numerous laptops, printers, phones, and other electronics.

Behind him, Rylee stood at a giant whiteboard that had been wheeled in on a stand. The marker in her hand flew across the surface, listing evidence and timelines, drawing diagrams, and collating links between people, places, and events.

While the seductive shape of her ass in those jeans tried to steal his attention, it was her mind that held him rapt, gripped in a state of awe. She'd managed to organize the tangle of conversations he'd just exchanged with his friends into an orderly, concise illustration.

As she worked, he made them both plates of food. Cole hadn't stopped messing with his equipment to eat, so Tomas made a plate for him, too.

Setting the heaping dishes on the table, he approached her back and dragged his nose through her soft hair. "You've done this before."

"Well, I've spent a lot of time holed up in cubicles with detectives, but they don't use evidence boards like this. Everything goes into advanced computer programs. It's a more efficient way to connect findings."

She tapped the marker on her chin, staring at her work. Her other hand absently drifted behind her to rest on his hip. It was a simple thing, just a casual touch, but it meant so much more. It was familiarity, comfort, and connection. It was everything.

"Right now, the one currency we have to work with is time," she said. "There isn't a serial killer on the loose or an abducted person held somewhere. No one's breathing down our necks. So I thought the board would be helpful to kick around ideas."

"Is this what you were discussing with Cole?"

"No." She laughed uncomfortably and turned around, her eyes watching Cole head toward the hall for more supplies. "I talked to him about you, me, my failed marriage, and the woman he built that dance room for. Relationship stuff. I did the talking. He indulged me by not kicking me out."

"He was listening." He stroked his thumb across her pillowy lips. "Listening to a beautiful, brilliant psychologist."

"Oh, my God." She laughed again. "I'm a terrible therapist. Therapists *listen*."

"You listened to me."

"And changed my major because I thought I could fix things." She touched his face, his gaze soft with affection. "Some things don't need to be fixed." With a small smile, she turned back to the board. "*This* has always been my dream. Investigation. Profiling. Criminal justice."

"You're in the right place for that. With us. I know it's too soon to make demands—"

She snorted. "You've been making demands since day one."

"Quit your job."

"Done."

"Just like that?"

"I took a sabbatical because I hate that fucking job.

The detectives pull me into their sit-downs when they have questions, but I'm never part of the analysis or action. I watch from the sidelines, bored out of my mind. When I drove into the desert, I was searching for so many things. A new life, friendship, happiness, possibilities..." She pressed her lips against his chest. "*You*."

He was a goner. Utterly, completely lost for this woman.

Pulling her close, he wrapped his arms around her and scoured his fumbling brain for something profound to say. "This is nice."

Lame.

"This *is* nice." She hugged his waist and perched her chin on his breastbone, smiling up at him. "I love the growly, aggressive, tough-guy thing you have going on, but it's also nice to just be able to touch you like this, to hold you without expectation or agenda."

Dishes clinked, voices murmured, boots scuffed — the din of family coming together for a meal.

He held her until she pulled away, turning back to her evidence board.

"Eat." He grabbed her shoulders and turned her toward the table.

She sat with a harrumph and ate with a smile in her eyes.

Cole returned a moment later, found his plate, and carried it to the board.

"This is great, Rylee." He took in her detailed lists and diagrams, the fork absently digging into his food. Then he went still. "What is this?"

"What?" Rylee wiped her mouth and joined him at the board.

"These words." Cole pointed the fork at the

guesswork she'd made from the hitman's dying gibberish. "What does this mean? The bridge?"

"That's what he said. I don't know." She stood taller, defensive, her expression tightening. "He said he was there because of the bridge. The rest...I don't know. It sounded like Thursday or thirsty or—"

"Thurney." Cole's whisper shuddered the air, and the plate in his hand slowly tipped.

"Yes. That's it. What—?" She grabbed the dish as it tumbled, unable to stop its descent. "Shit!"

Enchiladas and dishware exploded across the floor, but Tomas wasn't interested in the mess. He was interested in Cole's stark, ghost-white expression as the man spun, scanning the room for something.

"What does Thurney mean, Cole?" Tomas stood, his adrenaline spiking.

Cole's shell-shocked eyes landed on a pile of burner phones. He snatched one and turned away as he punched in a number and held it to his ear.

Who the fuck was he calling?

In the next breath, he barked into the phone, "Call me back on a secure line."

He hung up and stared at the device as muscles flexed across his back.

"Cole." Liv broke the silence. "What's going on?"

The phone buzzed, and Cole lifted it to his ear. "Your location?" A pause. "Lock it down. Where is she?" He gripped his hair, his voice plunging into a seething roar. "Fucking get her. Bring her to the safe house!" He pivoted, pacing, listening to whoever was on the other end. Then he slammed to a stop. "No, goddammit. I want her *here*. It's Thurney. Yeah, you heard me. I'll be in touch."

He disconnected, and a sharp, icy hush lanced through the room. Tomas didn't breathe. No one did as Cole stood frozen, staring at nothing.

Then he turned toward the table, slowly, too calmly, and slammed the phone down on the surface, smashing it into pieces. A collective flinch rippled the air.

"Thurney Bridge." Cole raised his eyes, divisive and chilling. "It's where I lost my life."

TWENTY-FOUR

A thousand questions piled up as Tomas put together everything he knew about Cole Hartman. It wasn't much. The man had more secrets than friends.

One question was answered, though. Thurney Bridge, wherever that was, wasn't Rylee's bridge.

As that detail clicked into place, her lips parted, her gorgeous silver eyes round and glassy. She had nothing to do with this. At least, not at the foundation.

Someone had connected her to Cole and put a hit on her.

Why? Who *was* Cole Hartman?

Tomas had learned some things about the man over the past two weeks, but nothing about losing his life on Thurney Bridge. Except he remembered a conversation they'd had in the desert.

I was sent out in the field for a while. Mistakes were made, and I was forced to fake my death to protect her. By the time I cleaned up the mess, quit the job, and returned home to her, she'd fallen in love with my best friend.

Whatever Cole was mixed up in — then and now — put Rylee and the entire team at risk.

"Are we safe?" Tomas met Cole's eyes. "Right now, in your house, are we safe?"

"Yes." Cole straightened and ran his hands down his face. "This is the safest place in the world." He surveyed the room, taking in the disbelieving expressions around the table, and sighed. "The man I just called was my handler. He was also my best friend until he married my fiancée."

"That sounds deliciously nasty." Van didn't smile.

"The point is, while Danni is no longer my…" Cole's hand clenched. "While she's no longer mine, I still protect her. She was a target during my last mission. A mission that ended with me taking a bullet on Thurney Bridge. Now she's in danger again, and there's nowhere I'd rather her be than in this house."

Tomas was surprised to finally hear the name of the mysterious woman who'd leveled Cole's world.

"Is she coming here?" Rylee tilted her pretty head, concern softening her eyes. "Did your best friend agree to bring her?"

"No." One word and Cole's face clouded over.

"Let's go back to the bullet," Tomas said. "Is that when you faked your death?"

"Yeah. I was wearing bullet-resistant clothing. High-tech stuff." Cole tapped his sternum. "The bullet broke skin, fractured ribs, but didn't enter my body. I fell into the river below and swam out of sight. If I hadn't faked my death, the perpetrator would've killed Danni."

"Where's the perpetrator now?" Rylee asked.

"She's in prison. *That* is a fact I can one-hundred-percent guarantee. I monitor her status. She'll never see daylight again."

"You were shot by a woman?" She arched a brow.

"She was my partner," he growled, his eyes dark and murky. "A traitor to the agency."

"Which agency?" Tomas leaned over the table. "No more secrets, Cole."

"Those aren't my secrets. It's classified, and sharing classified information is punishable by law."

Tiago's dark laugh turned all heads toward the corner of the kitchen, which was darkened merely by his presence and the deadly look in his eyes. "You can't scare this group with threats of your law."

"It's not my law."

"Who the fuck cares? The only law we follow is our own. You're one of us. Now tell us what you were involved in."

"Espionage."

"We need more than that," Liv sang in an eerily melodic voice that crashed into a spine-tingling command. "Trust us, Cole."

Cole paced to the windows and laced his fingers behind his neck. The entire room seemed to strain toward him, tense with anticipation.

He made them wait, building the silence into a volatile, rumbling thunderstorm. Fingers drummed. Shoes tapped. Molars sawed. Patience thinned.

At last, Cole turned and faced them, decision made.

"I retired from a special unit, a clandestine group, that goes by many names." He folded his hands behind him, feet braced apart, voice monotone. "OGA, ISA, Optimized Talent, Gray Fox... Whenever there's a classified spill, the designator changes. But those inside refer to it as the *activity*. I was a deep undercover operative, deployed to foreign nations to collect information. *Crucial* information. The kind that changes the outcome of wars. Or prevents them, as it were." He rolled his neck, cracking it. "I was the eyes and ears in the shadows, and I was fucking good at it. Until Thurney."

Tomas' head pounded as he came to terms with what they were dealing with. The Freedom Fighters had taken down some scary motherfuckers, solidified a trusted relationship with the Restrepo Cartel, and learned the ins and outs of the criminal underground. But top-secret espionage and government corruption? This was way out of their league.

"What happened on Thurney Bridge?" he asked.

"I was embedded deep within the enemy's ranks. But the enemy, as it turned out, was my partner. She was ambitious and power-hungry and turned her back on her country to make some money." He gripped his neck. "Everyone connected to her was apprehended. No stone left unturned. The *activity* was thorough in this."

"Not thorough enough," Van drawled. "Someone knows about Thurney and put a hit on Rylee, who happens to know everything there is to know about us."

"I can't even begin to guess who it is or what they want." Cole's gaze swept over the laptops and gear that littered the long table. "I need to sit down, pore through the findings, and make decisions on how to proceed."

"*We* need to do that." Tomas pointed a finger around the room. "We're not from your world, and we don't know shit about your tech. But we're your team now. Train us. Put us to work."

"All right." Cole nodded, his expression thoughtful, maybe even relieved. A split-second later, he snapped into full-on work mode. "We need to scrape through every detail of my last mission. Identify the actors — enemies, allies, informants, and everyone in between — and run a cross-connection between those actors and Mason Sutton, Paul Kissinger, and Daniel Millstreet."

"Daniel Millstreet?" Rylee asked.

"The cunt you killed in the motel room. I received confirmation on his identity an hour ago." He strode toward the mess of food he'd dropped on the floor.

"I'll get it." Tomas held out his hand, itching for something to do. "You'll tell us how you found his name?"

"I'll *show* you everything."

TWENTY-FIVE

Over the next two weeks, Tomas sat side by side with his team, absorbed in congressional documents, private phone records, and handwritten reports of Cole's undercover missions. Handwritten by Cole. Godawful penmanship. The scrawl was so terrible it made Tomas' eyes cross. It was also really goddamn impressive.

Under U.S. law, Cole couldn't make copies of briefings or anything related to his job. But on the heels of each operation, he'd written everything down by memory, filed it meticulously, and kept the notes in his armory.

Cole hadn't just given them the key to his entire life. He'd literally put details of national security in their hands. In the filthy hands of vigilante criminals.

If that didn't say *trust*, nothing did.

The first week of digging through reports was an eye-opening experience, the entire team engrossed in their newfound knowledge of government inner-workings.

The classified intel didn't interest Tomas, but it opened a portal into Cole's extraordinarily unique skill set. Bottom line, Cole was a master at milking information. He knew how to talk to informants, manipulate dangerous adversaries, and use social engineering to obtain what he needed.

He no longer had access to government systems and confidential records, but he never needed that access. He only had to identify who had the access and massage them into unknowingly leaking the information he was after.

That had been the core of his job in the *activity*. He slipped behind enemy lines, deep undercover, and went to work, befriending and inveigling.

That was how he'd learned the identity of the hitman. He'd convinced someone, a lot of someones, to feed him innocuous pieces of information until he had enough to put it all together.

Fucking mind-blowing.

Tomas pushed back from the table and rubbed his hands down his face. He'd been bent over documents for hours, and the words were blurring. Stiffness knotted his neck, and his body screamed for exercise.

The house was equipped with a weight room, and they all used it daily. But they weren't accustomed to this type of work. They were the feet on the ground, the fingers on the triggers, and muscle on the front lines. They weren't analysts.

Cole sat beside him, flicking that coin-shaped GSM bug between his fingers, eyes on his laptop. He'd been focused on the bug's technical components, reaching out to unknown contacts, subtly asking around about it, and collecting data. He was convinced the tech in that device held all their answers.

Tomas looked around the living space, taking in the bodies sprawled on couches and chairs, holding laptops and reading through reports. In the kitchen, Tiago and Van prepared lunch while arguing the finer points on how to properly chop cilantro.

Definitely not a typical day for this group. But not once in two weeks had anyone suggested going home.

They didn't know who the enemy was, what this entity wanted, or if it had anything to do with them. Maybe his emails were out there somewhere in the hands of someone who intended to exploit them. Maybe his emails didn't factor in at all.

It didn't matter. They were here, sticking together like wet on water.

His gaze fastened on his favorite brunette across the room. She lay face-down on a rug, her fingers clicking on a laptop and legs bent, rocking her delicate feet in the air. It was a girlish thing to do, reminiscent of Caroline lounging lazily on his bed. But that was the only similarity between the two.

The feelings Rylee stirred in him were so much deeper, darker, and deliciously grown-up.

He rose from the chair and prowled toward her. She hummed as he stretched out over her prone body, bracing his hands on either side of her shoulders and lowering into a push-up position.

"Take a break," he said at her ear.

"I could use some fresh air."

Outside, they took the bridge that led from the terrace to the dock below. The tree-lined shores wrapped around calm water that stretched for miles. Several boats bobbed on the horizon, too far to venture near this inlet.

As they made their way to the water's edge, her hand slipped into his, and he felt a pull in his chest, a breath of undiluted happiness.

At the end of the dock, benches faced the water. He lowered onto one and guided her onto his lap, wrapping his arms around her, warming her skin in the chilly air.

He'd fucked her on this very bench yesterday. Over the past two weeks, he'd taken her in every corner of this property, in every position. His need for her was unquenchable, and she had the enthusiasm to match.

Being cooped up together had given them a lot of time to explore. Not just their bodies. He'd never been one to vocalize his feelings, but she had a way of opening him up and riling not only his temper but also his fears, joys, and hardest memories.

She'd demanded to hear every detail of his mission with La Rocha Cartel in California, including an explanation about the girl on the meat hook. He didn't want to revisit that, but after he shared the story, he realized he could tell her anything. Not just in an email, but in person, while looking into her eyes.

It was another first for him.

They talked a lot, argued plenty, and sometimes, they communicated without saying anything at all.

She curled up on his lap, her nose buried in his neck, choosing the view of him over the stunning vista of the lake. She loved him. The words hadn't left her lips, but he felt them. He felt them in the weight of her stare, the caress of her constant touch, and the sigh of her breaths.

She leaned up, her gaze fastening on his. "I'm going to sell my house."

"Okay."

"I'll need a place to live."

"I'm your home."

She nodded, smiled, and her chin quivered.

He kissed her lips. "Scary, huh?"

She nodded again.

Her dirtbag of an ex-husband had put that fear in her.

Deep down, he hoped that Mason Sutton was behind the hit on her so that he would have an excuse to murder the son of a bitch. He might just gut the fucker anyway.

"Which is scarier?" he asked. "Living with me? Or living alone?"

"I don't want to live without you, so I'll take the scary. I'll take whatever comes as long as I'm with you."

"I know you will."

He kissed her, deeper this time. Then he removed her clothes and filled her until every drop of fear deserted her.

The fear would return again, and when it did, he would fight it with her. Fuck it out of her. Break through it piece by piece.

With every word, every touch, every passing hour, they were moving forward. Together.

Two days later, they were sharing an early breakfast alone in the kitchen when Cole darted in from the hall, carrying a laptop.

"I found the last link." He set the device on the table and pointed at the screen, his eyes tired and bloodshot.

"The *last* link?" Tomas knew Cole was making progress with the data they'd collected, but he had no idea how close they were. He squinted at the screen, which displayed some kind of ledger. "What am I looking at?"

"Mason Sutton's bank records."

"We already scoured those."

"This isn't his personal bank account." Rylee leaned over Tomas' shoulder, eyes on the laptop. "These are financial records for his orthopedic practice. I can't believe you got your hands on this."

"Look." Cole moved the mouse, highlighting a ten-thousand-dollar withdrawal listed under miscellaneous. "Six months ago, he wired this money to another account." He switched the screen to Paul Kissinger's bank records. "There. Ten-thousand dollars came into Paul's account on the same day."

"Goddammit!" Rylee straightened, her eyes aglow with fire. "Mason paid that man ten-thousand dollars? To do what? Kill me?"

"No," Cole said. "Mason hired Paul to watch you and report back your activities, specifically who you were fucking. That's all Paul did until the night Tomas left him in the desert."

The night Paul tried to rape Rylee.

A torrent of emotions flooded Tomas' chest, but regret from killing that man wasn't one of them.

"Mason didn't put a hit on me." Rylee released a slow breath and lowered into the chair beside him.

"I'm still going to kill him." Tomas gripped her knee.

"No, you're not." She ground her teeth. "I'm really fucking angry that he hired someone to stalk me for six months, but you're not going to kill him, Tommy. He's not worth the effort." She turned back to Cole. "How is Paul Kissinger connected to the hitman?"

"He's not. Paul was a run-of-the-mill private detective, skirting around the law and doing dirty jobs to make an extra buck. No question, he was a sleazeball, but he had nothing to do with the hitman." Cole looked at Tomas. "Daniel Millstreet worked for someone else, and he arrived in Texas on the same day that I did."

"How do you know?" Tomas asked.

"Data from the phone we found on his body. Someone dispatched him to Texas. For one reason only."

"To kill you?"

"No. To kill everyone close to me, starting with Rylee."

Her eyes widened. "I didn't even know you before all this started."

"They bugged your house the day you drove to the desert. The moment you walked into Tomas' life, they connected you to me." Cole paced in front of the evidence board, motioning at it. "I've been linking all the data you collected, putting the findings together, and the facts are these." He stopped and met their eyes. "Someone from my past, someone related to Thurney Bridge, wants to hurt me or pull information from me. Maybe both. If they wanted to kill me, they would've sent the hitman after me, not Rylee. I've been in hiding for the past seven years, retired from the *activity*, and they've been patient, waiting for me to return to the United States."

"You've been outside the country all this time?" Tomas pressed his fingers to his brow. "No, wait. You were here a year ago when Tate contacted you."

"I came here twice for Tate, staying only hours each time. And I joined the rescue mission last month to retrieve Luke and Vera in California. Again, I was in and out within hours. This visit is the longest I've been stateside in seven years."

"Why?"

"I've always worked abroad, and I'm always working." Cole released a slow breath. "Someone has been waiting a long damn time for me to return, and they know I'm connected to you."

The hairs rose on Tomas' nape. "They've been watching my house."

"Yes. They knew when we turned up there. You, me, Rylee, and Paul Kissinger." Cole resumed pacing. "The hitman called Paul's phone when he showed up at your house, which suggests that Paul was on the hitlist. Good thing, because that's how I was able to track the hitman's location the night he found Rylee."

"Jesus." Tomas leaned back in the chair, his mind spinning.

"I assume they have eyes on Mason Sutton and Detective Hodge, too." At Rylee's gasp, Cole shook his head. "If they were in danger, they would already be dead. Whoever is watching knows you're not close to them."

"Evan…" Her face fell, and she dropped her head in her hands. "Oh, God, they killed him."

Because she was close to him.

Tomas reached for her, pulled her onto his lap, and rested his lips against her brow.

"I was able to trace the tech on this." Cole held up the GSM bug he'd removed from her house. "Bad news. It's only available to the *activity*."

"What are you saying?" Tomas froze, because he knew. He knew exactly what that meant.

"Someone on the inside is behind this." Cole's

expression contorted, etched with barely concealed rage. "Someone inside my old group is after me."

"Someone you know?"

"Maybe. They could be retired, still employed, a rogue, who fucking knows? It's a long, classified list." His lips curled into a smile void of humanity and mercy.

"I don't know if I like that look on your face."

Tomas tipped up a brow. "I take it you have a plan."

"I'm going hunting."

TWENTY-SIX

Two weeks later, Rylee followed Tomas up the stairs that led to the top floor of her house in Eldorado, Texas. Every room had been swept for bugs and threats, the property deemed safe by Cole and the team. But her spine tingled anyway, her mood sullen and twitchy.

The place writhed with memories of Evan. She hadn't loved him, and in her heart, she'd said goodbye the day she drove away and left him standing on the porch. But he was a good man, an amazing friend, and hadn't deserved to die.

Pushing away those thoughts, she rubbed her chest and focused on her future.

Her future looked delicious as he strode down the hall in front of her, his gait steady and confident, his muscles flexing through the glide of his strides. Corded arms, narrow waist, chiseled ass—he was sexual heat and male potency, dominance and devotion, utterly loyal and all hers.

Turning his neck, he glanced over his shoulder.

Eyes of gold, reflecting the color of his heart.

He wasn't always good-natured, but that mighty heart of his made hers beat like nothing ever had before.

"This closet?" He paused at the door at the end of the hall.

"Yep."

He opened the door to shelves of towels and cleaning supplies. "Where is it?"

"If you were a bad guy—"

He gave her a glare that closed her throat.

"Fine." She coughed. "Since you *are* a bad guy, where would you look for a thumb drive?"

"Not in a linen closet." He glanced at the other doors. "I would search the underwear drawer first."

"Of course, you would. Panty-sniffer." She crossed her arms. "But I already told you it was in the linen closet."

He scanned the bottles of cleaning products and random clutter, his expression quickly transforming into boredom.

"You win." He grabbed her, lifted her off her feet, and kissed her hard on the mouth. "Show me where you hid it."

Wriggling out of his arms, she removed the vacuum from the closet and opened the dirt bin.

"You're kidding?" His brows climbed, widening his eyes. "How have you not accidentally thrown it away?"

"I don't use this vacuum. It's broken." She dug through the powdered dirt in the collector, removed the tiny stick, and blew off the debris. "My working vacuum is downstairs."

She handed him the thumb drive, which contained

all the photographed copies of his emails. Nine years' worth. She'd started snapping pictures of his messages after his captivity in Van's attic.

"Have you ever gone back and reread them?" He palmed the thumb drive, regarding her with affection.

"Never needed to. Your words stuck inside me on the first read-through."

His lips tipped up, taking hers with them. They stared at each other. Smiled at each other. Stared some more. These were her favorite moments, the private eye contact they shared. It wasn't a game to see who would look away first. It was a game to see who would *move* first.

This time, they moved as one, coming together with arms, breaths, and open mouths. He backed her against the wall, and she gripped his hair with greedy hands as his tongue chased hers, caressing and rubbing and drowning her in warmth.

The potency of his kiss was enormous, his love even greater. She threw her arms about his neck, mouths locked, holding him close, knowing she would never let him go.

When their lips melted into panting sighs, he touched their brows together. "The team is waiting."

Everyone had left Missouri to return to Texas. They weren't in her house, but they were in the neighborhood, in the shadows, watching and waiting.

Cole had a crazy plan, which involved baiting and hunting his unknown adversary. This stop at her house was just a detour to grab the thumb drive and her personal belongings.

She was going with them, wherever that took her. It was terrifying and thrilling, but for the first time in her life, she'd found her home.

"I forgive you." She slid her nose astride his.

"I forgive you, too." He dropped the thumb drive on the floor between them and crushed it with his boot.

"I need you."

"I need you, too.

"I love you."

A rush of air escaped his lips, and he grinned. "Wow, that's a great feeling." His grin widened. "I love you, too."

They were back to staring and smiling again.

"You," she breathed.

"No, you."

"How much time do we have?"

"Not enough." He checked his watch. "Twenty minutes."

Someone, probably Cole, had decided this was the ideal window of time to enter her house. She needed to pack the few things she wanted to keep. The rest would be donated and the keys turned over to a real estate company.

"Twenty minutes." He kissed her lips and stepped back. "Pack what you want from the bedrooms. I'll do the downstairs."

"You don't know what I want to keep."

"You sure about that?" He winged up a brow.

"I'll check your work."

With a chuckle, he pocketed the broken thumb drive and ambled toward the stairs. She watched him go with a flutter of hummingbirds in her belly.

He stopped on the top step and gave her a strange look.

"What?" she asked.

"I live a crazy, filthy, dangerous life."

"I know."

"Reading about it in emails isn't the same as living it. I make decisions and do things that sane people would never fathom."

"In case you didn't notice, I'm not the sanest person in the world. You're not going to scare me away."

"Prove it."

"Oh, I will." She pushed back her shoulders.

He nodded, smiled, and vanished down the stairs.

Maybe he was a bad guy, but he'd committed acts of bravery and self-sacrifice and made inconceivable progress in his efforts to decimate human sex trafficking. His victories weren't celebrated or recognized in the news. No one knew what he and his team did in the shadows of the underworld.

Many might consider him a ruthless thug. A villain, even. But in her eyes, he was an unsung hero.

Her hero.

Nightfall darkened her bedroom. She turned on the lights and went to work, sorting through clothes and collecting keepsakes. She didn't own much, hadn't kept anything from her life with Mason.

When her twenty minutes were up, she'd filled five large duffel bags. Grabbing two, she made her way downstairs.

She dropped the bags in the entry, turned the corner into the living room, and slammed to a stop.

Masked men. Armed. Three of them, all aiming rifles at a naked man who was gagged and restrained on her couch.

It takes three seconds to make a life-or-death decision.

She blinked, paralyzed, unable to believe her eyes.

Mason.

His bulging, watery gaze fastened on her, his cries muted behind a wad of cloth. Rope bound his arms and legs, crisscrossed his chest, and tied around the sofa.

Why was he in her house? Why the fuck was he naked?

Where was Tommy?

Her heart sprinted as she jerked her attention to the three gunmen. Black ski masks covered their faces and hair. Black jeans and shirts molded to muscular builds.

Familiar statures.

Safe.

The masked head in the middle turned in her direction, staring through the narrow eye opening. She knew him intimately, from the tips of those boots to the glint in those golden eyes.

She pressed her lips together, angry, worried, and intrigued.

Don't say his name.

Whatever this was, he'd masked himself to remain anonymous. Every word she spoke in front of Mason would need to be chosen carefully.

Looking closer at the other two men, she recognized Van's arrogant posture and Luke's towering height.

Tommy, Van, and Luke. Masked and armed. Terrorizing her ex-husband.

A sheen of sweat glistened on Mason's body. His belly, softer and rounder than she remembered, quivered with the heave of his muffled sobs. His dick shriveled between his legs as if retreating in fear.

The team wouldn't have lured him here. It was too risky. If she had to guess, he'd showed up unannounced to pester her *again* about coming back to him.

He didn't have Paul Kissinger to report her activity. She'd quit her job — a phone call she'd made two weeks ago — and she'd vanished after she'd called him from the motel room last month.

He had no way to track her anymore. But the team was tracking *him*.

They would've known he left El Paso, which was a five-hour drive away. The window of time to pack up her house made sense now. Tommy knew Mason was coming and wanted to make sure they were here when her ex showed up.

For what purpose?

It took her a few seconds to put this much together and another few seconds to force her feet into the living room.

Tommy's eyes followed her, studying her reaction.

She'd told him not to kill Mason, but she'd never put a limit on anything else. Threats? Torture? There were many levels of pain.

Blood whooshed through her veins as she stepped closer.

Mason bucked and thrashed, howling soundlessly behind the gag. From his perspective, they were both in danger. There were armed, masked men in her house, and he couldn't protect her.

Fuck him. He'd given up that right ten years ago. Besides, if she were truly in danger, he was helpless, naked, and shaking in terror. She would have to save *him*.

She paused by the couch and looked at Tommy expectantly.

Your move.

He lowered the rifle. Then he lowered into the

293

chair behind him.

Van and Luke spread out, taking up positions on either side of him, guns trained on Mason.

"You hired Paul Kissinger to monitor this woman." Tommy leaned forward, his mouth moving behind the mask. "Paul got a better offer and handed off the job to us."

Mason's eyes widened, and his thrashing went ballistic.

She remained quiet, uncertain where Tommy was going with this lie.

"I want my payment in advance." Tommy turned his cruel glare on her. "Undress."

Her heart stopped, and her limbs turned to ice.

What was he doing?

I make decisions and do things that sane people would never fathom.

That conversation had been deliberate. He was warning her. Testing her.

Was this a test?

He reclined in the chair and lowered his zipper. The fly opened, exposing the thick, swelling root of his cock.

Sex was the destination. In front of Mason, Van, and Luke, he expected her to undress and ride his lap.

I live a crazy, filthy, dangerous life.

His team lived openly in their sexuality. They had monogamous partners now, but they hadn't started that way. Tommy had watched Luke fuck Vera in California. Van had fucked half of the guys. They weren't shy about sex. If she was going to live with them, this couldn't be a sticking point.

It wasn't. Not for her.

She looked at Mason, taking in his traumatized misery.

This wasn't a test. It was punishment. Revenge. Tommy had set this up for Mason, the man who destroyed her trust and continued to harass her for the next decade.

She reached down deep and searched for something, a scrap of a feeling inside her that wanted to save Mason.

All she felt was heat. Fire. A burning desire for justice.

An eye for an eye.

"I watched you fuck another woman." She stepped toward him and removed her shirt. "Do you know how that feels to watch someone you love betray you so cruelly?" She unbuttoned her jeans and kicked them off with her shoes. "I'll show you."

She stood before him in a black bra and panties. A matching set. Lacy and sexy. She'd chosen wisely when she dressed this morning. But she hadn't selected her underwear for Mason. She was interested in one reaction, and it was searing a line of fire down the length of her back.

Pivoting, she found his eyes in the mask, and oh, Jesus, they smoldered.

Luke and Van kept their guns and their attentions on Mason as she made her way to Tommy. She circled his chair, savoring the track of his gaze. It stayed with her, turning his head until she stepped out of view behind him.

Bending over his back, she brought her hands around him, caressing his sculpted chest, dragging up the shirt, and exposing all that glorious muscle.

He moaned as she touched him. He slumped down in the chair as she reached lower, slipping her hand into the *V* of his open fly. Soft hair, swollen root, he was so hard, so long and thick. It took some adjusting and a lift of his hips to wrangle him free.

A muffled cry sounded from the couch, drawing her gaze to the tears leaking down Mason's cheeks. He was hurting. The emotional sort of suffering that stabbed deep.

She didn't rejoice in that. Didn't torment him with a smile. She might've been vindictive, but she wasn't inhumane.

Straightening, she walked around the chair, eyes locked on her man. He sprawled with a casual confidence that watered her mouth and soaked her panties.

His cock lay on his thigh, twitching as his golden stare violated every inch of her body.

She climbed onto his lap.

He did the rest, his hands roaming, pulling her close, and tugging aside the crotch of her panties. His mask prevented kissing, but his eye contact sealed their intimacy. He watched her as he guided himself into her body. He didn't look away as she gripped his corded neck and struggled for breath. He held her gaze as he lanced into her and broke into a hungry rhythm.

She was on top, but he controlled everything. The speed, the thrust, the tempo of her pulse. He owned her, dominated her, and brought her screaming and writhing into blissful completion.

With his forehead against hers, he grunted into her cheek, exploding, spilling himself into her with a deep, rumbling growl.

Mason was full-on sobbing behind her.

As she started to lift, Tommy palmed her backside, holding her to him.

"Thank you," he whispered, too low for Mason's ears.

His jealous-possessive nature had needed that bit of revenge. She'd needed it, too. For entirely different reasons.

Mason wouldn't bother her anymore, and he would think twice before cheating on another woman.

"Thank *you*," she whispered back.

She rose from his lap and quickly dressed while Tommy strode toward a weeping Mason, his wet cock hanging out of his zipper.

With a grip on Mason's hair, Tommy shoved him toward his semi-hard dick. "Lick me clean."

She froze, and Mason went wild.

"Nah, I'm just playing." His laughter sobered into cruel authority. "You will never taste heaven again."

Her lungs released a sigh.

She was done here. No more torment.

Luke and Van stepped forward, guns trained as Tommy cut Mason free from the rope.

"You won't talk about this." Tommy tossed Mason's clothes to him. "You hired us after all."

Free of the rope, Mason yanked out the gag and scrambled to pull on his pants. "I didn't—"

"Don't talk. Not a word. If we catch wind of you blabbering about what you witnessed here, we will find you. And we will kill you."

Half-dressed, Mason gathered the rest of his things and backed toward the door. His tear-soaked eyes jerked from the rifles to her, his expression ugly with accusation.

"Don't send any more men to watch me." She

stepped beside Tommy and placed her hand and her cheek against his muscled arm. "I'm keeping this one."

Tommy let Mason go. He stood at the door and watched her ex sprint toward his car and speed away. Van and Luke grabbed her bags and carried them outside.

"You knew Mason was coming." She touched Tommy's tense back.

"We'll be watching him for a while." He turned and searched her face. "You're not running."

"If you're trying to scare me, you'll have to try harder."

He grinned, blinding her with his gorgeous sex appeal. "We're going to war with an unknown enemy from Cole's world. Does that scare you?"

In a few minutes, they would drive to Tommy's property in the desert. There, Cole would activate the GSM bug he'd removed from her house and lure in the threat. The team would be in position. They would be ready.

"Yep." She shivered with excitement and fear.

Fear was good. It affirmed she was alive.

He leaned in and brushed his lips against hers. "It's going to be complicated."

"Then you definitely need me there."

"To dominate it?" He kissed her, lingering, controlling her breaths.

"We'll dominate together."

The DELIVER series concludes with:

COMPLICATE (#9) - *the final book*
Cole's story

OTHER BOOKS

LOVE TRIANGLE ROMANCE
TANGLED LIES TRILOGY
One is a Promise
Two is a Lie
Three is a War

DARK COWBOY ROMANCE
TRAILS OF SIN
Knotted #1
Buckled #2
Booted #3

DARK PARANORMAL ROMANCE
TRILOGY OF EVE
Heart of Eve
Dead of Eve #1
Blood of Eve #2
Dawn of Eve #3

DARK HISTORICAL PIRATE ROMANCE
King of Libertines
Sea of Ruin

STUDENT-TEACHER / PRIEST
Lessons In Sin

STUDENT-TEACHER ROMANCE
Dark Notes

ROCK-STAR DARK ROMANCE
Beneath the Burn

ROMANTIC SUSPENSE
Dirty Ties

EROTIC ROMANCE
Incentive

Made in the USA
Middletown, DE
15 April 2022

ABOUT

New York Times and USA Today Bestselling author, Pam Godwin, lives in the Midwest with her husband, their two children, and a foulmouthed parrot. When she ran away, she traveled fourteen countries across five continents, attended three universities, and married the vocalist of her favorite rock band.

Java, tobacco, and dark romance novels are her favorite indulgences, and might be considered more unhealthy than her aversion to sleeping, eating meat, and dolls with blinking eyes.

EMAIL: pamgodwinauthor@gmail.com